THE TEMPTATIONS OF CREMORNE

Sasha knocked at the door and a sweet young female voice called out, 'Come in!' I opened the door and we entered and what a delightful surprise greeted us. Lying on the bed, utterly naked except for the briefest pair of frilly white knickers, was perhaps the most voluptuous young lady it has ever been my privilege to see!

'Don't be shy,' said this ravishing beauty. 'Lock the door behind you and perhaps we can all have some fun!'

In the same series:
Cremorne Gardens

Also available from Headline:
Venus in Paris
A Lady of Quality
The Love Pagoda
The Education of a Maiden
Maid's Night In
Lena's Story
The Lusts of the Borgias
States of Ecstasy
Wanton Pleasures
The Secret Diary of Mata Hari
The Pleasures of Women
The Secrets of Women
Sweet Sins
The Carefree Courtesan
Love Italian Style
Ecstasy Italian Style
Body and Soul
Sweet Sensations
Amorous Liaisons
Hidden Rapture
Learning Curves

The Temptations of Cremorne

Anonymous

Introduced and edited by
Radley Marlborough

HEADLINE

First published in 1991
by HEADLINE BOOK PUBLISHING PLC

10 9 8 7 6 5 4 3 2 1

All characters in this publication are fictitious and any resemblance to real persons, living or dead, is purely coincidental.

ISBN 0 7472 3685 2

Phototypeset by Intype, London
Printed and bound in Great Britain by
Collins, Glasgow

HEADLINE BOOK PUBLISHING PLC
Headline House
79 Great Titchfield Street
London W1P 7FN

The Temptations of Cremorne

INTRODUCTION

This further, uncensored extract from the erotic novel *The Secret Lives of Modern Girls* by Max Dalmaine follows on directly from the narrative found in *Cremorne Gardens* (Headline Books, London, 1990). The book was first published privately by the All-England Society of Priapus in May, 1902 and was later serialised in revised form in *The Cremornites* magazine between 1904 and 1908.

In his interesting preface to *Cremorne Gardens*, the distinguished social historian, Dr Louis Lombert, confirmed that this bawdy tale enjoyed great popularity via the official fortnightly magazine put out by The Cremornite Society, a notorious group of libertines who flourished in the late Victorian and Edwardian eras. The publication was distributed not only to Club members, but also found its way to a wider public through a semi-secret network of eager readers who were more than willing to pay the non-members' price of ten shillings (fifty pence) for a copy of perhaps the most explicit of all underground Victorian journals – and this at a time when a newspaper cost only a few pennies. Yet we should not be surprised at this because behind the façade of stern respectability of those days, there also lurked a huge demand for The Cremornites' stories that are totally unfettered and unashamedly open in their varied accounts of sexual delights. Never of course on open sale, copies of *The Cremorne* magazine were then widely circulated amongst the cognoscenti, although original copies of the publication are now extremely rare. Indeed, the script of the novel upon which this book is based was taken from a set of *The Cremorne* discovered hidden in a locked cabinet found during the recent refurbishment of an old mill house in a tiny Oxfordshire village.

Who were the original Cremornites? The group was originally made up of former patrons of the infamous Cremorne Gardens pleasure park in Chelsea, where every evening members of the district's bohemian set of artists and musicians rubbed shoulders with Society 'toffs', along with a large number of ladies of pleasure who thronged the area looking (often very successfully) for trade. Coupling sometimes took place amongst the dark groves of trees away from the bright lights of the restaurants and bars, but brisk business was also conducted in such places as Mrs Gascoyne's dining rooms in the Fulham Road, or Lizzie Smyth's small hotel in Cathcart Street. And for those of a more *recherché* taste and who could afford a higher tab, there was always a welcome at the Rawalpindi Club run by Trenton de Berri at nearby Stamford Bridge which specialised in providing beautiful Chinese and Eurasian girls for the delectation of their guests. Whilst for those who practised 'the love that dared not speak its name' the Italian painter Carlo Massetto ran a secret homosexual circle that met in The Boltons until he was forced to flee the country after the downfall of Oscar Wilde in 1894.

When Cremorne Gardens was finally closed down by an outraged borough council, a small band of aficionados formed The Society of Cremornites, a private club of members devoted to the pursuit of the hedonistic pleasures which had attracted them to Chelsea in the first place. Amongst their number were several well-to-do men about town including the American Lieutenant Colonel Frederick Nolan, who is featured in this novel as a lover of Penny Arkley's friend, Georgina Burstine; Sir Terence Whitley, renowed for his robust private life and escapades with the Prince of Wales, who is also woven into the story; and Brigadier Leon Goldstone of the Fourth West Oxfordshire Rifles, a man of extraordinary sexual prowess whose secrets were later chronicled in The Cremornites' magazines by our author, the French born *bon viveur* Max Dalmaine, himself a regular contributor to the spectacularly rude scandal sheet *The Oyster* and a regular participant in the club's wild parties which were often held in the luxurious surroundings of the Mayfair mansion of Count Gewirtz of Galicia or at the raffish Jim Jam Club in Great Windmill Street in the heart of Soho.

A biographical sketch of Max Dalmaine (1852–1939) was provided by Dr Lombert in his introduction to *Cremorne Gardens*. To this, we might add that Max was Membership Secretary of The Cremornites from September 1893 until June 1898, the month before his marriage to Miranda, the youngest daughter of a fellow clubman, Sir Jasper Muttlebury. A wealthy country gentleman from Gloucestershire, he was, incidentally, the lecherous 'Sir Jasper' upon whom the eponymous rugby song is probably based. Naturally, after his wedding, Max must have found it more difficult to attend Cremornite functions but he continued writing for the magazine which was now under the editorship of Sir Michael Bailey, another well-known sybaritic *roué* who flourished around the turn of the century.

Interestingly enough, Max occasionally used the names of real people in his novel. This light-hearted private joke may have endeared him to such well-connected upper class personages as Sir Ronnie Dunn, Campbell Black or even the noted ornithologist Professor David Jackson, but whether any ladies involved appreciated Max's impish sense of humour is debatable. However, one of his long-standing mistresses, the famed Edwardian belle Estelle Quentonne, had no qualms about being named in Max's 'randy novels' as she termed them in a letter to a friend.

So here is writing often of an unexpected liveliness and wit which makes no bones about its revels in a myriad of sexual adventure. As Dr Lombert commented in his study of Victorian erotic fiction, *His Mighty Engine* (Thomas and Dibble, London, 1969): 'Max Dalmaine was perhaps the best of the scribes who put together the material in the naughty journals of our great grandfathers. He offers his readers a voluptuous assortment of endless arousals enhanced by some pulsating prose for which The Cremornites' magazine was justly famous, being produced for uninhibited men and women whose common aim was to glorify the pleasures of the flesh. Ignored for too long, these delightful chronicles of the Cremorne Club bare the erotic preoccupations that lay behind the public face of Victorian respectability.'

Lovers of gallant literature will surely be delighted that this saucy tale is once again in print. Social historians too may find much of value in this classic work of Edwardian erotica.

Radley Marlborough
Geneva
October, 1991

I can resist everything except temptation.

Oscar Wilde

CHAPTER ONE

Bob Goggin heaved a long sigh of relief as he slipped his rucksack off his shoulders and sat down on the bench that a local worthy had thoughtfully provided by the entrance to the village green. Bob drew a map out of his pocket and concluded that he was in the village of Uppark, a beautiful part of the country where the Sussex Downs merge into those of Hampshire.

The landscape was broad and breathtaking as Bob scanned his surroundings, and he noted with pleasure the wooded Weald laid out in a chequerboard pattern of cultivated hills and farmsteads. Although it was early September and the weather had been unseasonably warm, on this fine autumn morning Bob noticed that grey appeared to be the predominant hue – the grey-gold of ripened corn, the grey-brown of ploughed tracts, grey-green of the grassland in many shades and a grey haze in the distance.

'Well, this seems a good enough place to start,' he muttered to himself, rustling through his rucksack for the sketchpad and expensive set of Swiss-made artists' pencils that his love, Penny Arkley, had given him for his nineteenth birthday three weeks before.

[*Readers of* Cremorne Gardens *will remember that*

the aristocratic Penny, the youngest daughter of Sir Paul and Lady Arkley, enjoyed a passionate but highly secret romance with Bob Goggin, the youthful second gardener at Sir Paul's country home at nearby Treyford – RM]

It was Penny who, the previous evening, had persuaded Bob to spend one of his rare days off to rise early and use the time to make some sketches of the beautiful South Downs countryside. She had slipped out to meet him after the Arkleys had dined, using the pretext of a mild headache which would be cured by a short walk in the grounds. Her Mama had frowned but Katie, Penny's older sister, had guessed that the headache was only a ruse to escape from the house for a brief tryst with her beloved Bob.

So when the formidable Lady Arkley commented that a rest upstairs in bed would probably be more effective, Katie stoutly stood in Penny's corner and said: 'But, Mama, last week Doctor Danells urged us to make the most of the fresh air, especially during the evenings, whilst the weather is so nice. I'm sure that Penny will feel better after a stroll round the back garden.'

'I don't recall asking for your opinion, Katie,' said Lady Arkley icily. 'However, if this is what the good doctor recommended, then I suppose we must follow his advice. Be off, Penny, but don't be too long. Remember, we are all rising early tomorrow to go to London.'

Penny rose from the table and threw a quick smile of thanks to her sister. 'Don't be too long, Penny,' said Sir Paul, whose mind was in fact more concerned with how he would be able to slip into the bedroom of Selina, the fresh-faced new parlourmaid who had joined the household only three weeks before but who had already wriggled her pert young bottom provocatively in front of him and who had raised no objection, save for a tiny yelp, when he had managed to grasp her rounded bum cheeks for a moment as she passed by him earlier that morning in the hall.

When she judged she was no longer in view, Penny raised her skirts and ran towards the greenhouse where Bob was already waiting for her. The handsome lad engulfed the girl in his arms and they exchanged a passionate kiss as they wrapped their bodies together. Bob gently squeezed her breast but Penny pulled his hand away and said: 'Oh darling, don't do that – I'd adore making love with you but I haven't any time now, more's the pity.' His face fell, though he brightened up considerably as Penny continued: 'Now, Bob, you know that I am going up to London as we are all going to the theatre, but Katie and I are returning the day after tomorrow and so we will be able to have heaps of time to spend in bed!'

'That's marvellous news,' Bob enthused. 'I'll count the hours till then – it's just a shame, though, that Mr Durie had given me tomorrow off and I will have to spend it alone.'

'Make the most of this day,' advised Penny, hugging the disconsolate youth as she pressed herself even closer to him. 'You have a real artistic talent which it would be criminal to waste. Pack your sketchbook and pencils and walk across to Uppark. You will find some magnificent views around there to capture.

'No, I really want you to promise that you will do this – after all, Bob, you surely don't want to be a gardener all your life, do you? Wouldn't it be wonderful if you could make your living as an artist? I'm sure you would prefer it to digging up weeds and cutting lawns.'

Bob replied that he doubted if his work would interest any serious collector. 'Why, I haven't even been to art school,' he said gloomily. 'And whilst I appreciate your opinion, I'm sure that most people would say I have only a very small talent.'

'Now I wouldn't agree with you there,' said Penny teasingly. 'I think you have a very large talent when you choose to display it.' And as if to prove her point she rubbed her palm playfully along the outline of his cockshaft which swelled up noticeably under her smooth hand. 'M'm, let me take this talent in hand.'

Bob gasped as Penny added softly: 'We've no time to fuck but I could suck you off if you would like me to do so.' She correctly understood Bob's silence to mean that he agreed to the idea, and she commenced unbuttoning his fly as the lad sank back into a handily situated garden chair. His prick being at full stance she had no difficulty in pulling it out, thrusting back the material of his shirt to leave his stiff, naked cock quivering with desire in her hand.

'Well, indeed, let me pay my respects to Master Pego,' she whispered throatily as she continued to handle his swollen stalk, rubbing the shaft which caused the uncovered helmet to dance merrily up and down in her grasp. Penny glanced around to make certain that the coast was clear before sliding to her knees and, shaking a fringe of chestnut hair from her face, bending forwards to take Bob's rock-hard cock in her dainty little mouth. She sucked slowly, tickling and working around the tiny 'eye' as she washed the cap of Bob's tumescent tool with her tongue before sucking harder on his throbbing shaft, taking in as much as she could manage between her lips before the tip touched the back of her throat.

Bob was now well past the point of no return and his hips lifted off the chair as her licking and lapping increased in tempo. She cupped his balls and felt them harden which signalled to Penny that Bob was about to spend – and sure enough, within a few seconds his rigid rod twitched and jerked before spurting out a fountain of creamy spunk into Penny's mouth. The jet hit the back of her throat and she swallowed the wonderful flood of tangy sperm until the last dribbles of juice had been milked from his softening shaft.

Penny sat up and grinned saucily at Bob as she wiped her lips with her hand. 'Here, taste your spend, darling – it's finger-licking good,' she giggled. But before Bob could reply, the couple heard the patter of footsteps coming along the path. Hastily, Bob tucked his shirt inside his trousers and Penny looked out anxiously to see who was coming towards them. 'Don't worry,' called out a friendly female voice. 'It's only me, Katie. I appropriated the errand from Heavan the butler to call you back inside. H'm, from the flushed look on your faces it seems that it was as well I did so, though I do hope I did not interrupt the glory strokes.

'But, Penny, we have both been summoned to help entertain an unexpected guest, a Professor Graham Eames from Manchester who has arrived quite unexpectedly. It appears that he met Papa in France last month at that international conference on trade and Papa extended an open invitation to Mr Eames to visit Arkley Hall at any time. To be fair to the gentleman, he did write to confirm that he was passing our home this evening but his letter must have been mislaid in the mail.'

Whatever had happened to Mr Eames' letter was not a matter that exercised Bob Goggin's mind one whit – all he could think of was the obvious fact that he and Penny would have to say *au revoir* until the pretty lass returned from London.

And so that is how Bob Goggins found himself hard at work, sketchpad in hand, at eleven o'clock on a bright, though slightly cloudy September morning on the village green of the peaceful little village of Uppark. God knows how this comes to be called a village, thought Bob, for there were no shops, a very few houses and only one small tumbledown building of an inn which boasted a rickety home-made sign on its wall announcing its nomenclature of 'The Jolly Blacksmith', but which appeared to be closed and quite deserted.

He was interrupted from his gloomy reverie by an aristocratic gentleman of a somewhat portly disposition who had suddenly appeared at his side. 'Good morning to you, young man,' said the stranger. 'How good it is to find that this tiny hamlet boasts a talented artist in its midst.'

'Thank you for the compliment, but I think it undeserved – especially as I have only sketched out a few lines which surely can tell you very little,' said Bob with a smile.

'No, no, no, my dear chap, I grant that your sketch

is rough but unless I am much mistaken, you will use colour in your picture to show exactly what you see, to give an accurate rendition of the play of light and shade,' insisted the newcomer, tapping Bob's pad with his forefinger as he spoke.

Now Bob may have been only a lowly artisan, but Penny had provided him with several books on art and he was not overawed by the well-dressed young man's remarks. 'I suppose that I do follow this new idea of "impressionism",' he admitted, 'although some critics have railed against the movement.'

'Such critics are reactionary old fuddy duddies,' he declared vigorously. 'Though, ironically enough, it was just such a critic that gave the style its name – did you know that? When shown Edouard Manet's *Impression du soleil couchant*, the jackass disliked the painting as it intended to present an impression of what the eye can see at any given moment.

'But I for one applaud this rejection of the posed pictures of the neo-classical studio paintings. Give me rather the work of such giants as Monet, Degas and Alfred Sisley which capture the richness of actual everyday life.'

'You would appreciate the picture on the wall of Sir Paul Arkley's dining room,' said Bob. 'It's a von Menzel that Sir Paul bought twenty years ago in Frankfurt.'

'Ah, you must mean the one of a middle-class couple entertaining evening guests. Yes, it captures the true spirit of Impressionism, though I often think that the splendid insouciance of the style is so French that German or British artists will never attain the heights of the French masters.

'But what a coincidence that you should mention this picture. Why, I was at Arkley Hall myself only last night as a somewhat unexpected guest as it turned out. Obviously you are a very frequent visitor. Do you go there regularly?'

'Not exactly,' said Bob awkwardly. 'You see, I, er, well, not to put too fine a point to it, I'm actually employed there as a menial gardener.'

The garrulous gentleman threw out his arms and said: 'No need to be ashamed of that, my boy. My own father was a mere bookseller and I had to work at all sorts of jobs during the vacations whilst studying at university, I can tell you. Never forget the wise words of Crowquill: "The bread earned by the sweat of the brow is thrice blessed bread, and it is far sweeter than the tasteless loaf of idleness." I hope you would agree with that noble sentiment, Mr, er . . . – '

'Goggin, Bob Goggin, sir.'

'Eames, Professor Graham Eames at your service. But for heaven's sake let us dispense with formalities. Do call me Graham, Bob, as I am sure that our paths will cross again after today.'

'Thank you. Actually, your name was mentioned last night, if I recall correctly. Miss Penny Arkley and I were talking in the garden after dinner when Miss Katie rushed out to announce your unexpected arrival. You'd written Sir Paul a letter, hadn't you, but it had been lost in the mail and had never arrived at Arkley Hall.'

'Yes, yes, you are absolutely right,' chuckled the Professor. 'I had indeed written a letter but the Post Office must be absolved of all blame. You see, I had slipped the envelope into my jacket pocket and promptly forgot to post it! Don't tell the Arkleys, there's a good chap.'

Bob grinned and said: 'I know a chap who I regret to say deliberately uses the non-arrival of a letter to extract himself from tight situations, mostly concerning his rather erratic love life.'

'I must confess to having done this myself,' confessed Bob's new companion. 'However, since the wider use of the telephone, it has become rather difficult to pull that trick any more. Still, as my old friend, the famous theatrical impressario Mr David Zane is fond of telling me, the promise that "the cheque is in the post" is the oldest untruth in the business world.

'And the biggest lie in the context of another kind of business is: "I won't spend in your mouth, darling." Ha, ha, ha! But I expect you've heard that old chestnut before,' added the Professor.

The amusing if naughty anecdote put Bob at his ease and soon the two men were chatting away like old acquaintances. Bob told the Professor (or Graham, as we must now call him in deference to his expressed wish) how he had not wanted to join his family group which had decided to emigrate to far away New Zealand. At the time, there had been a girl in his mind, of course, but alas, his first experience of the opposite sex had not turned out well as the young lady in question had ditched him for the eldest son of the village butcher. 'My parents and I still write to each other regularly,' explained Bob. 'but I only have a small circle of friends and I do get rather lonely sometimes.'

Graham nodded sympathetically. 'You need a girlfriend to banish the blues. Aren't there any pretty young housemaids in Arkley Hall? Surely there is one special serving girl who blows you an occasional kiss.'

Bob blushed for he could hardly tell Graham that for the last six months he had been fucking the younger daughter of the master of the house! Taking Bob's embarrassment as confirmation that the lad needed female company, Graham said kindly: 'I have a splendid idea, Bob. I left the Arkleys this morning to stay for a couple of days with my sister Geraldine and her husband Timothy who live near Treyford, not five miles from here. Look, I have my motor car here, why don't you come back with me and join us for luncheon?

'Don't be shy, Bob, they live very simply and anyhow, my brother-in-law has his niece, Sarah, staying with them. She is a very sweet girl of about your age and I am sure that you will get along famously. Now then, I won't take no for an answer. First though, let me interrupt your work no longer. Whilst you continue, I will sit here if I may and finish reading my magazine.'

The die has been cast, thought Bob, who finally agreed to this plan. After all, he had little else to do with his day and Graham had also added that he would drive him back home to Arkley Hall that evening. He had never travelled in a motor car before and he was looking forward eagerly to this new experience.

But he banished all extraneous thoughts from his mind as for the next hour or so, Bob worked solidly, enjoying the quiet tranquillity of the scene. When he turned round to Graham, however, he saw that the Professor had fallen fast asleep in the hazy sunshine and the magazine he had been reading had fallen to his feet. Bob carefully picked it up and, to his great interest, noted that in his hand was the latest edition of *The Oyster*, a very naughty magazine indeed which he had heard about from Effie, the under-parlourmaid who had once found a copy in Sir Paul's library hidden between the pages of a Latin dictionary.

'This looks hot stuff,' murmured Bob to himself as he began to flick through the pages of this extremely interesting publication.

One of the tales was a thrilling description of a medical gentleman's exploits with a buxom young nurse. Bob devoured the text in which the dirty doctor excited the girl's amorous feelings, and the first illustration that caught Bob's attention showed the doctor raising her smock and feasting his eyes upon the snowy beauties of her voluptuous big breasts. He turned the page and there the nurse was now naked, her splendid cunt protruding its full rounded lips from the midst of a thick covering of crisp curly hair, while the crimson line of her crack gave a promise of a warm reception to the doctor's thick cock which she had in her hand, and on which she looked with shy pleasure.

Bob's heart began to quicken as he turned the page again and here were two photographs. In the first, the girl was lying across the man's lap, her exquisitely rounded bottom with its milk-white globes turned up to meet his amorous gaze. In the second photograph, the girl had climbed up astride him, just about to sit down on his huge flagpole of a prick whose knob had just penetrated the outer cunney lips and was about to luxuriate in the soft wet folds of her welcoming pussey.

'My God! This is far more exciting than *Gardening For Professionals*,' muttered Bob as he sat down and began to read through the 'Letters To The Editor' columns which were (if Bob but knew it) perhaps the most popular feature in the publication.

'Good heavens!' said Bob softly as, scanning the pages, he came across a letter from a Miss Cora Pelham-Sykes, a friend of Penny's sister Katie and the daughter of Dr Warwick Pelham-Sykes, Headmaster of Loynes Houses, a small though exclusive private school for Young Gentlemen. Bob had seen Cora often at Arkley Hall, the last time not more than a month ago at one of Lady Arkley's summer tea parties. What on earth is young Cora up to, writing about her experiences in a magazine like this?' thought Bob as he read with interest Cora's very personal plea for help from the magazine's famous advisor on *l'arte de faire l'amour*, Doctor Jonathan:

Dear Doctor Jonathan,

I would much value your advice as I have behaved foolishly and I am not certain as to how best extricate myself from a problem I freely admit is of my own making. Perhaps the easiest way of explaining my problem is to sketch out the circumstances of what occurred last Thursday evening.

My father is headmaster of a well known private academy for boys in Sussex. It is a most pleasant place with a fine house standing in large grounds of its own and surrounded by small fields of arable and pasture land, interspersed by numerous interesting copses through which run footpaths and shady walks where you are not likely to meet anyone in a month. I shall not give further clues as to the exact location as I have no wish even for fellow devotees of The Oyster *to contact me directly. However, should any readers wish to write to me, they may do so c/o The Editor, a gentleman whose name must never, of course, ever be mentioned in print for fear of police informers amongst us. In case there are any such weasels reading this letter, I would add that The Editor is a gentleman of quality who is welcomed in the grandest houses of the very highest in the land, many such members of Society subscribing* sub rosa *to our secret little journal.*

However, I digress. Let me return to the purpose of my letter. I am just twenty-two years of age and must admit that my daily workload is far from onerous. Occasionally I assist my Papa as a private tutor in French and German in cases where Mr Barber, our excellent teacher of foreign languages, believes that a pupil would benefit from individual tuition. So you will appreciate the fact that I am blessed with plenty of free time during the day to amuse myself – at least until the autumn when I leave Papa and Mama for London where I shall be living with my good friend Sally Randall and working alongside her on The Young Ladies Sporting and Athletic Journal.

Anyhow, my problem began last Thursday afternoon when I willingly agreed to deliver a message from my father to Denis Dixon, our groundsman who was preparing the pitch for the school's cricket match the coming weekend against Charterhouse. However, old Dixon was nowhere to be seen so I thought he might be in the sports pavilion. The door was wide open so I walked inside, to view a scene I could never have imagined to discover. For your readers could surely never guess, Mr Editor, as to what shocking sight awaited me when I peered through into the medical room set aside for those needing recuperation from injuries sustained on the field of play.

There, as bold as brass, standing in an amorous entwinement was Lucy Lapwing, the daughter of our local vicar, as naked as the day she entered this world in the arms of our captain of athletics, Colin Vernon-Smith, who too was nude except for a brief pair of running shorts. My hand flew to my mouth as I stood silently at the doorway. The young couple were oblivious to my presence, being so engrossed in their kissing and cuddling that they would have hardly heard the arrival of the Bengal Lancers!

I regained my composure and my first thought was to announce my arrival – but then, I reasoned, Lucy and Colin hardly wished to be interrupted and if their love-making was to be perhaps less private than they would have wished, they should have taken the simple precaution of bolting the door. So I stayed silent, enjoying the erotic tableau that was unfolding just eight feet or so in front of me.

Lucy was a tall girl blessed with long tresses of auburn hair, with a pretty face, set off by dark eyebrows and long dark eyelashes with richly pouting cherry lips and a brilliant set of pearly white teeth. Her body too was the very epitome of female pulchritude, with swelling young breasts that jutted out proudly, capped with large tawny nipples set in their circled aureoles below which lay a lovely whiteness of belly, itelf set off by a bush of silky auburn hair between her legs through which I could just make out the outline of her slit. Lucy's blood was up for her eyes were bright with passion and her nostrils flared out as she let her hand fall to stroke the huge bulge between Colin's legs which showed that his sporting equipment looked to be in the best working order! She gave the bulge an encouraging rub with her palm and this had the desired effect of setting a match to the tinder.

In a veritable flash, Colin pulled down his shorts and Lucy took hold of his thick prick with its enormous, uncapped red helmet which stood bolt upright against his flat stomach. She squeezed his rigid rod appreciatively and said: 'You've just run three miles round the grounds, so sit down on the couch and I'll ride a St George upon your big fat cock.' He obeyed her instruction and Lucy climbed onto his lap and slipped her knees along his muscular young thighs. She put one arm around his neck and felt for his cock with her hand, adjusting her position as she slipped his rock-hard tool between them, fitting it snugly into her pussey. When she was satisfied that she had inserted his shaft fully inside her cunney she hugged Colin tightly, kissing the corners of his mouth as she whispered: 'Push your prick inside me, there's a good boy – that's right, push up with your hips as I press down – you won't hurt me, don't worry, keep pushing!' She began to work her hips up and down, riding slowly but firmly on his erect shaft, letting it sink all the way into her engorged crack, holding it there until every last inch was completely engulfed as their pubic hairs matted together. Colin was hugely excited by this lascivious mode of fucking (in which he had not previously participated) and soon I saw him shudder as the love juice began to collect in his balls for the grand finale. Lucy ground her bottom down and round on his mighty cock and as she felt the lad begin to spend, she bounced quickly up and down on his glistening shaft as the sperm began to spurt out. 'I'm coming too, Colin, keep spunking, ah-re, ah-re, yes, yes, YES!' she screamed out as she, too, climaxed gloriously as he flooded her cunney with a copious emission of frothy white sperm.

Almost unknowingly, I had been rubbing my own pussey through the thin cotton material of my summer dress during this sensuous show, but I did not speak out as I quietly withdrew and left the pair to continue their love-making. I walked back to the school in a state of some agitation for the erotic performance had whetted my appetite. I was more than a little angry too, for though Lucy was also in her early twenties, she had obviously had no compunction in fucking with a boy at least three years younger than herself, whereas I had never dreamed of allowing this to happen, even though I had often yearned to experience the virile young pricks of the more handsome of the sixth form boys, all of whom would doubtless have been more than happy to oblige!

Now, in the normal course of events I would have simply walked straight back to my room – and in this case I would have wasted no time at all for I do have hidden in my bottom drawer one of Madame Nettleton's dildoes, purchased at Shackleton's Emporium in Tottenham Court Road on my last visit to London last April, and in my state of excitement at this time I would certainly have made use of this excellent godemiché.

However, as fate would have it, I realised that I had promised Papa that I would bring a bottle of Doctor Ounce's Golden Elixir into his study from the sanitorium as he was being troubled by an irritating summer cold. But when I reached the sanitorium I distinctly heard a rhythmic creaking of bedsprings. This was strange, for I knew that thankfully no pupil had reported sick during the previous few days. So I tiptoed to the door which I opened with care and there, for the second time, I was greeted by a sight of shocking sensuality! For lying on one of the beds, naked except for an athletics vest, was Peter Toddington of the History Sixth, a tall, slender boy who in one hand was holding a copy of your magazine, Mr Editor, whilst on the other was slowly frigging his standing prick, caressing his shaft until it stood in a fine state of erection.

I rubbed my eyes in disbelief. A wild thought struck me that Mrs Bickler, the new school cook, must have added some kind of stimulant to the porridge this morning as a practical joke. Equally quickly I dismissed the idea from my mind. Not only had Mrs Bickler entered our employment with the highest possible references – but what possible motive could she have to play such a prank which, if she were to be found out, would result in instant dismissal. Well, whatever was causing this wave of lewdness which was apparently coursing round the school, I decided that there was no earthly reason why I should not partake of the joys being offered . . . but how best to take the plunge into this sea of lubricity? How indeed?

Well, as the saying has it, nothing ventured, nothing gained so I quite simply entered the room without as much as a by-your-leave and closed the door sharply behind me, making poor Peter leap down from the bed with a look of abject fright on his face. The magazine slid to the floor as he hastily attempted to hide his erect cock and balls in his hands.

'Don't fret, there's nothing to worry about,' I exclaimed hastily as I did not want to alarm this good-looking young man. I hastened towards him and pulled

his hands away from between his legs and took hold myself of his naked, red-knobbed cock which stood in all its manly glory, as stiff and hard as marble with the hot blood looking ready to burst from its distended blue veins. He blushed and cleared his throat but I put my finger to his lips and said: 'Now you don't have to say a word. It is quite natural to want to frig yourself when you read such an exciting publication as the one lying at your feet. Would it surprise you to know that there isn't a boy at Loynes House with hair round his prick who wouldn't do exactly the same? No, the only thing you should be ashamed of is not closing the door and locking it – unless, of course, you were hoping to be disturbed!'

'Oh no, Miss Cora,' said the lad falteringly. 'I had no idea that the door was unlocked. I was just carried away by the photographs in my magazine. I do apologise most profusely and I hope that you will not report me to your father.'

'That depends,' I said with as much severity in my voice as I could muster, for I was desperate to take hold of Peter's lovely-looking young prick which was still standing at half mast and looked good enough to provide me with the excitement I craved.

'Depends on what, Miss Cora?' he asked nervously.

'On how many marks I award you on your ability to fuck,' I said unashamedly, unbuttoning my blouse and shrugging off the offending garment to expose the swell of my breasts to this sweet boy.

Peter caught his breath and he looked on with a mixture of delight and disbelief as I quickly stripped off the remainder of my clothes to stand naked in front of him. 'There is no need to be shy,' I murmured, taking his hand and placing it on my pink-tipped nipple which rose to the touch of his fingertip. Yet although his cock rose up back to its full, proud stiffness, my young man still held back. Was I losing my attraction? Was he perhaps attracted to members of his own sex – a phase most boys go through at his age but through which, thank goodness, the vast majority pass unscathed?

Suddenly, Mr Editor, I realised the obvious cause of his hesitation, which perhaps your readers have already guessed. Yes, of course, Peter must be a virgin! Now the question was how best to put him at ease . . .

I ruffled his hair with my hand and murmured: 'Peter, it is my turn to make an apology. I think this is the first opportunity you have had to make love to a girl. No, no, there is no need to deny it. After all, what opportunities have you had to do more than play with your prick? But now, you lucky boy, I will help you lose your unwanted virginity. Please, please, do not worry about anything – it would be grossly unfair to mark you like I said just now. Just do your best, which I am sure will be quite marvellous. And you can be sure that I will not be informing my Papa about anything that takes place here this afternoon!'

Gently pulling him to me, our bodies met and we kissed – he needed no instruction to put his tongue inside my mouth, and we stayed glued together as we fell upon the bed. I took hold of his swollen cock again and how exciting it looked with its foreskin pushed back because his purple knob had grown so large. I pulled down the foreskin even further and exposed his crown completely. It looked irresistible, already shining with pre-cum, and I took the tip of his helmet in my mouth and felt its heat on my tongue. Lingering on the tender underside with my lips, I took his balls in my other hand and gently scraped the hairy sack with my finger-nails. My pussey was now already damp as I continued to massage his thick shaft, taking pleasure in how his helmet swelled up as I drew back his foreskin along the shaft. I could see that he was more than ready to cross the Rubicon, so I reached down to guide his throbbing cock into me as I lay on my back, and he thrilled to his first experience of having his tool enter that slippery pathway to bliss. His huge knob slid inside me and I spread my legs well apart to enable him to push further downwards. He trembled, overcome with the emotion of putting his prick inside his first pussey, and he lay motionless for a moment.

'There, that's nicer than pulling your own prick, isn't it?'

'It's wonderful, Miss Cora, and it's what I have yearned for since I was thirteen. But, to be quite honest, I'm not too sure about what to do next.'

With difficulty I suppressed a giggle and said, 'All you have to do is to push your darling prick in and out. You'll soon feel the spunk rushing up from your balls, but don't worry, you can shoot inside me today as I will have my monthlies tomorrow or the next day at the latest, and you will do me no harm.' My hands slipped down to clasp his firm young bum cheeks. 'Come on, Peter, I know you can do it,' I said encouragingly, delighted at being the first girl ever to receive his prick's liquid libation. He needed no further urging as his arms went under my shoulders and, as his pelvis jabbed down, I eagerly lifted my hips to welcome his thrusting tool which slid so slickly in and out of my cunney. Well, what Peter lacked in experience, he cer-

tainly made up for in enthusiasm, bouncing merrily up and down as I clutched his jerking bottom and heaved myself upwards, doing my best to pull him even deeper inside me.

Peter plunged deeper and deeper and the excitement of his shaft being caressed by the slippery membranes of my cunney proved too much for him and his cock suddenly popped out of me and slid wildly across my pussey as it spurted a jet of creamy sperm all over my pussey hair and belly. I rubbed his shaft to milk the last drops of white froth and happily his cock stayed stiff in my hand. I gave him some time to recover and told the young scamp how well he had fucked me. 'But this time, let yourself go, Peter. You have now fucked your first girl, so now that you know you are capable, you do not have to worry about anything except enjoying yourself,' I assured him.

This time I did not need to guide his prick for he took hold of it himself and pushed his gleaming knob between my squishy cunney lips. Heavens, how his thick cock pounded in and out of my pussey with the speed and power one would expect of a fit young lad of not quite seventeen years. This time, as soon as he had finished his initial phase of fucking, I told him to rest with his cock fully inside my cunt. Directly every inch of this monster shaft was ensconced in my cunney I closed my thighs, making the handsome boy open his own legs and lie astride me, his prick trapped sweetly inside my pussey. What a deliciously lewd sensation for us both!

Peter could not move his cock forwards or backwards as the muscles of my cunney were gripping his shaft so tightly and, to add to our pleasure, I ground my hips round, massaging his shaft as it throbbed powerfully in my juicy love-channel which was now dribbling our juices in little rivulets down my thighs. He took hold of my bum cheeks and I eased the tender trap to allow his pulsing cock to move and he began to drive wildly in and out, again fucking at a truly incredible rate of knots. 'Oh, what a gorgeous fuck!' I panted as, with insatiable desire, I wrapped my legs around his shoulders and quivered in anticipation of a crescendo of luscious orgasms. As my clitty hovered on the brink of a spend I felt Peter's body go rigid and he moaned loudly as his stiff, jerking cock shot massive spurts of hot love juice inside me. I pushed my pussey hard up against him and just let all that wonderful white froth bathe the inner walls of my cunney until my whole body glowed with an intensity of sensuous joy.

We lay still and Peter then slowly pulled out his now shrunken cock. 'Was that all right?' he asked anxiously. I gave him a big smile and answered quite truthfully that I had enjoyed myself immensely.

'If you reach a standard in your academic studies similar to your abilities in the art of fucking, you may well gain entrance to Oxford University,' I said truthfully, which pleased my young lover immensely.

Now, believe it or believe it not, but as I gave his prick what I imagined would be one last farewell stroke, his shaft began to swell again! Surely he could not rise to the occasion for a third bout! However, his cock was already more than half way up to a full erection when he said: 'Miss Cora, please do not think me selfish, but in the Sixth Form common room I overheard Wingate tell Hutchinson that having one's prick sucked was perhaps even nicer than fucking.'

'Y-e-e-s-s, maybe so, although not having a cock myself hardly gives me the right to judge whether that statement is true or false. Mind, I assure you that as pleasurable as it can be to have one's cunney sucked, I do feel that fucking is just that much better.

'But from the look in your eye and the stiffness of your cock I would imagine that you would like to make this judgement for yourself.'

'I would simply love to find out for myself,' agreed the young rascal who, emboldened by our previous intimacies, took my hand and pressed my fingers firmly around his engorged staff.

I took my hand away for I did not want him to spend too soon, and we locked ourselves into a lingering, erotic kiss. I then kissed him all over until my lips found their way to the tip of his lovely long shaft.

Then I took the smooth dome between my lips, jamming down his foreskin and lashing my tongue around the now rigid shaft. I sucked hard, taking at least a third of his hot shaft into my mouth whilst I played with his hairy ballsack. Peter moaned softly as I drew my wet tongue from his balls right along the shaft up to the little 'eye' on the gleaming red-mushroomed dome. He clutched at my hair as I circled my tongue all around the flesh of the uncapped helmet, paying particular attention to the ultra-sensitive ridge.

I paused for a moment and, looking up to the lad whose eyes were shut in an ecstasy of erotic enjoyment, I said: 'Well, have you made up your mind what you prefer – fucking or sucking?' He groaned for an answer and pushed my head back towards his throbbing tool. So I took hold of the pulsating shaft again and sucked up as much of this thick sweetmeat as I could. He was close to spending so I bobbed my head up and down, slurping noisily on the twitching flesh which, as I thought, very soon exploded jets of frothy spunk into my mouth. Greedily I swallowed every tangy drop of his copious emission before his truncheon began to shrink back to limpness.

Now, Mr Editor, this stimulating tryst has remained secret from my parents and I know that Peter has never spoken of what happened that afternoon to anyone. But I must confess that I enjoyed teaching the joys of sex so much that since then I have taken the virginities of three further youths from the Fifth Form. I think I am now sated as far as younger lovers are concerned, but do you think any harm has been done?

Bob Goggin expelled a deep breath and muttered: 'The only harm done is that there will be some very jealous Fifth Form lads if it ever comes out that the Headmaster's daughter was offering a special private course to a chosen few.

'But wait! What did Doctor Jonathan advise?'

Bob turned the page to find out what the dirty doctor prescribed for Cora: 'No harm has been done whatsoever, and the lads lucky enough to have been tutored by you in *l'arte de faire l'amour* were fortunate indeed to have such a wise and caring teacher. You are part of a time-honoured tradition of the older girl who initiates younger boys into the joys of intimacies.

'However, whilst the experiences have been enjoyable for all concerned, enough is enough and whilst it may be that with boys younger than yourself you feel more in control, generally speaking it bodes better for a relationship if you are sexually involved with someone of your own age or older who is as sexually competent as yourself.'

Bob nodded his agreement with Doctor Jonathan and smiled wryly as he remembered his own rites of passage, accomplished rather uncomfortably with a kitchen maid in a broom cupboard not all that many years ago. Bob wriggled uncomfortably, for the erotic magazine he had been reading had naturally affected his prick which was threatening to burst out of the confines of his trousers. So he took three or four deep breaths, exhaling slowly as he climbed to his feet. As he took up his sketchpad to continue his work, the Professor suddenly stirred and stretched out his arms. 'Ah, there's little to equal a nice nap, is there? Now then, let me see what you have accomplished while I have been in the Land of Nod.'

Bob blushed and said: 'I'm afraid that I haven't actually done anything at all except read your copy of *The Oyster*.'

'Ha! Ha! Ha! No wonder you were diverted from your work, Bob,' chuckled Professor Eames. 'But I do hope that you were not offended by its explicit contents.'

'No, not at all, I found it both entertaining and instructive, although it has put drawing completely out of my brain.'

'Never mind, young man,' said Graham Eames heartily. 'Look, my motor car is about half an hour's walk away in South Platts. Let's take a brisk stroll there and go on to Treyford for luncheon.

'Now don't be shy – like yourself I am dressed for a ramble in the countryside and I assure you that my sister Geraldine keeps a most friendly and informal home.'

A more retiring man than Bob Goggin may well have refused the invitation, but our young hero was blessed with a spirit of adventure and he needed no further cajoling to accept the invitation. They climbed Telegraph Hill, the site of one of the old semaphore stations, and stopped a while to take in the picturesque landscape that stretched in all directions – to the north, the pleasant Weald; to the east, unending Downs, rolling beyond Beacon Hill. As Graham Eames commented, they could not have wished for a better time to view the scene as the panorama was now at its best, when a September sun was shining brightly through a cloudy sky, for the plain is then lighted in patches of sunlight and patches of shade that meld so beautifully with the patchwork effect of the cultivated farmland fields.

The two men enjoyed their exercise, but both were glad to reach the Professor's motor vehicle for both had been tired by the walk and longed to rest their feet. As has been noted, this was to be Bob's first ride in a horseless carriage, a fact he mentioned to his companion as they meandered along the winding land towards Treyford.

'It won't be your last,' said Graham, slowing down to give two equestrians a wide berth, 'And I will wager that in a very few years horses will generally only be ridden for sport. The internal combustion engine will drive them all off the highways, mark my words.'

As it turned out, the modern forms of transport dominated the pre-luncheon conversation at the home of Timothy and Geraldine Wendover after Graham

Eames had effected the necessary introductions. His sister was a gracious hostess and took pains to make Bob feel at home. Neither she nor her husband were at all bothered about Bob's lack of social standing – indeed, both were deeply involved in radical politics and were friends of the likes of Lloyd George and Ramsay MacDonald. With her husband's blessing, Geraldine spent much of her time campaigning for Mrs Pankhurst's militant Suffragette Movement which was calling for the immediate introduction of votes for women.

But as Bob sipped at his whisky and soda, he was only half listening to the talk around him for he could hardly take his eyes off Timothy Wendover's beautiful niece, Sarah, who, announced her uncle, had only the day before yesterday celebrated her eighteenth birthday. What a stunner, thought Bob as he watched the tall, willowy girl move gracefully across the room to ask the butler for a glass of orange juice. He could hardly tear his gaze from her pert, pretty face and bright brown eyes that matched her long, exquisitely soft hair that fell down in ringlets almost to her shoulders. Although coltish in figure, she appeared to be amply endowed with high, rounded breasts. Bob's lascivious thoughts were suddenly interrupted – fortunately perhaps as his prick had already begun to stir – by Geraldine Wendover who said: 'And so what are your views, Mr Goggin? Do you think we need lay down fresh regulations to keep both the drivers of horses and motor vehicles happy?'

'I'm hardly qualified to speak on the subject, Mrs Wendover,' he stammered.

'Oh, don't let that stop you. Why, such a caveat has

never prevented my brother opening his mouth on any matter you can think of!' she laughed.

'That's quite unfair,' protested Graham as the company joined in the merriment. 'Though it so happens this is a vexed question which I cannot see being easily resolved. Maybe if every motorist was as thoughtful as he should be towards those who still prefer to drive horses, perhaps in time the animals would take as little notice of motor cars as they do of bicycles. But I fear that even in the hands of the most skilled coachmen, it will be many years before the horse will stop shying away from any vehicle that is travelling at a speed over twenty miles an hour.'

'I'm afraid you are right,' said his sister. 'Even though my own mare is of a placid temperament, she still objects to the few cars we see here in the heart of the country. I do not think that even the most patient coaxing could ever make her reliable in town. So will we be forced to ban horses from our highways?'

'It won't come to that,' responded Graham. 'Before long, motor vehicles will become the standard means of conveyance and they will be produced so that the travellers can arrive at their destination in the same state of cleanliness as if they had been for an old-fashioned carriage drive.'

'Do you really think so?' said Sarah, entering the conversation for the first time. 'I hate the horrid things, although I admit that it is exciting to travel at speed along the open road.'

'You obviously take after your father,' grinned Graham. 'Why, I've been a passenger in his car when we must have touched fifty miles an hour up at your estate in Buckinghamshire.'

Mrs Wendover leaned forward to confide in Bob. 'Sarah's father is the sportsman, Sir Norman Stevenage. You may have read of his various achievements in the illustrated newspapers.'

'He's quite a chap,' said Bob with genuine admiration. 'Didn't he come third in the Grand National steeplechase a couple of years back, and then went on to play cricket for England?'

'That's the man – but he has retired from all sports now except golf, and now he is besotted by the motor car. He is arranging a race of British, German and French cars next month along a special circular track Lord Wane is having built near Guildford,' said Mr Wendover.

'Now if you are all ready, come outside on to the patio where Mrs Critchley has prepared an *al fresco* buffet for us. Isn't it delightful to be able to eat out of doors in September?' he added.

Lucky Bob found himself next to the divine Sarah. He found the sweet girl a delightful luncheon companion and they chatted animatedly about horticulture, for it turned out that Sarah was a keen amateur gardener. Bob tried hard to keep his eyes from wandering over her delicious breasts which were covered only by a frilly lace blouse and appeared to be far larger than one would have expected in such a slim, lithe figure. So he tried to stop his attention from straying from the conversation about the difficulties of growing raspberries, although he could not prevent himself thinking how much happier he would have been sucking her rosy titties than eating a plate of that succulent fruit.

After coffee had been served, Mrs Wendover suggested that after a rest, perhaps her guests would like to play tennis. Graham Eames accepted her husband's challenge to a game but Sarah turned to Bob and said quietly: 'I'd rather take a walk in the woods.'

'So would I,' said Bob gratefully. 'I've never played tennis before and I'd much rather not show myself up on the court.'

Sarah giggled and took hold of his hand. 'Come on, let's walk off our meal now whilst the weather remains so fine. Aunt Geraldine, Bob and I are going to take a constitutional around Linehead Wood.'

'Jolly good,' said her uncle. 'Don't be too long, though, as your aunt has invited Colonel Grosvenor and Miss Hennessey over for tea and I'd appreciate it if you made an appearance.'

'We'll be back in good time, Uncle Timothy,' promised Sarah as she led Bob through the garden. Once they were out of the back gate and on their way to Linehead Wood she said: 'Oh, it's so nice to talk to somebody of around my own age. My aunt and uncle are charming people but I'm not all that interested in political affairs and though the neighbours they have invited over for tea are also very nice, I do get bored occasionally.'

'Why, for how long are you staying here?' asked Bob, boldly taking her hand in his as they strolled slowly along the dusty track.

'Just for a fortnight whilst my parents are abroad with my young brother visiting some old friends who live in France. I'm going back home when they come back next Tuesday.'

They walked on unhurriedly through the beautiful woods of Linehead. The afternoon was warm and calm, the foliage soft with mellow sunlight and the trees were red and rusty with early autumnal tints. In the woods the beeches were inclining to russet; an elm or two was bright in green and gold and a crisp carpet of brown leaves, whose fall had not as yet left the branches bare, crackled pleasantly under their feet.

After a while they paused and sat down in a leafy aisle, leaning against a dry hillock of earth, and suddenly Sarah whispered: 'Bob, dear, there is something troubling me. If I confide in you, will you promise never to reveal what I say to a living soul?'

Bob's heart beat a little faster as he gallantly replied: 'Of course! I would never betray a confidence.'

The pretty girl wriggled deliciously and lowered her head. 'I believe you, Bob, you look like a kind man and I know that you won't break your word.

'Well, the truth of the matter is that one of the reasons I am so out of sorts here is that my boy friend, Andrew, cannot visit me. He is studying for the Bar and unfortunately he performed so poorly in his examinations that he will have to resit them in December. So his father has insisted that he studies throughout September with a private tutor in London, and Andrew has to go home every weekend to his parents as they say that he spends too much time with me instead of with his law books. And I'm afraid to say that they are probably right!'

Bob tut-tutted sympathetically. 'I say, that does sound like bad news, Sarah. What a rotten summer you must be having.'

She nodded her head. 'Yes, I miss Andrew and it isn't as if I have anyone else to be with, so to speak.'

'To be absolutely honest with you, dear Bob,' she

added shyly. 'More than anything else I miss being fucked.'

Bob started. 'I beg your pardon, what did you say?'

This time she giggled. 'I thought that might surprise you. Why don't men realise that the female of the species also has needs and desires? I miss being fucked, Bob. There, I've said it again and I don't care a damn. It has been more than three weeks since I've had an opportunity to indulge myself in the joys of love-making and I can hardly tell you how randy I feel. At lunchtime I thought I noticed a bulge between your legs but now it seems to have vanished. Don't I appeal to you? Without wishing to sound immodest, I have often been told that I am very attractive to men.'

A look of concern flitted over her face. 'Bob, you are not a nancy boy, surely. I mean, you do like girls don't you?'

'I should say so,' said Bob hoarsely. 'I've had a hard-on almost since we met, but your words shocked me so much that I need a few moments to pull myself together.'

Sarah's tawny eyes gleamed and she said: 'I'll gladly help you as far as the pulling is concerned! Oh Bob, do you know I've been having the most intense erotic dreams! I'm sure I've actually climaxed in them as I wake up all hot and sweaty. Foolishly, I forgot to pack my dildo so I don't mind telling you that I'm almost at my wits' end!'

For a fleeting moment Bob thought of Penny Arkley, but when Sarah peeled off her blouse and revealed her bare breasts to him, the young man could simply not hold back and with a strangled cry he took the lovely girl in his arms and crushed her unresisting soft body against his own male hardness. He held her in his arms and gently pressed his lips against her. She responded immediately, her tongue forcing their lips apart, and they thrilled to an animal passion with the fire of pure lust destroying any lingering traces of shyness or fear. With a burning urgency they eagerly tore off their clothes and in no time at all were writhing naked in each other's arms.

Bob delighted in the wondrous feel of this passionate creature as her high pointed bare breasts swelled to his roving caresses and her nut-coloured nipples rose to erectness as he rubbed them against his hand. Sarah slipped her hand around his thick cockshaft and rubbed the straining staff which excited them both to boiling point.

'Fuck me, Bob,' she said softly, lying back with her long legs open as she sensuously let her hand stray into the silky brown fleece of hair that covered her cunney. In a trice Bob was on top of her and his bursting tool tasted the delights of her wet cunt. He drove deep against her belly and, clinging madly to each other, they groaned in ecstasy as Bob pumped fiercely in and out of her sopping crack. 'Faster, faster!' she panted, her love channel gripping his rampant prick which slicked its way in and out of her juicy pussey.

They writhed lasciviously together, groaning in mutual ecstasy as Bob's thrusting prick rasped up and down the cat's tongue roughness of her supple cunney walls. Sarah came first with a deep throaty cry of satisfaction as her whole body stiffened whilst the force of her orgasm raged through her. Yet very soon she was ready for more, her body arching up to receive

Bob's frantic pumping prick. She sank her nails into his back as her love channel squeezed deliciously around his throbbing shaft. With every thrust she counter-thrust until Bob felt the hot sperm boiling up inside his balls. He tried to hold back but nature could not be denied and he crashed powerful jets of milky spunk into her cunney as she moved her hips faster and faster.

'Oh, yes,' she gasped. 'Oh, I'm coming again, yes. Ohhh!' As she jerked into another frenzied spend, the thrilling feel of her exquisitely formed young body rocking to and fro caused Bob's cock to discharge further copious discharges of white cream, filling her crack to overflowing as with one final convulsive heave Sarah finally lay still, arms and legs splayed out and only her breasts quivering with the tremendous energy she had expended.

Bob slid his still semi-hard shaft out of her dripping pussey. Their combined juices were now dribbling down Sarah's legs and soaking into the moss on which she lay. They were both spent and exhausted and all seemed very still around them as they lay motionless, billing and cooing with delight as they rested their warm bodies tenderly together. There were at least two hours left before they would have to return to the Wendover household for tea, and Bob breathed slowly as if in a trance as he stared at the gorgeous girl who lay snuggled inside his arms. Her sheer animal loveliness was so intense that it seemed to shimmer in the sunlight. He kissed her high, proud breasts, marvelling at the rich red of her nipples and at the dark luxuriant fleece between her thighs. One last belated drop of spunk hung momentarily on the end of his knob before dropping to the ground as the lovers closed their eyes and ears to the world and slipped gratefully into the arms of Morpheus.

CHAPTER TWO

Dear reader, let us leave the young lovers to their sated slumbers and retrace the day as it had so far affected Sir Paul Arkley, Bt, Master of Arkley Hall and, as those of you who have followed previous adventures of this randy baronet [see *Cremorne Gardens*, Headline Books, London, 1990 – RM] will know, a gentleman who was extremely fond of fucking. Indeed, his friends at the exclusive Rawalpindi Club in London were often heard to remark that Sir Paul would poke anything in a skirt except a Scotsman, when Sir Paul was seen escorting yet another lady to his permanent *pied à terre* at the Club's sumptuous premises near Buckingham Palace [so very conveniently placed, we may note, for the Rawalpindi's Honorary President, His Royal Highness King Edward VII, who enjoyed the company of Mrs Keppel and other royal mistresses in the Club's discreet *salles privee* – RM]

Let us hasten to add that whilst somewhat envious of Sir Paul's sexual prowess – on one wild night he fucked the Club's cook, two chambermaids and Lady Olivia Scott-Wilson – the clubmen were generally tolerant of having their facilities used for this extra-mural activity. As Count Gewirtz of Galicia said to the Duke of Cambridge, who once complained of the noise emanating from Sir Paul's bedroom: 'We must allow special latitude in this case – why, at home the poor man is allowed his conjugal rights only twice a month at best. And I am reliably informed that Lady Arkley sips her tea and reads the newspaper whilst Paul is heaving away, so it's no wonder that the man looks elsewhere for passionate pleasures.'

As aforesaid, readers of earlier escapades will recall Sir Paul's sexual involvement with the saucy Charlotte, a wench who had relieved his prick of pints of spunk during the eighteen months she had stayed as a servant in the Arkleys' residence in Hyde Park Gardens. Alas, Charlotte had rightly decided that she was sitting on a fortune and resigned her position to chaperone lonely gentlemen in London for Mrs Messina's 'Employment' agency in Soho. So Sir Paul looked even more lasciviously than usual at the pert bum cheeks of Selina, the new second chambermaid at Arkley Hall, who was bending over not a yard away, busily sweeping away with a dustpan and brush. There could never be a better time to try his luck, he calculated, as the place was almost empty. His wife and daughters had left for London; his unexpected house guest Professor Eames had also departed; whilst even Bob Goggin, the under-gardener, had been given time off, leaving only Hamilton the butler and a skeleton staff at home to attend to his needs.

But would Selina be interested in some slap-and-tickle? There's only one way to find out, he decided and he reached out from the depths of his armchair and pinched the lovely bum cheeks that wriggled so invitingly in front of him.

'Oooh, Sir Paul! You naughty man!' she squealed in mock anger. 'How would you like it if I pinched your cock?'

The baronet's face brightened – obviously this fair little filly would gallop all the way to the winning post! 'I would raise no objection whatsoever, m'dear,' he rejoined, placing her palm on his swelling prick. Selina giggled saucily as her lusty employer cupped the firm swell of her fine young bosoms in his hands, before pulling open her blouse to uncover her naked breasts. 'That's nice, Sir, very nice indeed. Please allow me to return the favour,' purred the little minx, unbuttoning his trousers and taking out Sir Paul's sizeable shaft, cradling the twitching tool. Her silky stroking soon had his shaft as hard and erect as a truncheon.

With a throaty growl, Sir Paul Arkley ripped off his jacket and trousers, but as he began to pull down Selina's skirt, the cheeky maid wriggled out of his grasp and said: 'Now, now, Sir Paul, I would really love to have you fuck me but I hope you'll leave a little something under my pillow tonight for me to spend on my day off next Tuesday. And also, talking of spending, you mustn't come inside my pussey today. I'll suck you off if you like, or you may use the tradesmen's entrance. Is that understood?'

'Indeed it is, my proud beauty, and I will be extremely careful to accede to your wishes,' he promised. 'Let's go up to your bedroom and take off the rest of these damned clothes.'

In no time at all Selina was stretched out in all her glorious nudity upon her bed, her legs invitingly open whilst the equally naked Sir Paul clambered up between her knees to pay homage to her pretty little pussey which was covered in a sweet little growth of fine, fairish hair from which the cunney lips protruded in all their erotic splendour. He leaned forward to kiss the pink pouting lips of her crack and worked his mouth all around her bush, inhaling the pungent female aroma as he licked all around her pubic bush, sending Selina into a frenzy of desire as lovingly he continued to eat her, forcing his tongue deeper and deeper into the warm wet pit.

'A-h-r-e, that's wonderful! Now suck my clitty, there's a good boy,' she begged, as she pulled her inner thighs further apart. Her cunney was already wet and he slipped first one, then two and finally three agile fingers in and out of her dripping pussey. He replaced his fingers with his mouth and he felt his own excitement mount with hers as his tongue flicked and stroked around her cunney lips. He licked around her erect clitty that was now bursting from its hood and stood up like a tiny little cock. Her hands pulled his head closer to her as he grasped her delicious buttocks and lapped all around her juicy wetness. He slurped noisily as he nipped her little clitty playfully with his teeth and she slid her hands through his hair, urging him on as he tasted the sweetness of her love juices that were now freely running from her dripping crack. Selina's hips and bottom now moved in synchronised rhythm with his mouth and tongue and suddenly her body stiffened and she cried out with joy as she spent profusely, her juices drenching Sir Paul's moustache as he continued to frig her clitty with his tongue until she climbed down from the summit of pleasure.

The baronet straightened up and knelt in front of

her. His thick, gnarled cock stood out large and hard, nudging between her smooth thighs. She reached out and pulled it towards her as she sat up and opened her mouth, easing his purple-domed knob between her rosy red lips. With one hand she grabbed his hairy arse and with the other she massaged his soft ballsack as she sucked lustily on the red, throbbing shaft that was now firmly jammed in her mouth. She first teased his smooth rubicund knob, running the tip of her tongue around the ridges of the springy cap whilst gently manipulating his balls through the soft wrinkled skin of their bags.

The girl gave a grunt of satisfaction as he began to thrust his gleaming wet shaft in and out between her lips. With surprising dexterity she managed to position her tongue so that as he pushed forward his helmet, she washed it all around his crown. The exquisite sensation was simply too much for Sir Paul and he groaned with a mixture of both frustration and delight as he felt himself fast approaching the supreme summit of pleasure. His prick began to twitch and tremble and the moment of truth was but seconds away . . . Selina jammed her lips as tightly as possible over her fat sausage of cock as the first spurts of salty spunk crashed into her mouth, which was immediately filled with the lovely gushing foam as his cock bucked uncontrollably as she lightly held it between her teeth. Sir Paul's face contorted with effort as his massive cock continued to hurtle his cream into Selina's mouth which she gulped down greedily, milking the last drops of spunk from his gushing prick until he fell back, exhausted from the invigorating exercise.

'Oooh, your spunk is really tasty, Sir Paul,' said

Selina brightly, as she rolled over onto her tummy, to present the panting baronet with a bird's eye view of the fleshy *rondeurs* of her delicious young buttocks. 'As soon as you have recovered, you may fuck my bottom if the fancy takes you.'

'I'll need a little assistance to start me off,' confessed her Master. 'Perhaps you would be good enough to give me a helping hand?'

For reply she took hold of his limp shaft in her hands and bent her head down until it rested on his thigh. She looked across at the sad little shrunken member and permitted herself a tiny smile. 'This cock is a suitable case for treatment,' she declared, curling her fingers around the shaft and rubbing her hand sensuously up and down it, drawing back his foreskin and capping and uncapping his now swelling purple knob.

She continued to rub his prick briskly, murmuring lewdly: 'Come now, Mr Pego, let me see you rise up stiffly again. I want to feel your helmet pressing its way between my bottom cheeks and then for you to shoot a nice thick pressing of juice up my bum!'

This vigorous frigging produced the desired effect and soon Sir Paul's meaty cock was jutting out like an arrow ready to fly. Selina chuckled as she scrambled round the bed and knelt forward, presenting the delectable white globes of her rounded bottom cheeks. The baronet massaged those marvellous mounds with his big hands and then his eyes alighted on a pot of cold cream on the bedside table. 'Ah-ha, that's just the ticket,' he murmured happily, dipping a hand in the jar and smearing the white lubricating cream all around and inside Selina's rear dimple.

He stroked his pulsating prick and then took hold

of the sturdy weapon which was pressing against her. Gently but firmly, he then proceeded to guide his glowing knob between her bum cheeks which were waiting to be split. He pushed forward and had little difficulty easing his uncapped helmet into her wrinkled little bum-hole. He continued to push forward and his veiny stalk was soon enveloped between the in-rolling cheeks of that lovely backside and completely sucked up inside her. Once he was fully inside her arse, Sir Paul began to work himself in and out of the tightly clinging orifice, pushing his whole body forwards and backwards, making her bum cheeks slap loudly against his belly as they now moved in sensuous rhythm. His thick prick was now fully ensconced in her back passage and their motions became ever more frenzied as the girl appeared to suck even his swinging balls into the dark depths of her *derrière*.

'What a great bum fuck!' he yelled as Selina wriggled to and fro, opening and closing, clenching and unclenching those snowy white buttocks. Sir Paul leaned forward to fondle and clasp her lush breasts and erect titties. As she waggled her bottom she turned her head and there was no doubt of her total enjoyment of having the stiff cock pounding in and out of her bum. He continued to slew his staff in and out of her juicy hole until, with a hoarse shout of 'I'm going to spend,' he flooded her arse with spunk as they shuddered to a glorious mutual climax, falling forwards together in a heap of tangled limbs.

Selina pulled her bum away from her employer's shivelling shaft and both would have preferred to stay in her bedroom fucking and sucking the day away, but Sir Paul suddenly remembered that he was expecting a visitor for luncheon, the distinguished Spanish lawyer and travellor Senõr Antonio Ribalta. This gentleman was an old friend of Sir Paul, who was, as perhaps we should have noted before now, himself involved in legal affairs, being amongst the most senior officials in the office of the Lord Chancellor.

So the lewd couple dressed themselves and Sir Paul reiterated his promise to slip a five pound note under the pillow of Selina's bed later that day – he was not an ungenerous chap and, as Selina knew from the gossip in the servants' hall, was also known to be very much a man of his word. The pert young parlourmaid returned to finish her chores whilst Sir Paul wandered into the library to pour himself a small schooner of sherry whilst he waited for the arrival of his guest. He sat quietly in his favourite chair and was about to raise the glass to his lips when the edge of a piece of writing paper wedged between two books on the sideboard caught his eye.

What was this curious paper? Sir Paul set down his glass and pulled out not one, but three sheets of paper that were nestling between *David Copperfield* and *Great Expectations*, two volumes from his expensive leather-bound set of the works of Charles Dickens. He noticed that, most unusually, the papers were covered in type-script. Well, despite this, it hardly needed Sherlock Holmes to discover who the author might be, for only his eldest daughter Katie possessed one of these new-fangled typewriters and, in any case, the lovely girl was the only person in the house who ever wanted to read any of Charles Dickens' novels!

It appeared, however, that he had stumbled not on a piece of correspondence from Katie, but a letter his daughter had received from her best friend Georgina Burnstine. At first Sir Paul was inclined simply to put back the letter from where it had been half-hidden from view – or perhaps, he thought, he should go upstairs and place the letter on Katie's dressing table, for she had probably left it in the library by mistake. But then a line of type caught his eye and he sat back muttering: 'Good god, I don't believe it! What are girls coming to these days!' He took a large swig of his sherry and, putting the three sheets in correct order, he read from first to last the letter sent by Georgina who, like Katie, was twenty-one years old and living with her parents. Let us look over his shoulder, dear reader, at the contents of this rather personal missive:

Dear Katie,

As you know I have been marooned in the wilds of Buckinghamshire for six whole days now. I thought I would die of boredom but fortunately my parents entertained a house guest last night, the American military attaché Lieutenant Colonel Frederick Nolan, and my ennui was shattered in a most delightful way by this gallant gentleman.

I should say at the start that Frederick is more than twice my age and is by far the oldest man I have ever encountered with regard to l'arte de faire l'amour. *Mind, this experience now leads me to give support to our mutual friend Hilary Holmes who has often told us that, in her book, the best tunes are played by older fiddles! Anyhow, I am sure you are eager to know all the details of last night and I am just as eager to furnish them to you!*

Only Papa, Mama, Frederick and myself sat down to dine. Perhaps it was the Aragosta Siciliana *– lobster grilled with parmesan and a touch of Sambucco – prepared by Signora Bertolucci together with the vintage champagne that we consumed so liberally that set off the scenario that was about to follow . . .*

To cut short the story, Papa and Mama retired to bed whilst Frederick and I decided to take a stroll around the grounds as the night air was still pleasantly warm and we both felt we needed some exercise after our heavy meal. Now Frederick is very well-connected and is a self-confessed shameless gossip. He regaled me with many amusing stories about Sir Terence Whitley, Lord Arthur Pine and other dashing young men around town. I laughed heartily at Frederick's witty tales which I must confess I only recall somewhat hazily. But I do remember that when we reached the stables he said: 'And so, Georgina, that was my week and you're welcome to it!'

And I also remember with complete clarity that as Frederick turned to walk back to the house he was unfortunate enough to place his foot in some very fresh evidence of a horse having recently passed by. He executed a wild ballet – complete with the utterance of a suitable oath for which, in the circumstances, he could hardly be reproached – before falling heavily to the ground. He attempted to rise to his feet but alas, his right ankle had been badly twisted. He crawled for a yard or two and then I assisted him to his feet. He could walk only with extreme difficulty and, as fate would have it, the wind began to freshen appreciably and a cold gust sent a shower of leaves scurrying around us.

'I think your ankle is swollen and it would be best if

you rested awhile before we make our way back to the house,' I said. He grimaced with pain and said: 'Georgina, I'm afraid you're right. Can you just help me inside the stables?' With one arm round my shoulders, he hobbled into the wooden building just as the first drops of rain pattered down upon us.

'I fear we are in for a summer squall,' he declared in his pleasant American drawl. 'So you are best to stay here until the storm passes over. It is fortunate that your father had the foresight to install electric light.'

I told him that the grooms often work after dusk and rather than risk a fire through negligent application of gas lamps, Papa decided to pay for this most modern and convenient form of lighting. 'Now what shall we do?' he asked, and I suddenly realised that here was the perfect opportunity to practise the technique of healing massage you may recall Madame de Montparnasse, the Chinese wife of the French painter, showed us at Sir Lional Trapes' soireé *last year. I explained to Frederick that he should remove his jacket and trousers and lie in the clean straw that had been thoughtfully piled up in a corner.*

Frederick looked somewhat dubious at this instruction but he complied, perhaps relieved to be able to divest himself of his trousers which were completely covered in manure. He lay back clad only in his shirt and drawers and I began to massage his leg as Madame de Montparnasse had shown us.

'You have healing hands,' said Frederick after about five minutes. 'Do you know, my ankle feels better already?'

'That is very pleasing to hear,' I replied. 'It is a simple technique to learn and in the East it is given regularly

by friends to each other to ease away aches and pains.

'They also say that it is a wonderful way to enhance friendships and get to know each other better,' I added, moving my hands to stroke Frederick's smooth inner thighs. His cock shot up against the waist-band of his drawers and I began to feel the first stirrings of passion . . .

Our mouths clamped together and his tongue thrust sinuously against mine as we rolled together in the straw. His hand strayed to my breasts, cupping them and stroking them whilst he ripped open my dress to expose their firm swell to his lustful gaze. I helped him to ease off my bodice which caused dear Frederick to pass his tongue lasciviously over his top lip.

Now his head was moving down towards my titties and I shuddered with desire as his wicked tongue curled over the hardening tip, his teeth dragging so tormentingly against the nipple that I gasped in an audible agony of need. My nipples have always been terribly sensitive and I started to juice down below as he continued to tweak my titties between his long, tapering fingers.

His hardened shaft rubbed against my leg and I reached down to pull down his drawers. And Goodness! My dear Katie! What an enormous cock sprung up to attention. It must have measured at least nine inches and was so thick that I could only fully grasp it if I used both my hands.

'What a truly magnificent prick you have been blessed with, Frederick,' I breathed. 'Tell me, are they all as big as this in California?'

'I really don't have a clue, Georgina,' he said honestly. 'But if you have no objections, I would prefer to declare exactly how I would love to fuck you.'

'Oh yes, that would be divine,' I said as clasping each other's buttocks, we pushed our bodies together, he thrusting his arse in little short jabs while I rotated mine in small circles. The uncapped mushroom knob of his cock pushed against my cunney lips causing a rapturous tremor to rotate from between my legs to my breasts, to my neck and shoulders and all over my body.

'I'm going to fuck you at the gallop, Georgie,' he began, 'And I'm going to cram my cock into your crack and pump my spunk inside you if the time of the month allows.'

'Yes! Yes! Yes!' I cried out. 'My cranney will suck your cock inside me and we'll come together in a glorious spend – so come on now, Frederick, I want action not words!'

He rolled me over on my back and I lay with my legs apart as, grasping his glistening cock he brought the huge head to my cunney lips. Now although I have sampled perhaps more than my fair share of pricks, I must tell you, Katie, that Frederick's massive weapon looked so formidably large that I was genuinely worried that I might not be able to accommodate this tremendous tool – surely it would split me in two! I spread my legs further as he pressed his tremendous tool forward and, of course, there was no problem at all. My own cunney juices assisted him as he gradually gained entry to my cunt. I was overwhelmed by this lustful sight and I reached down to diddle my clitty as slowly but surely every inch of this wonderful shaft was pressed inside my eager, sopping little sheath. Our groins touched, pressed together, our strands of pubic hair entangling as for a moment he lay quite still.

He whispered: 'I'm fully in you, every inch of me –

all the way. And now I'm going to fuck you, my English rose.'

'Go on, Yankee Doodle, fuck my arse off if you can!' I retorted saucily.

I wrapped my legs over his round, tight arse as he eased his super shaft in and out and we began a leisurely movement together, lingering over each sensation. I lifted my pelvis to meet him and then he started to fuck me in earnest, fucking me quite beautifully as his cock slurped in and out of my cunt, making that unique squelching sound as my juices freely flowed out of my excited pussey. His rock-hard rod slammed in and out of my cunney and we wriggled around until we were both set for some truly wild fucking. Frederick started to pump faster and faster, his big balls banging against my bum cheeks as he pounded that proud prick in and out of me again and again as I squealed with delight. My pussey pulsed furiously around this colossal column as we fucked away in perfect rhythm.

'What a truly great fuck,' I panted, 'but I'm almost ready to spend, Frederick, so you can spend whenever you want.'

'I'm ready to give you my spunk now. Watch out, Georgie, here it comes!'

As his huge cock began to tremble I felt the first tiny spasms and then whoosh! I screamed with joy as spasm after spasm of hot love juice filled my pussey and my own climax arrived almost immediately as my saturated slit sent shudders of delicious delight throughout my frame.

But Frederick Nolan was not yet finished and suddenly I felt a further hot gust of spunk in my cunney as the handsome American shot a second jet of frothy love juice inside me. What a man! What a cock! I do believe that he could have brought his mighty weapon up to attention for yet another joust, but the rain had stopped and if we had stayed later, my parents might have sent out a servant to look for us . . .

Later that evening Frederick crept into my room and we spent most of the night sucking and fucking to our mutual pleasure. Incidentally, Frederick's ankle was much better in the morning and only a large bruise advertised the accident which in fact turned out very well in the end, don't you agree?

I must close now, Katie. Do write back soon and tell me all about Walter Stanton, your handsome new lover. Is he a good fuck? As I heard my Aunt Clare say to Mama recently, a hard man is good to find.

All my love,
Georgina

Sir Paul Arkley laid down the letter and mopped his brow. Gad! Hector Burnstine was an old chum whom he had known since they shared rooms at Keble College, Oxford more than thirty years ago. How could he ever look his friend in the eye again without thinking of his pretty daughter who had obviously sampled the joys of lovemaking not once, not twice, but many times. And what of his own first-born, the lovely Katie? 'I'll horsewhip that scoundrel Stanton within an inch of his life,' he muttered, but then saner thoughts presented themselves to him. After all, what harm was being done? Katie was happy with Walter, of that he was sure, and Walter Stanton was a nice enough chap, so as long as they took any necessary sensible precautions against Katie getting in the family way, he could not in all conscience object to her enjoying a sexual liaison. 'And anyway, you're a fine one to pass judgement,' he muttered, thinking of the many pussies his prick had entered just over the past twelve months alone. So he took another large swig of sherry and picked up a copy of the morning newspaper to while away the time until his guest made his appearance.

He had only ten minutes to wait before the door was opened and Hamilton announced: 'Sẽnor Antonio Ribalta, Sir Paul.' He rose to greet the Spaniard and, as the swarthy, well-built Señor Ribalta entered, Sir Paul held out his arms and said: '*Buenas Dias, Antonio, mi amigo viejo, que tal?*

'*Gracias, soy muy bien*, and all the better for seeing you, my dear old friend. Let us talk in English as I have an appointment with your Lord Chief Justice tomorrow and as you may know, the old gentleman practically prides himself on the fact that he cannot converse in any other languages but English and Latin.'

'A typically British stance, I regret,' sighed Sir Paul who spoke Spanish and French fluently and could make himself understood in German and Italian. 'My countrymen are under the impression that all foreigners should speak English and to hell with those that cannot do so.'

'Yes, generally speaking, I am afraid that is the position. Now you have the greatest Empire in the world upon which the sun never sets, but in the future things may be very different and no longer, as the common man says, will wogs begin at Calais.'

[*Despite his well-founded criticism of the poor linguistic capabilities of the British and of their arrogant insularity, Señor Antonia Ribalta (1863–1937) was a true friend of Great Britain. He headed an intelligence net-*

work for the British Ambassador in Madrid during the Great War and was rewarded with an honorary knighthood from King George V in 1919. Although a wealthy landowner in Andalucia, he remained loyal to the legitimate Republican government during the Spanish Civil War. Together with his British-born wife, he was killed during fierce fighting three days after his seventy-fourth birthday – RM]

Sir Paul sighed as he handed a glass of sherry to his distinguished visitor. 'We haven't seen you for months, Antonio,' he complained. 'Have you been off to far and distant shores?'

The lawyer smiled and replied: 'I've been to the Canary Islands, Paul, to settle some fractious legal business. I hadn't been there before, even though my country owns the islands, and I must say I was most pleasantly surprised by the beauty of the place.'

'Did you go to Tenerife? Mrs Patrick Campbell stayed for a fortnight there a couple of years ago with General Godfrey as they wanted to get far away together where no-one would bother them, if you catch my drift.'

'Yes, I know all about that – you must have heard the tale going around the Rawalpindi Club that the General came back with a bandage around his prick where the divine lady had nipped his shaft with her teeth rather too enthusiastically. But in answer to your question, no, we steamed past Tenerife for my destination was Lanzarote.'

'Lanzarote, eh? Isn't that a volcanic island?' hazarded his host. 'Quite striking scenery to be enjoyed if I am not mistaken.'

'Yes, and a very beautiful place it is too – Lanzarote is an island of very great charm with a unique lunar-like landscape caused by the black volcanic ash which is distributed all over the island. But the soil is fertile and tomatoes, potatoes and onions are all grown there whilst there are even some vinyards, although the wine would hardly grace your cellar, my friend.

'The weather is almost always sunny but the cool sea breezes keep the temperature to what you would expect on a good day in June or July here in England. Anyhow, few visitors come to Lanzarote [*how times change*! – RM] except for the fortnightly call of French merchants and the monthly touching of Forwood's boats from London.'

'What exactly brought you there?' said Sir Paul, rising from his seat as Hamilton entered the room and announced that luncheon was ready to be served. 'Some legal affair, I think you said.'

'Yes, yes, my old friend, and perhaps after luncheon I will tell you the unexpected and extraordinary events in which I became involved there,' said Señor Ribalta with a smile.

The two men lunched sumptuously and after Hamilton had brought in the port and wheeled away the remains of their meal, Sir Paul and his guest settled down in two comfortable armchairs for a post-prandial rest. It was then that the Spaniard began to recount his fascinating story of sexual shinnanigans in the Canary Islands.

He began: 'I settled the contretemps between the two merchants' houses relatively easily – as you British say, a little give and take goes a long way in resolving any dispute. Unfortunately, saving face means a great deal to my people but once I had managed to find a formula that enabled honour to be satisfied on both sides, it was all plain sailing and we celebrated the settlement with a grand dinner at the house of the Governor of the island.

'And talking of sailing, this brings me nicely to the point of my tale. At this dinner, I sat next to Maria, the pretty eighteen-year-old daughter of the Mayor of Arrecife, the small town that serves as the island's capital. When she heard that my visit would be short, she offered to take me sailing around the coast of Lanzarote the next morning. I was more than happy to accept this kind invitation and we journeyed by horse and cart from her home along the road down to the fishing village of Puerto del Carmen.

'This was most enjoyable as Arrecife is built close to the sea, in the middle of a plain completely surrounded in the background by a semi-circle of low volcanoes. A road runs along close to the sea and owing to some recent beneficial rain, the plain was unusually green, though the mountains in the background were bare and rugged and trees were few and far between. We were in no hurry and the old grey mare between the shafts plodded happily along at a slow pace. As you know, I always travel with my camera, and I had my big Kodak, tripod and all the necessary equipment in the cart.

'I asked Maria if she minded if we stopped for a moment so that I might take some photographs of the view. "But of course," she said. "What a shame, though, that we have not yet invented cameras that can capture scenes in colour. After all, the scenery is so green just now, but soon it will all change to a parched brown for it may be months until we have some more rain."

' "What would happen if the rains fail?" I asked. "No matter," she replied. "Every house of any size has a large tank beneath the patio and all the cisterns are full of water. Mind, if we have a terribly dry year like 1877 we would have to rely on ships bringing in the precious fluid. That was a shocking time and several hundred people emigrated to Spain."

'How unfortunate to have to leave this beautiful island, I thought, as we pulled up some four kilometres out of town. I looked back and saw that I was well placed to capture the splendour of the eighteenth century Palace of Spinola.

'I set up all my apparatus and I have the results with me which I will show you later. If I say so myself, these are excellent photographs, full of interest.'

Here Antonio Ribalta paused and Sir Paul looked somewhat puzzled. 'Well, that all sounds very nice, Antonio, but I don't see what is so unusual about all that.'

'Ah ha, I am now coming to the crux of the matter,' said the Spaniard. 'Maria stood watching as I took my photographs and then out of the blue she said: "Would you like to photograph me, Señor?" "Of course," I said, little knowing what she had in mind. "I should have told you I was taking a camera for you could then have chosen a favourite dress."

' "Oh, that doesn't matter," she said carelessly. "I have many photographs when I have on all my finery. No, what I should like very much is you to photograph me in a classical pose. Look, we are only two hundred metres from the sea. You could set up your camera on the beach and photograph me as Venus rising from the waves." I was staggered at her precocious words – did she really want me to capture her beauty in what would surely be its glorious nudity?

'Maria must have read my mind for she added: "Surely I have not shocked you for I cannot believe that the sight of the naked female form is unknown to your eyes. Of course, if the idea offends you, please ignore my request and we will say no more about it."

' "The idea gives no offence at all," I said truthfully. In any case it would have been ungallant to say anything else, and besides, like yourself, I could never be accused of prudery! So I tied up the horse and Marie helped me carry my equipment down to the small pebbly beach. She disappeared behind some rocks to change whilst I set up my camera. In two minutes Maria came skipping happily towards me, completely nude, and I caught my breath at her sprightly beauty. She was well proportioned in leg and limb, with a graceful olive-skinned face and large black eyes, lips as red as cherries which when parted revealed gleaming, pearl-white, even teeth.

'Oh, my friend, she was a perfect specimen of celestial Spanish beauty. My heart began to beat faster and faster as she brushed the long tresses of dark hair from her face as her superb youthful breasts, standing partly upwards with their high-tipped, red-berried nipples, jounced up and down with the movement. her flat belly led down to long, long legs as sweetly shaped as any sculptor might have fashioned them, the calves and ankles slender and the thighs fulsome.

'And between those thighs nestled a dark mass of curls that frothed all about her mount and I could make out the shell-like lips of her cunney pouting out as I dived beneath the black cloth to adjust my lens. As you might imagine, the fit of my trousers also needed adjusting as my cock rose to salute this goddess of desire.

' "Shall I go into the sea straightaway?" she asked, striking a coquettish pose. "Or would you like to take some pictures of me beforehand?"

'Trembling, I adjusted the camera as she pushed up her pert breasts even higher, cupping the firm white globes in her hands. Then she was still as I clicked the shutter. But the saucy Maria was far from finished – I was held transfixed with my face underneath the cloth as she slid her hand lasciviously between her legs, letting her fingers slide across those pouting pussey lips that stood out inside their covering of silky black hair. I could see her slipping her index finger in and out of the now moist channel which opened as if by magic to her touch. She began dipping her fingers in and out, rubbing her thumb knuckle against her engorged little clitty which popped out at the top of her crack like a miniature penis. She began to pant as this sensuous frigging drove her to a self-induced ecstasy.

' "Well, don't just stand there!" she said breathlessly. "Have you no red blood in your veins or don't you find me attractive?"

'The question was unnecessary for the sight of this gorgeous creature had already sent my senses reeling. I ripped off my clothes and threw myself upon the lovely girl who sank down on the sand – which luckily was on a part of the beach free from pebbles – and covered her rich red lips with mine as we exchanged a burning, passionate kiss. Our tongues were flying around in each other's mouths as she guided my hands to her breasts and I squeezed her erect titties up to a grand stiffness. I trailed my hand downwards across her smooth belly to the glistening dark bush until I found her cunney lips and slid my finger between them, causing her to shudder with unslaked desire. I soon found her clitty and began to massage the ribbed flesh as she whispered to me that she wanted to be fucked.

'I was more than happy to oblige and I plunged my throbbing cock into her squelchy wetness as our bodies locked together. I fucked her vigorously with long, sweeping strokes, sliding my prick in and out of her now sopping cunney, pushing in with all my might so that my balls banged against her bum. Maria responded magnificently, joining my rhythm and managing to contract her vaginal muscles around my shaft, sending delightful pulses of pleasure all along my staff. I felt myself about to spend so I withdrew all but the knob of my cock which I teasingly slipped between her cunney lips, popping it in and out until with a moan, Maria threw her arms around me, pulling me deep inside her as I arched my lips forward so that our pubic hairs meshed together and every last millimetre of my cock was firmly embedded in her cunt.

' "Spunk your juice into me!" she screamed as her own climax was almost upon her. That was an easy command to obey for this frantic fucking had set the sperm boiling up in my balls and I was ready to spend. For a moment I held back until I felt her tremble in anticipation of her own spend. So I relaxed and, with a gasp, my body exploded into action and I shot spasm after spasm of love's liquid into her willing womb.

'I lay back exhausted but I was only given a minute

or so to recover! With a gay laugh, Maria straddled her legs over me with her back to my face. Then she leaned forward and pushed out the glowing cheeks of her shapely young backside which set my heart beating even faster with anticipation. I was not to be disappointed as I slipped my hand between her legs and fingered her sopping pussey as those velvet lips kissed my cock which somehow found the strength to rise up again to meet this sweet embrace. She began to jerk my shaft up and down in her hand, frigging me deliciously as she capped and uncapped my bulbous red helmet that was still liberally coated with our mingled love juices.

'Her moist tonguing brought my prick standing up to full erection as she licked and lapped around the sensitive knob. Then she opened her mouth wide and sucked in most of my cock, slurping with gusto in long satisfying bursts as her busy fingers gently stroked my balls. As I busied myself with running my hands up and down her back, she sucked thirstily on my swollen cock until I felt the first hot waves of spunk flood along my shaft to burst out into her waiting mouth. Swallowing quickly, she managed to milk my prick dry until, squeezing the last drops of cream from my knob, she carefully took my happy but exhausted member in the palm of her hand, watching with interest as it lay there, inching its way back to its normal sleeping state.'

'Gad, Antonio, you lucky fellow. I envy you, a good cocksucker is worth her weight in gold,' commented Sir Paul, trying hard to keep a note of envy out of his voice. 'Well, what happened next?'

'Well, we dressed and continued our journey. We made our way along the road for another kilometre and there I saw a sparkling white new dwelling gleaming in the sun. Although not large, the villa looked well cared for and Maria told me that it was owned by a Lebanese merchant, Sheik Babani of Beirut, who had it built some six years ago. "The Sheik is a strange fellow," Maria told me. "He does not venture very often from his house, which he visits only once a year, or travel around the island or even much into Arrecife but spends most of his time inside his house, being attended to by a bevy of servants who he brings with him. Actually, he arrived here ten days ago and I must say that I would love to meet him, though he keeps very much to himself."

'Just as she spoke, the front door opened and the Sheik came out to take the morning air. He was a handsome, dark-skinned man dressed in flowing, brightly coloured Oriental robes and although perhaps a shy fellow, he returned my wave of greeting. "Perhaps your wish is about to be granted," I said as we approached the dusky stranger.

' "*Buenos dias*," I called out. "*Habla usted Espanol*?"

"*Si, senor*," he replied, and Maria's face brightened for at least we would be able to conduct a civilised conversation in our own language.

'Well, the Sheik turned out to be a charming gentleman, well travelled and most cosmopolitan in his outlook. It turned out that we even had a friend in common, the famed Count Gewirtz of Galicia, whose special parties in Mayfair are renowned for *récherché* entertainment.'

Sir Paul coughed discreetly and said: 'That's true enough, I was fortunate to be invited to such a gathering earlier this year.' [*for full details of this wild party, see* Cremorne Gardens, *Headline Books, 1990 – RM*]

'Were you now?' said Señor Ribalta. 'You must tell me about it later. Anyhow, the Sheik asked Maria and myself to partake of morning coffee inside his home. And when he entered, I could immediately understand why he kept himself aloof from the many joys this sunny island could offer.

'Inside his villa, the main room downstairs was laid out in cool, white Carrera marble that the wealthy Lebanese merchant had ordered to be shipped in from Italy. The furniture was of the finest whilst painted on the walls were pictures of the most lascivious that nature could conceive, women in every variety of posture and position, nearly all of whom were represented in some mode or other of fucking. There was one picture that particularly caught my attention – a beautiful, dark-skinned girl is lying naked across the lap of an equally nude gentleman who looked the spitting image of our Oriental host. Her beautifully rounded bottom with its chubby globes is turned up to meet his amorous gaze and he is shown patting her cheeks. Meanwhile, in front of them, another dusky unclothed beauty is kneeling down in front of them, her hands holding his huge erect prick and her pink tongue just about to lick his purple-mushroomed knob.

' "That's a splendid picture," I commented as we passed it.

"I am so pleased you like it," the Sheik replied, clapping his hands as we sat down. And who came in bearing coffee cups on two silver trays but the two very same girls as depicted in the painting! They were dressed in white robes that set off their colouring quite exquisitely and the Sheik murmured: "These are my two companions, Leila and Ibzaidu. As you may have noticed, I use them for my models for as you see, I am a poor but enthusiastic painter."

' "You are an accomplished artist, Señor," said Maria, finding her voice. "But how did you manage to paint yourself into the scene?"

' "Very easily," he replied. "I have a good camera and I set the time exposure so I could photograph myself *in situ*. However, I must admit that I found the position so exciting that I first had to *shtupi shtupi* the girls before I could continue to pick up my palette and brushes."

' "I am hardly surprised, for they are two gorgeous Eastern beauties," I said. "You think so?" he replied. "If you wish they are yours. In my country, an honoured guest is enjoined to delight himself in whatever he so pleases." I looked at him with astonishment. "Please do not be shy," he insisted. "Your friend Count Gewirtz fucked Leila last year in Marseilles. She enjoys men immensely and it will be her pleasure as much as yours, I do assure you."

'I looked towards Maria, for it would hardly be good manners to fuck another girl so soon after tasting her sweet fruit, but the generous girl insisted that I should avail myself of this Eastern delight. "Do go ahead, Antonio," she begged. "So long as I may stay and watch the performance."

'So she and the Sheik reclined on the couch and he shouted out some instructions in Arabic. Moments later Leila reappeared, dressed this time only in the briefest of lace knickers (which I was later to understand had been purchased for such occasions by her master). Her luxuriant tresses of black hair fell over her shoulders as she danced her way towards me. Her slim, lithe body was now next to mine and, raising her head, she slipped her arms around my neck, gripping me tightly and pressing her lips to mine. Her tongue shot out, right down my throat and her slim, lithe brown body writhed in lascivious passion as my hands wandered across her velvety skin, cupping her firm young breasts which I then kissed, toying with them with my tongue and making the rose-coloured titties rise up to greet me.

'My kisses went lower and lower as, with trembling hands, I pulled down the silken covering which hid her soft little downy mount which was covered in a dark fleece of silky hair. Now on my knees, I kissed it and opened her legs and buried my face there, my tongue working furiously as I licked and lapped her dampening crack. Still in the kneeling position I parted her lightly scented pubic locks with my fingertips to reveal her swollen clitty. As I worked my face into the cleft between her thighs I could not help but drink in the delicious feminine aroma from her clean and appealing cunney.

'By this time I had arranged my head between her quivering legs, with one hand under her firm bottom for a little elevation and the other reaching round her thigh so I could spread her pussey lips with my thumb and forefinger. I placed my lips over her clitty and sucked it into my mouth where the tip of my tongue began to explore it from all directions and I could feel it swell as her legs twitched up and down along the side of my body. I let my teeth nibble gently over her clitty as my tongue teased her slit with long, rasping licks. This made her gyrate wildly though I kept her clasped firmly to me as I licked and lapped at her succulent cunt, and her now freely flowing juices drenched my face as I continued to play with her pussey.

'Leila shuddered to her climax and then she wriggled her way out of my embrace and helped me to my feet. It was her turn now to kneel as she unbuttoned my trousers and bared my straining prick which leaped out to greet her. With difficulty she took my knob in her mouth and I quivered all over as her tongue washed my helmet with her saliva. She did not touch me with her fingers but continued to run her tongue all around my crown as gradually she managed to get all of my shaft into her mouth, almost to her throat. Now she let her hands play with my balls as somehow she endeavoured to move her lips from the stem to the tip of my cock which I found so stimulating that I spent profusely, sending a torrent of spunk inside her mouth. She gulped down my spend and not until my prick had eased itself down into limpness did she withdraw her lips.

' "Come now, Antonio, you must fuck this poor girl. She deserves full satisfaction after sucking you off so superbly," scolded Maria. And of course, my friend, her rebuke was fully justified. Leila lay back on the carpet, her legs apart and her hands provocatively rubbing her dark-haired mount. My cock, however, still stayed limp and I told Maria that I was in need of help! So she kindly came over and, pulling down my foreskin, took the uncapped knob into her mouth and began to suck lustily upon it. This had the desired effect and my prick swelled up again as I hastily removed the rest of my clothes before joining Leila on the floor, slipping a finger into her soaking pussey and rubbing harder and harder until her little clitty turned as hard as a tiny cock at my touch.

'Then the fiery girl struggled to her feet and stood over me, her legs apart, straddling my body. Her teeth flashed in a lustful smile, her eyes twinkled and then she slowly began to lower herself upon me. Carefully, she opened her cunney lips as she slid downwards and my stiff shaft slid straight and deep inside her at the first attempt, and our pubic hairs were soon enjoined. Momentarily she paused, like a jockey testing a new mount, clamping her cunney muscles around my staff, testing me for size and girth, wondering maybe what pace to set, or how long I might last before I would shoot my seed right up into her.

'I flexed myself, willing my cock to recover, delighting in the exciting nipping of her love sheath. I jerked my hips upwards but she put a finger to my lips and the weight on my thighs left me in no doubt as to who was taking charge of this fuck – not that I was inclined in any way to argue.

'She pumped her tight little arse cheeks furiously up and down, digging her fingernails into my arms as she held on for dear life and started to ride me so voluptuously. Each shove was accompanied by a wail of ecstacy as the tip of my cock tickled her clitty, and I grabbed her breasts and brought the rosy tipped nipples down to my mouth to suck. She moved even more quickly under this extra stimulation as I aided her in her ride, pushing her up and letting her drop hard on my stiff shaft. Her head jerked up as my cock sunk into her love channel to the full extent. She pushed back her bottom cheeks and called out something in Arabic in the direction of the watching couple on the chaise longue.

'Out of the corner of my eye I saw the Sheik rise and pull off his robe. His large circumcised cock stood proudly upwards against his belly and he moved swiftly behind Leila. I distinctly felt the parting of her bum cheeks as Sheik Babani slipped his crimson knob between them and pushed forward. 'A-h-r-e! Ha-a-a-a-r!" cried Leila as the Sheik wriggled his cock slowly but surely into her wrinkled brown bottom-hole. His face was now laid sideways between her shoulder blades whilst, bit by bit, her bottom yielded its firm richness to his cock. She writhed and twisted so fiercely under this joint assault that I could hardly keep my prick inside her – but soon I could feel my staff rubbing against Sheik Babani's prick, for only the thin divisional membrane separated the two straining shafts.

' "Har-ah! *Ahchambya! Ahchambya*!" Leila cried out in triumph as our joint spendings deluged both her cunt and arse, and she too spent copiously, her tangy juices oiling my embedded cock and trickling down between us to lubricate my balls with the fragrant liquid of her spend. I felt her small white teeth nip my ear as she leaned forward to receive the double dosing of spunk in front and rear. Her hips squirmed in the final raptures before the Sheik withdrew from her bottom, his cock emerging with an audible plop as Leila slid across me, panting with exhaustion.'

Sir Paul Arkley expelled a deep breath and said enviously: 'I suppose that Maria and the other Arabic girl now joined in the fun. Some people have all the luck!'

Señor Ribalta chuckled and replied: 'No, no, Paul, my God, I don't think I could have fucked any more that morning if Mrs Keppel, Lily Langtry or the Duchess of Warwick [*three distinguished mistresses of King Edward VII – RM*] had entered the room stark naked! No, I dressed and Maria and I bade farewell and continued our walk down to Puerto del Carmen. I took the girl out for an hour's sail around the coast and we returned for a late but delicious luncheon at her parents' home.

'But now, Paul, here is the interesting coda to this tale – Maria wants to come to England to learn English. She has studied diligently for two years at the home of Mr Topham, the British Consul, but there is no better way of learning than to visit the country where the language is spoken. So I wonder, my dear friend, whether she could attach herself to your household for a month or so next spring? Count Gewirtz is paying her fare to Britain, for she will break her journey to spend a week in Spain to check on some business interests the old devil has there. When she arrives in London she will stay at his house in Mayfair for two weeks in April, but after that I thought she would enjoy a period in the country down here in Sussex. I assure you, she will be keen to show her gratitude!'

Sir Paul's face broke into a large grin. 'By George, that would be absolutely capital! Write to Maria this very afternoon, Antonio, and inform her that she is welcome to stay at Arkley Hall for as long as she pleases. Tell her, *mi casa es su casa* and all that sort of stuff.'

'Yes, your house will be her house, and your bed will be on offer as well, I'll be bound,' rejoined Señor

Ribalta with an equally large smile. 'Especially, if I recall correctly, your wife and daughters plan to be in Italy at that time to attend the wedding of the Prince of Umbria to Lady Caroline McNab.'

The ever-randy baronet nodded and proferred the cut glass decanter of cognac to his guest. 'Let's hope that these arrangements remain unchanged,' he murmured softly.

CHAPTER THREE

Whilst Bob Goggin and Sir Paul Arkley were enjoying this fine autumn day, dear reader, let us not forget to recount the doings of the beautiful young Penny who had been forced to accompany her sister and Mama on a visit to London. All Penny could think of as she fidgeted in her seat was how much she missed being with her Bob. So she took little interest when, as the train pulled into Victoria, Lady Arkley announced that a change had to be made to their plans.

'I must tell you both that we have been forced to change our arrangements for tonight,' she announced. 'As you know, we are all supposed to stay with Lord Gerard Horn in Belgrave Square but alas, he sent me a telegram to say that he has been called out of town. Katie, you and I have been invited to stay the night with Lady Podger, whilst I have arranged for Penny to spend the night at your father's club after the theatre.'

'At the Rawalpindi?' cried Katie. 'Oh, but Mama, I am the eldest and surely I should be the one who stays by herself.'

Lady Arkley looked icily at the pretty blonde girl. 'If I remember correctly, Katie, Mr Walter Stanton is a member of the Rawalpindi Club and in all probability he is in town. I am certainly not allowing the risk of scandal by letting you stay overnight in the same building with Mr Stanton with whom, however much you deny it, I suspect you are enjoying some kind of secret liaison. No, do not even attempt to refute me.'

Katie blushed and bit her lip. Her fond Mama was quite correct and indeed, had Lady Arkley known that this lusty young scamp [*see Cremorne Gardens, Headline Books, 1990 – RM*] had indeed fucked her daughter many times and in many ways, she would not have let Katie stay within ten miles of the handsome rascal! However, fortunately for Katie, Lady Arkley could only guess at what might be happening and had no hard facts to back up her suspicions.

So the hansom's first stop was the Rawalpindi Club in Great Titchfield Street where Penny's trunk was unloaded. Lady Arkley came in with her and told Garrick, the club secretary, to take especial care of Penny. 'Take luncheon here at the club, Penelope,' she ordered. 'I will return with Katie at half past six and we will go straight on to the Globe Theatre where we will see the great actor Mr Tagholm play the title role in *Richard III*.

Unlike the majority of social clubs, the Rawalpindi was open to both sexes, although there were rooms set aside for those who preferred to dine solely with members or guests of their own sex. Penny decided to sit in the mixed lounge, but before she could even look for an armchair, a voice at her side enquired: 'Miss Arkley, Penny Arkley, it is you, surely?' She turned round and who should be standing next to her but Alan Brooke, one of the gayest young blades in London and a man known to have won the hearts (and bodies) of almost as many girls as Sir Terence Whitley, who was generally reckoned to be the most busy cocksman in London.

Penny knew of Alan Brooke's reputation, but though a mite suspicious of this silver-headed Romeo with his twinkling blue eyes and sparkling repartee, she gave him a warm smile of recognition.

'So what brings you to London, Penny?' asked this known Lothario of London's clubland. 'I thought that you were down in Sussex until the beginning of the Season.'

'My mama had brought my sister and I to see the ballet at Covent Garden tonight,' she replied politely. 'I believe that *Spectre de la Rose* is being performed and it happens to be perhaps my favourite ballet. Unfortunately we could not obtain tickets, so we are going to see Shakespeare's *Richard III* at the Globe.'

He nodded sagely and said: 'All ballets are charming in their different ways. To say that this ballet or that is the best is, I feel, like pulling a dinner to pieces and saying that this dish or that dish was the best, though it is often the sequence and contrast that gives them their value.

'However, I do enjoy your so-called favourite ballet myself – it is quite a gem. Such a simple idea, so short embodied all in the figures of a man and a woman and in the result the quick sense of life, the assurance of delight in a perfectly understood, perfectly rounded whole. Last year I saw the ballet performed by the great Diaghilev at St Petersburg. Let me assure you, Penny, that when the Russian ballet finally comes to London, the whole artistic world will be turned upside down.'

[Alan Brooke's prophecy was absolutely spot on. When Sergei Diaghilev's company visited London in 1911 it created a sensation. One critic summed up the general feeling by writing that the Russians 'have extended the realm of beauty for us, discovered a new continent, brought a positively new art and revealed new faculties and means of salvation in ourselves'! – RM]

The conversation turned to a discussion of other matters and Penny asked if Mr Brooke had enjoyed any luck at the racecourse, for she knew that, fucking apart, the sport of kings was his prime passion.

'Yes, as a matter of fact, I was at Leicester last week and by the time the penultimate race was about to be run I was down by some three hundred pounds to the bookies. I was cursing my luck when all of a sudden who should appear but my old friend Sir Michael Bailey. We broke open a bottle of champagne in the refreshment tent and I bemoaned my bad luck that afternoon – after all, two of my horses were beaten into second place by distances of less than one length. "Don't worry, Alan," he told me. "Put everything you have on Radlett Farm. It's a certainty, old boy, you may safely put your shirt on it."

'I looked at my form card and I wondered why Michael was so sure of this horse's worth, for it had been defeated by four lengths by the probable favourite five weeks before and had been beaten by a neck by another runner. I said as much but my good friend advised me to follow his advice. "For the first time, the jockey will be really trying his best to win," he whispered. "I am currently fucking the owner's wife and she assures me that the horse has been kept back for today when her husband hopes to obtain excellent odds for a substantial wager. He has five men around the course who will put on bets just before the race so as not to spoil the starting price. I have had ten pounds on the horse myself – follow me and you won't go wrong. But don't tell anyone else or we'll lose the long odds."

'Well, I have always trusted Sir Michael's judgement, so I waltzed right out and popped a tenner on the nose at fifty to one. Penny, Radlett Farm ran as if someone had squeezed a pot of mustard up its arse, if you will pardon the expression, and romped home ten lengths ahead of its nearest challenger. So I left Leicester two hundred pounds to the good, which is yet another good reason why I insist that you take luncheon with me, for I need someone with whom to drink some celebratory champagne!'

Penny laughed and said: 'That is hardly the most romantic proposal put my way, but as I have no prior engagement, I accept your kind invitation.'

They sat down in the Club's ornate dining room and Alan Brooke ordered the following celebration luncheon:

Huitres Natives
Saumon d'Ecosse Fume

Coupe de Tortue Verte
Brindilles Diablees
Creme Ambassadeur

Faisan Roti a l'Anglaise
Coeur de Celeri au Jus

Pommes Fondates

Poire Roxanne
Biscuits Sec

Café
Liqueurs

Perhaps it was the oysters and champagne that made the conversation so animated and Mr Brooke's wit so sparkling, but Penny, like so many women before her, found herself sexually attracted to the handsome Mr Brooke. She felt a magnetic energy connecting them and a little voice inside her head presented the thought of how nice it would be to lunge across the table and kiss this marvellous man. How exciting it would be, continued this devilish voice, to ravish him and take his stiff delicious cock inside your cunney.

They exchanged heated glances across the table and Penny just knew that Alan Brooke, too, was feeling almost uncomfortably randy. Just the thought of this sent her large titties standing erect and just longing to be sucked. As they gazed into each other's eyes, the handsome rogue confirmed her thoughts by slipping off his shoe and insinuating his foot between her ankles. Slowly but surely, and with admirable coolness, for he moved just as the waiter refilled their coffee cups, Alan Brooke's toes had moved up along her calf and were rubbing sensuously along her inner thigh. Of course, within a short space of time, his foot had moved to the very epicentre of all her desires and Penny's silk knickers were soon dampening with her aroused juices.

'Now let us drink to friendship,' said Alan Brooke as the smooth-tongued rogue carefully filled two glasses with champagne. 'But really we ought to seal our friendship with a kiss!'

Penny blushed as they drank the toast, but the pressure of her companion's foot on her aching cunt caused her to spill some champagne over her dress. 'Dear, dear, what a shame – you will have to go upstairs and change,' said the sophisticated gentleman opposite her. 'Come, I will accompany you.' And with those words he stood up and walked around to stand behind Penny's chair.

Of course, once safely inside Penny's bedroom, he took the trembling girl in his arms and kissed her with a burning passion. 'I shouldn't really be doing this,' said Penny softly as Mr Brooke unbuttoned her blouse and gently cupped her delightfully proportioned breasts which swelled so voluptuously under the luxurious silk of her chemise. Soon he had pulled off her skirt and she stood solely in her underclothes. Penny could not resist this easy-mannered seduction and she inhaled the lovely scent of his cologne as he lifted her up and placed her gently on the bed. She lay still as he rolled down her stockings and put her hands over her head so that he could ease off her chemise to leave her nude except for pale blue French knickers.

He now tore off his clothes and kicked off his shoes, leaving on only his drawers as he jumped up to lie beside her. 'What a delicious little filly you are, Penny Arkley,' he murmured, running his hands across her naked breasts, tweaking her hardening nipples. He kissed her again as his hands travelled downwards to lower Penny's knickers, the sweet girl aiding and abetting him by lifting her firm young bottom off the sheet so that she could kick them away. As their mouths glued together, his hand slid down further, her thighs fell loosely apart and his searching fingers took possession of her cunney. With one bound, he gave her a final kiss on the lips and replaced his fingers with a tremendously powerful kiss squarely on her cunney.

The champagne, the thrill of his skilful loving and her desire to be fucked by this good-looking rake was too much for Penny to bear. With a low moan she grasped his head between her hands, as his greedy mouth sucked and tongued her cunt as expertly as one would expect from a man praised as perhaps the finest pussey-eater in London. He first parted her swollen pink cunney lips with his hands and his tongue traced a warm wet trail along the insides of her soft thighs. Then, teasingly, he began to lap at her crack until he found the hard, pointed little clitty which he playfully nibbled between his strong teeth. Penny writhed and squealed, her hips rotating as he brought her quickly to a most exciting little climax.

She lay panting with her thighs parted to his eager gaze as he lifted his head. 'Now fuck me, Alan,' she commanded and so, ever eager to please a lover, he pulled down his drawers to release his straining shaft from the confines in which it had been imprisoned. Now Penny was no stranger to pricks, but the upstanding girth and length of Alan Brooke's enormous tool was beyond all her previous encounters with the male organ.

Penny's hand stole downwards to grasp this huge organ, but she could not span it with her fingers. She thrilled with the thought that her pussey would soon be engorged by Alan Brooke's monster cock. She was relatively well-informed regarding the size of prongs and she knew that here she was in possession of perhaps the largest prick in London. As she was later to confide to her friend Patricia Miller: 'My dear, you will hardly believe this but it could not have been even a fraction under eleven inches from base to tip. Oh, it was a real beauty, at least fully two inches thick and set in a bed of thick, crisp hairs. His balls filled my hands and is there any wonder that I found it so difficult to resist his amoratory advances?'

So Penny was filled with keen anticipation when she rolled over onto her back and parted her legs invitingly for the equally eager young man who began the proceedings by rubbing the knob of his tremendous tool against her rolled cunney lips.

'Just lift your bum a trifle, my love,' he murmured, and obediently she raised her bottom two inches so that his hands, gliding beneath, could clutch her delicious arse cheeks. He wriggled up so that the lusting bulb of his huge cock could now slip between her pouting pussey lips as the subtle lubrication of her cunney allowed him to push forward with ease. He eased in about four inches of this splendid shaft and for a moment lay still.

Then, without further ado, he plunged the entire length of his great prick into her warm wetness and immediately they were locked into a superb rhythm of long sweeping strokes as Alan Brooke's trusty truncheon slurped its way noisily in and out of her juicy cavern. Penny squealed with pleasure as he continued to thrust in and out, keeping hold of her rounded bum cheeks in his hands as his lean body slewed one way and then the other and her excitement was further increased by the fact that she had a marvellous view of this grand fuck from the large mirror high up on the side wall. She pushed vigorously to meet every hot thrust of this stupendous instrument and her cunney spent time and again, squeezing the thick shaft buried in her love channel, nipping it as tightly as possible until they were both utterly consumed in a veritable frenzy of lust. His cock emerged gleaming at every long, plunging stroke and when he pushed back in, Penny whimpered with delight as she heard that sibilant, squelchy noise that is the very music beloved by all devotees of *l'arte de faire l'amour*.

Now it must be recorded that Alan Brooke was as proficient at fucking – as had been rumoured throughout the best houses of Belgravia – for he continued to pleasure Penny for a full seven minutes before he gasped: 'I'm going to spunk into you, Penny! Brace yourself!' And with a happy shout he jetted a fountain of white love juice deep inside her willing cunney. She milked his twitching shift of every last drop of spunk and he rolled off her exhausted, though his extraordinarily large member was still semi-stiff as it lay flopped over his thigh.

At this point both protagonists would happily have brought down the curtain, but in their haste to partake of these sensuous delights, neither had taken the precaution of locking the door – a foolishness from which others, in this narrative have not proved immune. For just as they were preparing to enjoy a post-coital rest, they were disturbed by an unexpected visitor . . .

Their uninvited guest was a pert little chambermaid named Lizzie who, upon seeing the name 'Arkley' on the reservation slip kept by the housekeeper, had naturally assumed it was the jolly Sir Paul who was booked in for the night. So she had already slipped off her knickers in readiness for a happy (and profitable) little joust with Penny's father, and Lizzie was more disappointed than embarrassed by her mistake for, it was a fact known to all the girls on the staff at the Rawalpindi, that Sir Paul tipped at least a sovereign for a swift little session during which the girl would toss off the randy baronet whilst he played with her pussey.

Lizzie was a pretty girl, just nineteen, with straight brown hair cut short, just above her shoulders. Her lively brown eyes illuminated a fair-skinned face with clear, strong nose and chin. And despite (or perhaps because of) her chambermaid's uniform of white blouse and black skirt, it was obvious to any who viewed her that Lizzie enjoyed a luscious figure with well-rounded breasts and a delectably rounded backside.

'Oh, I do apologise, sir, madam,' Lizzie blurted out as she saw immediately that the gentleman in question was not Sir Paul Arkley.

'How dare you burst into a room without knocking?' snapped Penny, holding one arm across her breasts whilst covering her pussey with the other.

"I'm terribly sorry, I thought it was another gentleman staying in this room,' she said, still rather confused by her mistake.

'And would you have also come in without knocking if he had been here?' asked Alan Brooke with a grin, not seeming to care at all that he was speaking to the chambermaid whilst he was lying naked on an equally nude girl's bed.

Lizzie blushed but the rascal of London Society had a kind streak for he added: 'Well, lucky old him, I say. Look here, Penny, don't be too cross with the girl, she obviously made a genuine mistake.'

Penny was nothing if not quick-witted. It was her name, not Alan Brooke's, which was registered for this room. 'You were expecting Sir Paul Arkley to be here, weren't you?' she said to Lizzie. 'He is the only other Arkley who stays at the Rawalpindi. Come on, girl, out with it.'

'Well, yes, but please don't say anything or I'll lose my position here,' begged Lizzie.

It did not take long for Penny to make up her mind. 'Very well, we won't tell on you – on the understanding that we can expect similar discretion as far as Mr Brooke and I are concerned.'

'Oh yes, Miss Arkley, we never tell tales at the Rawalpindi Club. You can ask anyone and they will all tell you that I never kiss-and-tell. Why, a man from the newspapers once said "Lizzie, I'll give you five pounds to tell me who shared Lord Baum's bed last Thursday, "but I told him to piss off" said Lizzie, trying hard to keep her eyes from straying too obviously to Alan Brooke's gigantic prick which was now stirring slightly from its limp position.

'Very commendable, Lizzie, but that will be all,' said Penny, but the pretty maid lingered in the doorway, still feasting her eyes on the enormous prick which was now rising majestically between its owner's thighs.

'I said you may go now,' added Penny. 'Or is there something you wish to do whilst you are in here?'

The girl licked her lips and replied: 'Well, Miss, to

be honest, I just can't take my eyes off Mr Brooke's prick. My friend Jane told me it was the biggest she had ever seen but I didn't realise just how huge – ' Her voice faltered but the kindly young man cleared his throat and said: 'Lizzie, would you like me to fuck you? If Miss Arkley has no objection, I am quite happy to oblige.' Penny frowned but as her cunney was still a little tender from the engorgement of this monster tool, and as she enjoyed watching erotic entertainment, she had no real objection to Alan Brooke pleasuring this pert servant.

'I don't mind at all, Alan,' she shrugged, moving over to the side of the bed and motioning Lizzie to come forward to sit on it.

Without further ado, Lizzie unbuttoned her skirt and the two lovers were treated to the sight of her furry-bushed pussey, for as you will recall, dear reader, Lizzie had been prepared to be frigged or even fucked by Sir Paul Arkley. But instead it was Alan Brooke who unbuttoned her blouse as his lips brushed her throat and his hands gently caressed her as she arched back her head, feeling the sense of pleasure beginning to course around her body. She stood gloriously naked and Penny too admired this well-made girl whose taut, well-muscled thighs and creamy beige breasts now sent the famous Brooke shaft sky high, slamming up against his tummy as he sat up to slide his hands over her rounded bum.

'May I come and join the party?' said the little minx, and on receiving the nod of approval, she clambered up and took hold of the tremendous tool that stood up proudly before her in both hands.

'Give him a good suck to begin with,' advised Penny,

and so Lizzie began by licking his balls, flicking her tongue all round the hairy sack. Then she opened her mouth wide and somehow managed to take both of his testicles inside her mouth. As he gasped with excitement, she grabbed his stupendous staff and held the uncapped, domed crown in front of her lips, nibbling and sucking noisily upon it. Then she smiled and, opening her mouth as wide as possible, she stuffed the rubicund helmet inside and her sweet lips worked furiously to gobble as much of this unique cock as was possible before bobbing her head up and down and gradually swallowing almost all of his pulsing pole.

The pretty young maid paused and looked up enquiringly at her excited stallion as if to ask whether she was pleasing him. 'Carry on, my love, you're doing a great job,' said Penny encouragingly, for even Alan Brooke – the man whose awesome feat of fucking Lily Langtry, Dame Jenny Everleigh and Lady Edna Bristolle one after the other in under fifty minutes is still talked of with bated breath in and around the West End of London – was panting too fiercely to reply.

Lizzie smiled and resumed the good work, wetting her lips before dipping her head back and running her tongue along the veiny shaft of his monster prick. At the same time she gripped the base and closed her mouth around the hot, gleaming helmet, sucking and swallowing, her eyes clamped shut, and soon his balls began to tremble inside their hairy covering and Penny could see that he was about to spend. She reached forward, tickled him underneath his ballsack and immediately a stream of warm, frothy spunk spurted into Lizzie's mouth and his cock buckled uncontrollably as Lizzie held his giant knob lightly between her teeth. Somehow she managed to swallow most of the copious jets of sperm that flowed from Alan Brooke's tremendous truncheon, and Penny looked on admiringly as Lizzie's tongue lapped round the spongy knob, licking the last drops of juice from around the little 'eye' until even that noble tool began to droop.

Penny's pussey had now recovered and she asked whether she could reclaim her rights to suck and fuck with her lover. But alas, despite her kissing and rubbing the tamed tool, it refused to stand up again, leaving Penny feeling frustrated. 'There are ways in which we can enjoy ourselves without men,' said Lizzie, whose voracious appetite for the pleasures of the flesh were still unsatisfied.

'Are there now,' said Penny, who knew full well what was being hinted.

'Certainly, Miss, and I would be delighted to show them to you,' said Lizzie, running her hands idly up and down Penny's naked thighs. Penny nodded her head approvingly and licked her lips as she saw the gleam of desire in Lizzie's eyes. Alan Brooke, too, guessed what was about to happen and he obligingly rolled over to give the girls room to come to grips with each other . . .

Lizzie and Penny were both on their knees and were busy caressing each other's silken-skinned bodies. Penny was particularly taken with the younger girl's firm, uptilted breasts which were topped by two rosy nipples that were already pushing outwards like two miniature stalks. 'You are so lucky to have such beautiful bosoms,' she said, cupping the firm globes in her hands. Now Lizzie loved her breasts being sucked so she slipped her hands under Penny's bottom and repaid the compliment by declaring: 'And you have such wonderful bum cheeks, ooh, how gorgeous it is to knead them with my fingers!' As she gripped Penny's arse she thrust her delicious titties up in front of her face and Penny manoeuvred one up to her lips, sucking and licking it up to an even further erection as both girls let their hands roam around each other's bodies, exploring the soft curves and murmuring lewd, appreciative endearments to each other.

Lizzie's unbridled lust was now at its highest pitch and she rolled Penny onto her back. She kissed the soft, hungry lips as she leaned over her before beginning to tongue Penny's ear in rapid rhythm. This excited Penny almost beyond endurance as she squeezed her legs together and pressed her nipples repeatedly between her fingers as Lizzie moved her tongue downwards, drawing circles across her belly until she came to Penny's soft nest of dark, silky cunney hair. Dipping her face close, Lizzie inhaled the heady aroma of an excited, wet cunt. Spreading the swollen cunney lips with her tongue, Lizzie explored for a moment, gauging her partner's responses; then, sliding her arms around the trembling girl's thighs, she adjusted her position and relaxed into a flowing rhythm, licking and lapping Penny's pulsing pussey, her tongue flicking and nudging the erect little clitty which was now pushing out of its hood. Lovingly, Lizzie began to eat her, forcing her tongue deep into the quivering wet crack, sliding up and down the slit, pushing and probing as Penny rubbed herself off against Lizzie's sweet mouth.

'Oooh! Ooooh! Lizzie, that's lovely!' panted Penny

in a frenzy as the young tribade continued relentlessly to stimulate her cunney in such lascivious style. 'Suck harder now and make me come!'

Lizzie responded at once, clutching the other girl's firm, rounded bottom cheeks as she thrust her face even deeper between Penny's legs, sucking and slurping with great ardour, rolling her pink tongue round and round, noisily lapping up the sweet juices that were now freely flowing from Penny's juicy pussey. This made Penny quite wild with passion and she clawed at the sheets, dragging Lizzie across the bed as she stayed determindedly with her task, her mouth seemingly glued to Penny's cunt. But Penny was fast climbing the pinnacle of pleasure as she gripped Lizzie's head between her thighs. 'A-h-r-e! Lizzie, you devil, I'm going to come!' she screamed, and then the floodgates opened as she came off with a huge shudder, deluging Lizzie's mouth and chin with her profuse spend.

This tribadic tableau had hardly gone unnoticed by Alan Brooke who now knelt by the girls, holding his unfeasibly large cock in his hand and Lizzie took hold of the glistening veiny shaft, drawing back the foreskin to make the purple crown swell and bound in her hand. She heaved herself up and Penny unselfishly rolled to the side to allow room for Lizzie to kneel forward and push out the cheeky white globes of her glorious bum to give the lithe lad an excellent view of both her arsehole and cunt. This presented a momentary problem for Alan Brooke – to use a sporting metaphor from the world of snooker, should he play the pink or the brown? Lizzie must have guessed that this question was going through his mind for she turned her pretty head towards him and said: 'Please fuck my cunt, Mr Brooke. Your prick is far too big for the tradesmen's entrance!' Ever the gentleman, he grabbed a pillow and inserted it under her belly so that her hips and plump arse cheeks were raised up into the air.

He then moved between her legs, nudging her knees further apart and, taking his enormously thick cock in his hand, he capped and uncapped the ruby-coloured helmet. Carefully, he guided the massive knob slowly into her dripping pussey from behind and began to fuck her in a slow yet steady rhythm. He was kneeling now between her legs and bending forward so that his hairy chest brushed against her back. He reached under the panting girl and cupped her pert breasts, holding them in a firm grip as he continued to pump in and out of her juicy honeypot.

Lizzie's plump bum slapped nicely against his thighs as she fitted easily into the rhythm of this fine 'doggy-style' fuck. [*This method was much favoured by Alan Brooke and was used seven years before in 1896, when he was awarded the Order of Mustapha Pharte by the Rajah of Chukerjee, after seeing the athletic young stallion fuck six of his concubines in a special libidinal entertainment especially arranged for the Indian potentate by Mr Gladstone – RM*] His gleaming shaft see-sawed in and out of her sopping cunt, above which the little brown, wrinkled rosebud of her arsehole quivered and winked with each fierce stroke. Reaching behind her, Lizzie caressed his big ballsack as she rocked to and fro, her head thrown back and her hair whipping from side to side. Desperately, she wriggled her bottom, working it round and round, her hips rotating to achieve the maximum penetration, and she threw her head back again in total abandon as a primordial sound came from deep within her and her climax coursed through every fibre of her being.

This was all too much, even for Alan Brooke, whose torso suddenly stiffened as he felt the sperm boiling up in his balls. With an anguished cry he managed one last thrust forwards, his balls banging against the back of Lizzie's thighs before his cock spurted spasm after spasm of hot, frothy spunk inside her. His climax was so powerful that it appeared that his very body was being shaken to pieces by the force of the orgasm, and he gave a last drawn-out cry before he collapsed on top of Lizzie, his frame bathed in perspiration.

'Goodness me,' said Penny anxiously. 'Alan, I would suggest that you bathe before we dress or you may well catch cold. I'll turn on the taps for you.'

'And I'll soap your back if you'd like,' chimed in Lizzie, giving Penny a sly wink.

'That is extremely civil of you,' said the young rake. 'I do enjoy luxuriating in a hot bath, especially since coming back from a weekend in the country at Lord Nottsgrove's seat in Herefordshire.'

'Why so? Surely His Lordship has all the necessary facilities available for his guests?' said Penny as she slipped on a dressing gown and padded across the room to the bathroom.

'Oh yes, but like so many old country houses, the hot water system was seldom reliable,' he answered as Penny switched on the taps. 'My own room boasted a large iron tank encased in mahogany in which three people might have sat with ease. At one end there was a brass dial on which was inscribed the words "Hot" and "Cold", and a revolving handle manoeuvred an indicator into position.

'Well, when I pointed it to "Cold" there was a free response of a flow of sharp, clean water which made its appearance through a small circle of perforated holes in the bottom of the bath. But when I tried to obtain a hot water supply, all I managed to achieve was a series of sepulchral rumbles and the appearance of a trickle of rust-coloured fluid, heavily charged with dead insects! And the water was stone cold! Luckily Lady Quintonne allowed me the use of her bath, a deep tin tub which was filled with immense cans of boiling hot water by the servants, or I would have come back with the odour of the country clinging to me.'

Lizzie frowned. 'Lady Quintonne, did you say? Would that be Lady Helene Quintonne, a pretty blonde lady probably in her late twenties engaged to be married to Colonel Gunsthorpe-Jarfield?'

'Yes, that's the lady. Why, Lizzie, do you know her?'

'I'll say I do! She stayed here at the Rawalpindi last month and I won't forget her visit in a hurry.'

'How so?'

'Well, funnily enough, this story begins with a bath. Look, let's go into the bathroom and I'll tell you about it whilst you're having a nice warm soak.'

Obediently, he followed the girls into the bathroom and settled in the large bath, then the scamp asked Lizzie and Penny to wash his back. In no time at all the two girls had somehow managed to squash into the large tub and once they were all comfortable, Lizzie continued her story about Lady Quintonne.

She snuggled down beside Penny and began: 'It all

began one day last April – Lady Helen Quintonne and her friend, the Russian Princess Alexis of Volgograd, had booked in at the Club as they had planned to stay a few days in London. I happened to be the chambermaid assigned to their room. On the first evening they went out to the theatre and, after dinner, Mrs Allendale the housekeeper – gosh, what stories she could tell if she had a mind to do so – told me to make up their room. As I walked down the corridor I wondered why they had not booked separate rooms, especially as I knew that the Club was only just over half full. And in any case, their room, number 73 had only a double bed in it so what sleeping arrangements did the ladies have in mind?

'Anyhow, whilst I was tidying up, I was intrigued to find a small box covered in a rich, red velvet cloth on the dressing-table. The lid was only partially closed and I admit that my curiosity led me to open it. To my surprise – though looking back I suppose I should have realised immediately that Lady Helene was a tribade despite her forthcoming nuptials – in the box I discovered an exquisitely manufactured dildo lying on a soft cushion of red velvet. It had been glazed with a remarkably true-to-life flesh coloured tint and I noticed a tiny G marked near the base which meant that it had been made at Mr Burbeck's pottery near Birmingham. Many ladies collect these hand-made dildoes that are modelled from pricks of their lovers. I know all about this as I was fucked by the Duchess of Merseyside's footman last year and he told me all about this latest fashion amongst Ladies of Quality. His mistress, the Duchess, already possessed dildos cast from moulds made from the cocks of Sir Ronnie

Dunn, Mr Harry Cust and Major Aspis of the Belgian Embassy.

'The particular dildo in Lady Quintonne's box was a particularly fine specimen and, holding it in my hand, I admired the artistry of manufacture and wondered upon whose cock it had been fashioned. Now this made me feel more than a little randy and, as Lady Helene and the Princess would not return for at least two hours, I slipped off my skirt, pulled off my knickers and lay down on the bed. I clutched the dildo in one hand and let the bulbous head nudge my pussey lips, whilst with the other I rubbed my dampening slit. I enjoy playing with my clitty and soon I was damp enough for the knob of the dildo to slide into my love channel. Oh, how deliciously rude, I thought as I slid this substitute shaft in and out, taking care that it rubbed my clitty at every stroke.'

'Very interesting, Lizzie. Pour in some more hot water, there's a love,' said Penny, idly letting her hand stray down towards her soapy cunney and letting her fingers play around her wet crack.

'Yes, but what followed was even more interesting,' Lizzie continued, turning the tap so that a flow of warm water cascaded over the trio from the shower opening. 'Mr Brooke, you come into the story in a minute!'

'Do I now! Well, do continue, my dear girl.'

'My, my!' Lizzie giggled. 'Don't be worried, as you don't come out of the affair too badly. Anyhow, the point is that there I was, happily playing with my pussey, when in flounces Lady Helene and Princess Alexis! At first I was so lost in my erotic reverie that I did not even hear the door open, but then Lady

Helene cried out: "Alexis! Look here at this cheeky girl diddling herself with my dildo on our bed!'

'I blushed crimson and hastily covered my pussey with one hand as I dropped the dildo on the eiderdown with the other. "Get out of here, you impudent hussey, I'll have you dismissed!' shrieked Lady Helene.

'I was about to jump off the bed when the attractive blonde Princess Alexis came forward and laid a hand on my shin. " *Nye byespokoyscya*," cooed the Princess. "Do not be too harsh on her, Helene, she was simply enjoying herself. No doubt she saw your lovely dildo and the temptation was simply too great. Let me see your *flagalishe* my dear, is it all nice and juicy?" Well, I was so embarrassed – and worried too for I didn't want to lose my job. As you probably know, Mr Brooke, there are so many people like Count Gewirtz and Lord Peter Kingsley who are renowned for their generosity in dispensing gratuities. On the other hand, I had heard all about Princess Alexis, who was an out and out tribade and greatly sought after by women who were solely of that persuasion. She was known to frequent the theatrical dressing rooms of the ballet, and between scenes pop her face between the thighs of any girl who took her fancy or who would accept a golden rouble for letting the Princess lick her out.

'What should I do? Although I enjoy occasional sex with girls, I prefer fucking with men. Still, the Princess was an attractive woman and it would hardly have been an imposition to let her suck me off. So I smiled and said: 'You are very gracious, Your Highness."

' "Not at all," she said throatily. "But why do you lie there half clothed. Come, let me help you take off the rest of your clothes." I made no objection as she unbuttoned my blouse and I pulled off my chemise, so I now lay stark naked in front of the two women. "Is she not beautiful, Helene?" said the Princess, breathing heavily. "Wait there – what is your name? Wait there, Lizzie, let me show you something." She ran to the wardrobe and dragged out a painting which she had commissioned from Sean Thomas, the noted Irish artist. It was a nude portrait of the Princess and Mr Thomas had certainly done his work well, bringing out every detail of her body and limbs, especially her big breasts and the patch of golden hairs on her lower belly and pink-lipped cunt.

' "Does it look like me?" she asked, sitting down on the bed and running her hand along my arm. I made some complimentary reply and her answer was to stroke my breast and rub my nipple up against her palm. "Would you now like to see the original upon which this picture was based?" she murmured, and I nodded my head in assent.

' "Well, it is rather warm in here," she commented and quickly slipped off her clothes until she stood before me in all her glorious nudity. Her hair was corn-yellow, her nose rather small and her well-formed mouth was undeniably Russian. Like women of her race she was big-boned, though not too much so. Her breasts were full and well-formed and, I thought, unusually erect, while the nipples were pointed and stiff and quite cherry-red in colour. Her waist was trim, her bottom cheeks were beautifully rounded and plump and her thighs were really beautiful. Round as apples and as smooth as ivory to the touch as I smoothed my hands across them whilst she joined me on the bed.

But what took my interest most was her flaxen-haired pussey all around her full-lipped cunt.

'I kissed her lovely love-pouch and soon she was gasping with pleasure as my fluttering tongue licked and lapped around her dampening slit. "A-h-r-e, my pussey is on fire," she cried. "Now suck my cunney and smack my arse – that will make me come!" I did as I was told, gently slapping her gorgeous bum cheeks. "You may hit harder than that, Lizzie!" she added, so I entered into the sport and struck her so smartly that her buttocks assumed a rosy hue. "Oh! Oh! Oh! I am coming!" she screamed and how right she was, for with a stiffening of her limbs her cunney disgorged a creamy emission of love juice all over my mouth. I sucked in as much of her tangy liquid as I could but she spent so profusely that much of it rolled down her legs.

'In the meantime, Lady Helene had disrobed and had joined us on the bed and was already burying her head between my own thighs. She began to lap at my wet pussey which sent me into fresh paroxyms of desire and wanting desperately to be finished off. She was licking along the lips of my love box but not putting her tongue inside my sopping crack. "Ah! That's delicious, but do suck my cunney and make me spend," I begged her. "Fuck me with your tongue." But then the Princess said "Don't worry, Lizzie, I'll do that for you."

'She lay down behind me, the dildo in her hand, and inserted the head of this man-made cock between my pussey lips from behind whilst Lady Helene sucked and nibbled on my clitty and played with my erect red titties by rubbing her hands all over them. The three of us fucked away in rhythm and it only took a few minutes before I came, splashing Lady Helene's face with my spend. Then we changed positions and I stuck my tongue up Lady Helene's crack, and rubbed my face all around her tender wet crotch and lapped her erect clitty until she spent. Then the Princess came round to my front and eased her hands under the cheeks of my bum as I raised my pussey towards her sweet face. She buried herself in my bush before sliding out her tongue and finding my clitty. Nibbling delicately at it, she brought me in an instant to the very verge of coming. Then she withdrew her lips and tongue and ran a finger down the length of my cunney lips. "See, the parting of the ways, as you British say," she giggled before diving back to bring me off into a further copious spend.'

This tale had fired both Penny and Alan Brooke, whose tremendous tool was now jutting up out of the bathwater like the periscope of a submarine. Lizzie took hold of this monster shaft and planted a kiss on the uncapped knob.

'Just a minute, Lizzie,' said Penny, taking both hands to encompass the great thickness of Mr Brooke's shaft. 'Let's not waste this stiff prick. I would like to have it up inside me and I am sure you would as well. So let's get out of the bath as the water is cooling off and we can fuck in comfort next door.'

The others agreed and, after wrapping themselves in the luxuriant folds of the special Rawalpindi Club bathtowels, they padded back to the bed. Penny was first to dry herself and she leaped onto the bed with her legs spreadeagled and lasciviously rubbed her cunney lips as she murmured: 'Oooh, I'm still wet down here, Alan. I'm more than ready for your fat sausage!'

The lusty rogue drew a deep breath and stroked his immense prick. Lizzie bent down and gave it an encouraging kiss and both girls admired his enormous tadger that glistened like a white pole, gleaming in the light, before he launched himself forward and almost the entire length somehow managed to force its way inside Penny's pussey. They rolled around in bed until Penny found herself on top and her cunney was now on fire as Alan Brooke's gigantic cock trembled and twitched in a manner that Penny knew heralded a spending. She felt his body go rigid and then he arched his back upwards and shot once, twice and then a third time and his semen jetted out with such intensity that Penny could imagine it splashing off the rear wall of her cunt, and this lewd thought sent her off into an intense little orgasm. Indeed, so abundant was his spurting that her thighs were well-lathered until his tingling staff withdrew, still semi-stiff, and rubbed itself amorously in a final salute against her sticky cunney lips.

But of course Penny was not so selfish as to keep this great cock for a second engagement. She rolled off his lithe frame and it was now the turn of the lissom Lizzie to take hold of the pulsating penis and suck lustily upon it until it stiffened up again back into its previous hardness, standing up straight against his flat belly. Lizzie lay back, her legs parted and raised, as Penny took hold of the monster in her hands and Alan Brooke raised himself over the trembling maid. Penny placed his purple helmet against Lizzie's pouting cunney lips and with a deep groan he thrust his steel-hard ramrod straight into her slippery abode of love. His balls slapped against her bum cheeks as she wrapped her legs around his back and dug her nails into his shoulders. 'Aaaah! Aaaah!' she choked as his lips settled on her risen titties, sucking at them strongly, as she bucked beneath him, her cunney muscles struggling to encompass the mighty member that slewed in and out of Lizzie's luscious love box. His balls swung heavily as he reamed the very back of her juicy cunt, her bottom cheeks writhing ardently upon his palms as one intoxicating spasm followed upon another. His prick shunted, thrust, emerged and then thrust in again, and Penny noticed how the lips of Lizzie's cunney somehow managed to swell and grip around the veiny pole that pumped between them.

They were fast approaching the summit of desire as Lizzie offered her lips to his, and they made a merry dance with their tongues.

'Shall I spunk now, my darling?' he cried out, withdrawing his gleaming wet cock. 'Or would you like me to continue?'

'More!' she shrieked with uninhibited passion. 'I must have more!'

Lizzie could feel the seat of her yearning dampening with every second. She smoothed over her cunney lips and this merest touch set her trembling with barely suppressed passion, rendering the girl helpless with erotic emotion. Eyes blazing and with parted lips, she crushed her body next to this handsome man, enjoying to the full the thrill of feeling his iron-hard cock against her thigh. Her arms snaked around his shoulders and her mouth opened to receive his questing, darting tongue. Quivering, he took her delicious arse cheeks in his hands, kneading the soft flesh with his strong fingers, pressing her cunt even more firmly against his pulsating prick as her breasts jiggled up and down and their bodies moulded into an all-enveloping embrace.

At first he teased her dripping snatch with the tip of his huge red-knob, rubbing it all along her pouting crack, smearing her juices which were already freely flowing all round her cunney lips. Then he lowered himself gently into her so that his throbbing tool was totally enclasped in the folds of her heated pussey. He rode the happy girl like a champion jockey, almost savagely thrusting his gleaming wet shaft in and out, and Lizzie screamed with pleasure as the downward plunges caught the edge of her clitty. His noble cock pumped in and out of her juicy slit whose velvet lips opened and closed over his glistening shaft. Madly they rocked together until, in a splendidly powerful release, Alan Brooke managed to spend a second time, his copious emission drenching the walls of Lizzie's womb with a deluge of frothy sperm as the delighted girl shuddered her way to her own ecstatic climax.

Amazingly, Alan Brooke, this grand cocksman of old London town, was still not completely finished as his sticky shaft was still hard. He rolled over onto his back and both Lizzie and Penny licked the crown of his cock until it rose back to its full, magnificent height. The girls gobbled furiously, lashing their tongues around his now rampant truncheon and Lizzie manoeuvred herself on top of him so that she could lower her own sopping pussey onto his face. Ever eager to please a lady, he licked and lapped at her dripping muff, expertly sliding his tongue in and out of her quivering cunney lips as Penny managed to cram his uncapped knob into her mouth whilst Lizzie concentrated on sucking his balls.

Even though he had spunked twice before in this torrid session, his shaft was soon signalling that a third gush of spunk was on its way from his large, hairy ballsack. This time, however, Penny did not have to contend with a stream of sperm but nevertheless was pleased enough to swallow delicious gobs of creamy foam, and she slurped up every drop of his love juice, milking his great cock and licking the last blobs from the 'eye' on the tip of the knob, until at last Alan Brooke's amazing prick finally began to shrivel down and rest limply upon his left thigh.

They lay exhausted after this feast of fucking until Penny summoned up enough energy to ring down for a bottle of champagne and some sandwiches, for their worship of Venus and Priapus had made them both hungry and thirsty. They had too little time, however, to enjoy their amorous langour. But as they rested, Penny asked Lizzie why Lady Helene and Princess Alexis had returned from their entertainment so early.

Lizzie laughed. 'I forgot to tell you, didn't I?' Well, the lusty ladies had obtained two best stalls to see Faust at Her Majesty's Theatre, but after just three scenes there was an interruption to the performance. The scene-shifters, ballet girls and extras came onto the stage and told the audience that the management had defrauded them of their wages and that they had not received them. They were showered with silver and copper thrown to them by the audience, Lady Helene told me, but a general commotion broke out and the performance had to be cancelled.

[This extraordinary occurrence was noted at the time

by the newspapers, and almost without exception the press condemned the management who had tried to cut the stagehands' wages by half as they had been forced to pay higher than expected fees for the principal singers – RM]

Penny looked at the bedside clock and, with a smile, said that she must ask her guests to leave as she had to change for the theatre.

Penny's guests dressed themselves and made their farewells. Lizzie was the first to leave and Penny noticed that Alan Brooke slipped a couple of sovereigns in the chambermaid's hand before she left the room.

'That was generous of you, Alan, especially as I understand that there are several titled ladies who are happy to pay you for the privilege of being fucked by an expert in *l'arte de faire l'amour*,' commented Penny, wryly.

He grinned wickedly. 'That's not true, you know. I may have no objection to receiving some token of appreciation for any prowess I may possess between the sheets, but I would never fuck for cash – nor indeed would I expect to pay for my pleasures. However, Lizzie is only a servant and depends upon tips to make a decent living. And like several girls here, in all probability she sends money back home to help her family.'

Later the couple sat in conversation at the Club bar, which is where they were met at half past six precisely by Lady Arkley and Katie. Penny's elder sister looked a little enviously at Alan Brooke for she guessed that her sister had probably enjoyed the charms of the noted fornicator during the afternoon, whilst she had been subjected to a most boring time shopping with her Mama at Fortnum and Mason's emporium in Piccadilly.

Lady Arkley was none too pleased to find Penny sipping champagne with a gentleman whose reputation was not entirely unknown to her, but she mellowed under the influence of Alan Brooke's charm as he asked the formidable matron about the play the Arkley entourage was about to see.

'Ah, you are off to the Globe, then, Lady Arkley? Yes, I've already seen Mr Tagholm's interpretation of the crook-backed tyrant. I thought the production to be first class. Of course, every Shakespearean actor owes it to himself to develop new ideas and Mr Tagholm has perhaps been bolder than his predecessors.

'He certainly manages to convey the tragic gloom and bloody horrors of the playwright's brain, and his Richard is a martial figure to which is added a fiendish, bloodthirsty temper. I am sure that you will enjoy yourselves.'

'Perhaps you would like to join us for supper after the play?' enquired Penny. 'We could book a table here or at Romano's.'

'Nothing would give me greater pleasure but, alas, I am dining at Lady Bracknell's tonight, and if I did not turn up there would be thirteen at table which Lady Bracknell would never allow.'

'How could she overcome the situation?' asked Katie curiously.

'Oh, quite simply by banishing Lord George to the nursery for his meal. But as George and I are friends I am loath to let this happen,' he replied with a roguish twinkle in his eyes.

'Indeed not,' said Lady Arkley frostily. 'Come, girls, we must be on our way. Lord Horne has kindly allowed me the use of his carriage tonight and it is waiting for us outside.'

The girls sighed as they followed their Mama to the waiting landau. In fact Mr Tagholm's performance was as good as they might have expected, although Alan Brooke omitted to mention that the famous actor had inserted quite a number of scenes from the Bard of Avon's Henry VI which made it a very, very long evening indeed.

During one of the intervals, however, Katie was amused by an incident that occurred just after she went to the ladies' cloakroom to pick up a handkerchief she had left in her coat. Two usherettes were deep in conversation behind the counter and had not heard Katie come in. Katie could not help smiling as she heard the following piece of gossip from the two unsuspecting girls:

'Yes, dear, I decided I'd had enough of Fred going boozing every night and leaving me all alone in the flat. And when Mrs Belsize told me that she had seen my old man with his trousers down screwing some young floozy against the garden wall of number 73, I thought to myself, right girl, that's it! What's sauce for the goose is sauce for the gander.'

'So what did you do, Mary?'

'What did I do? Well, I'll tell you, Annie. I've always fancied the young man next door. He's a big lad too, with wavy light brown hair and lovely brown eyes. He works on the railways and it must be all the physical work he does, 'cos he's so lean and muscular.

'Anyhow, I called to him last Sunday evening just

as he was going out. "Jim, could you help me for a minute. I need help with something and Fred's gone out and it's too big a job for me to do by myself." He's a good natured boy and he said straightaway that he'd be pleased to help me. So he followed me inside and I sat him down in the front room. "Make yourself comfortable, love. I just want to change my clothes and I'll be back in a moment." Jim looked puzzled, for why should I need to change? Well, I took everything off and wrapped myself in a bathtowel. I came back inside and poor Jim fairly jumped from his chair with shock.'

The other girl laughed. 'Too much for him was it? Blimey, Mary, you're only thirty-two and I wish I had your big titties!'

'Thank you, dear. Well, young Jim was startled but I noticed he couldn't keep his eyes from the tops of my breasts, and I lowered the towel a little so that my titties were only just covered. "It's such a hot night, Jim, that I thought it would be more comfortable without clothes. I love walking around the house naked – have you ever tried it?"

' "No, Mrs Hollingberry, I haven't," he mumbled. "Call me Mary," I said encouragingly. "Do try it, I think you'll enjoy it."

'Well, Annie, my young fellow-me-lad blushed as deep a red as I've ever seen but he was keen all right. He ripped off his shirt and then I unbuckled his trousers and pulled them down. Underneath he was wearing long johns and I licked my lips, I can tell you, when I saw what he had between his legs. I could see the shape of his thick cock and the outline of his balls and I stood there transfixed for a time, just staring at his crotch and warming to the idea of getting my hands on his wedding tackle.

'I slowly let the towel around me fall to the ground and stood naked in front of young Jim. He stammered out something when I unbuttoned his long johns and at first he tried to cover his bulging prick in his hands. "Don't be shy, lad, there always has to be a first time," I said as lightly as I could, for my pussey was now as wet as could be.'

Annie chuckled. 'Big lad, was he? You lucky girl! I bet he crammed your cunney with his cock!'

'Not the very first time, love. I think he could hardly believe his good luck, because he was so eager that he humped himself over me on the carpet, if you please, and came off so fast that I had hardly even started. Still, Jim's prick was hot and hard and I knew he would make a good fuck if I slowed him down a bit and taught him how to use it properly.

'So for the second half we popped upstairs into bed and began kissing. He was very good at that, making a meal of it with his tongue and teeth and he went wild when I began to fondle his balls. This time, though, when he climbed on top of me I told him to take it easy. "Just push in and out slowly, Jim," I told him as my hands slipped down his back to clasp his dimpled bum cheeks. "Come on, darling, fuck me," I breathed, feeling an odd tingle go through me as I realised that I had taken this big boy's cherry.

'He needed no urging after that, Annie. His arms went under my shoulders as he bucked to and fro. What Jim lacked in experience he made up for in enthusiasm as he bounced up and down on me as I clutched at his jerking bum and heaved myself upwards to meet his thrusts, doing my best to pull him further into my seething pussey. I closed my eyes and I felt myself spend all over his slippery shaft.

'Then, all of a sudden, I was rudely jerked back out of my sexy thoughts as Jim suddenly screamed. We'd only just begun the ride and he hadn't spunked yet so I wondered what was up. Annie, I almost died when I saw what had caused him to cry out! Fred had come back from the pub as he'd forgotten to take his pipe and was standing not two feet away from us! Ruddy heck, Annie, I thought he was going to kill us! But would you credit it! Fred cleared his throat and said: "Go on, son, fuck the arse off her while she sucks my cock!" as he unbuttoned his fly and took out his donger. It looked bigger and harder than usual, Annie, and when I clutched hold of it I felt it throb in my hand.

' "Do as he says, Jim, and feel my tits at the same time, there's a good boy," I said, thinking that having his wife fucked by a young chap obviously turned my old man on.'

Mary Hollingberry paused and the two usherettes cackled with laughter. Katie continued to listen intently to their conversation, fascinated by this lusty tale, and she took no notice of the tinkling bell that warned patrons that the interval was coming to a close. She did not have to wait very long for Mrs Hollingberry to continue. . . .

'So I took hold of Fred's shaft and began to toss him off before popping the knob in my mouth. I sucked greedily on his fat helmet whilst Jim continued to give my cunney a good seeing-to. Annie, it was so sexy, you just can't imagine. I went off almost straightaway and Fred spunked a great splodge of salty sperm into my mouth just as Jim let fly with a great gush of cum into my cunt.'

A second bell rang out and Katie was startled out of her reverie. She gave a discreet cough and Mrs Hollingberry turned round and saw her standing at the counter. 'Yes, Miss? And what can I do for you?' Katie giggled inside as she thought of two or three unsuitable replies to that innocent question, but she contented herself with merely asking for her coat so that she could retrieve her handkerchief.

The play dragged on for another hour and a half and both Katie and Penny clapped enthusiastically at the final curtain in relief that a tedious evening was drawing to a close. Lady Arkley and the two girls retrieved their coats and were about to step into their carriage when all of a sudden they heard a familiar voice cry out: 'Lady Arkley! Lady Arkley! Just a moment if you please?' The three women turned round to see none other than Alan Brooke pushing through the crowd to reach them. They waited until he finally arrived and Lady Arkley said: 'This is a surprise, Mr Brooke. I seem to recall that you told us you were dining at Lady Bracknell's.'

'So I was, my dear Lady Arkley,' beamed the great cocksman, flashing his snow-white teeth at her. 'But when I told my hostess that you and your daughters were in town she charged me with finding you to cordially invite you back to Belgrave Square for an after-theatre supper. Her Majesty, Queen Alexandria, is there and Lady Bracknell suggested that you might be interested in joining the charity formed under Her Majesty's patronage to swell the coffers of the

Children's Hospital in Great Ormond Street.'

Lady Arkley's eyes lit up. 'How kind of Lady Bracknell to think of me. Please give the coachman her address and we will make our way there immediately.'

'With pleasure – but may I add that the young members of the household are round the corner in Jackson's Mews where Gwendolen Bracknell is entertaining some friends, and she would be delighted to have your daughters join her there. I will chaperone them myself and ensure their safe return.'

'H'm, I'm not so sure,' said Lady Arkley doubtfully.

'Oh, Mama, Penny and I will be perfectly all right with Mr Brooke to look after us,' said Penny.

Her Mama considered the matter further and, to her daughters' delight, finally gave her consent with a warning not to stay out too late.

And there we will have to leave our excited girls and return you, dear reader, back in time and in place to the heart of rural Sussex. . . .

CHAPTER FOUR

So, reader, let us transport ourselves back to Lineham Wood where in the heat of the afternoon our youngster, Bob Goggin and Sarah Stevenage, are lying naked and fast asleep, entwined in each other's arms after a most enjoyable post-prandial fuck.

Sarah was the first to stir and she nudged her lover into consciousness. 'Come on, Bob darling, we must be getting back for tea.'

Bob gave her a gentle kiss and, as they put on their clothes, he asked Sarah about the guests who Mrs Wendover had mentioned were expected for tea.

'Oh, you won't know them,' she replied carelessly. 'Colonel Grosvenor's a country gentleman and a local magistrate, and Ann Hennessey is one of our nicest neighbours. She's about thirty-five or so and a pretty woman, but to the best of my knowledge she's not married. They say in the village that the Colonel stays overnight at her place, but then he's probably fucked more girls than Professor Eames, which really is saying something!

'Miss Hennessey writes poetry and some of her verse has actually been published in the newspapers. She might recite some of her latest work to us this afternoon. Tell me, Bob, do you like poetry at all?'

Bob gave a small laugh. 'I can't say I've read much, to be honest. Mind, I know some limericks, but I could hardly recite them at the tea-table.'

Sarah threw out her hands and said: 'It's quite extraordinary, Bob, how that particular verse form has become the chosen vehicle of sexual humour. Oh, yes, I know that Edward Lear and Langford Reed have written inoffensive limericks, but they are poor stuff. No, don't blush, I love limericks, for at their best they are genuine folk poetry of the highest quality. Come on, Bob, recite one to me.'

'You really want me to recite a naughty poem?' said Bob incredulously.

Sarah shook her head. 'Just a minute. We're not talking about rude verse here but a comic seven-line stanza in spondaic hexameter, alternating with amphibrachs and amphimacers.'

Bob gawped at her and she laughed. 'Yes, really, I would love to hear your poem and then I'll read you a verse I wrote myself.'

'Well if you're sure,' he said doubtfully. 'Very well, here goes. Have you heard this one?

> *'There was an old parson of Lundy,*
> *Fell asleep in his vestry on Sunday.*
> *He awoke with a scream:*
> *"What, another wet dream!*
> *This comes of not fucking since Monday."*

'Or how about:

> *'There was a young man of Penzance*
> *Who rogered his three maiden aunts.*

Though them he defiled
He ne'er got them with child
Through using the letters of France.

'Our old butler, Mr Hutchinson, used to know hundreds of nursery rhymes, as he called them, but I've forgotten them all. But I'd love to hear some of your verse, Sarah.'

'Would you really?' said Sarah as they walked back to the Wendover household. 'Well, I went to Arundel last week and before I left, whilst I was sitting on the banks of the River Arun admiring the view of the undulating Downs the muse came upon me:

'Farewell, Aruna, on whose varied shore
My early vows were paid at Nature's shrine.
Sighing I resign
Thy solitary beauties, and no more
Or on thy rocks or in thy woods recline,
Or on the heath, by moonlight lingering, pore
On air-drawn phantoms.'

'Very nice,' said Bob, who enjoyed the sounds of the words even though he was not too sure what they were about [*neither am I! – RM*] 'but we had better step lively now if we are not to be late.'

In fact, Colonel Grosvenor and Miss Hennessey had already arrived by the time our young couple had returned to the Wendover home. The subject of conversation was the present condition of art and Colonel Grosvenor was holding forth. 'The age is analytical and unsatisfied. Childlike enjoyment in anything for its own sake has almost departed, giving place in art at least to querulous questioning or frantic admiration. The fever of the great French Revolution of 1789 still infects the blood of Europe and it is this consciousness which is perhaps the greatest characteristic of modern time.'

'So you would have preferred to live in another age. Peter?' asked Timothy Wendover.

'Most certainly,' replied the Colonel. 'About one hundred and fifty years ago in London, when one could discourse with the great Doctor Johnson and the literati without being bothered by the whine of the ignorant masses.

'I don't suppose I'd carry you with me, would I, Geraldine?' he added roguishly to his hostess.

'You really are a fat-headed old reactionary,' said Geraldine Wendover. 'I don't know why I even let you come into this house, let alone be as fond of you as I am.'

Colonel Grosvenor laughed and Miss Hennessey said placatingly, 'Now, now, everyone. Don't let's argue. Remember that yesterday is but today's memory and tomorrow but the dream of today.'

'Why does she allow the old boy house-room if she so strongly disapproves of his politics?' murmured Bob to Sarah after they had been formally introduced.

'Oh, Peter doesn't really believe all that tosh, he only does it to annoy Aunt Geraldine. Anyhow, I think they are both far too sensible to let any political squabble spoil their friendship. And it is a close friendship, believe me.'

'Really? You make it sound a little mysterious.'

'Unusual would perhaps be a more appropriate word. I heard Uncle Timothy tell his friends, the

Russian businessman, Monsieur Labovitch, a very naughty tale indeed about Auntie Geraldine, Colonel Grosvenor and himself. I was sitting in the library and the two men were playing billiards next door. The door was open and I could not help but hear the drift of the conversation. Yes, I know I could have got up and closed the door, but truthfully I was so enthralled at what I was hearing that I stayed silent and enjoyed the anecdote.

'Come with me and sit in the corner. I can tell you all about it and we won't be disturbed,' she added with a wicked glint in her sparkling eyes.

After they had made themselves comfortable, Sarah recounted what she had heard. 'Last summer, Uncle Timothy and Auntie Geraldine decided to take a camping holiday in the Scottish Highlands. They journeyed up to Inverness by train, and found themselves a quiet site. Soon, however, another caravan rolled up and who should it contain but Colonel Percy Grosvenor and the pretty Mrs Stevens, who is the wife of the notorious business tycoon. Now it seems that Mrs Stevens was unwell – nothing serious, just an annoying feverish chill – but more of this later in the story.

'Auntie and Uncle were pleasantly surprised to come across Colonel Grosvenor there, and invited him over to take dinner with them that evening as Mrs Stevens was confined to bed. The next day dawned and as it was nice and warm, Auntie Geraldine decided to go off on a ride, and after she had changed her clothes, Uncle Timothy could not fail to see how the Colonel's eyes became riveted to Auntie Geraldine's breasts, which are very large, and how he could not refrain from gazing at her bottom cheeks encased in their tight riding breeches. Remember, Auntie is only in her late thirties, being much younger than Uncle Timothy, and she still possesses the fine figure of a woman in her prime. Well, as Auntie jumped up onto the horse, her titties were bouncing up and down quite provocatively and as she was not wearing a bust-bodice, her dark, pointed nipples could be seen outlined against the thin white material of her blouse.

'Uncle then noticed the bulge in Colonel Grosvenor's trousers. His interest in Auntie was obvious for he went back to his own caravan and sat in the front. Only the top half of the door was open but Uncle Timothy could see that whenever Auntie came galloping by, his arm began to move and it was a pound to a penny that he was playing with himself.

'Uncle Timothy told Auntie Geraldine about this and half jokingly suggested that she may as well give him full satisfaction. He knew she had always been an exhibitionist but I don't think that he was prepared for what actually happened. For she slowly stripped off all her clothes except for her blouse and knickers and walked out and stood right in front of Colonel Grosvenor's caravan. She looked at him with a naughty glint in her eye and slowly peeled off the blouse so that the Colonel had full view of her bare breasts. Then she quickly pulled down her knickers and stepped out of them. She walked over until she was only a yard or so away and then she stood with her legs slightly apart, massaging herself suggestively between her thighs.

'This was too much for the Colonel to take and he stood up smartly, showing both Auntie and Uncle his erect cock which he was rubbing violently with his hand. They watched as he brought himself off, sending a colossal shower of spunk that splattered over Auntie Geraldine's toes. He was obviously embarrassed for without a word he turned on his heel and nipped back smartly inside his caravan, shutting the door behind him.

'Auntie Geraldine came back inside her own caravan and she and Uncle were so worked up that after he had pulled off his clothes, his shaft had only been inside her cunney for a few seconds before he shot off his sperm. But they both managed terrific spends and Uncle told Mr Labovitch that if he fancied being sucked off by Auntie, he should not be ashamed to tell him and the necessary arrangements could be made. The only proviso would be that Uncle could watch the erotic tableau take place.'

'What an extraordinary tale,' murmured Bob. 'I would not fancy letting my wife or girl-friend perform with another man. Still, I suppose that so long as the couple both really want to live their lives in such a fashion they should be allowed to do so.'

'Quite so,' said Sarah firmly. 'As Mrs Patrick Campbell has said, consenting adults should be able to do what they want so long as they don't copulate in the streets and frighten the horses.'

Bob nodded his head in agreement and the young couple rejoined the others and listened to Miss Hennessey talk about her recent visit to Scotland. However, unknown to Ann Hennessey and the other guests, the sly Colonel Grosvenor had liberally laced her tea with whisky so that her account of her journey to Edinburgh was somewhat more free than expected.

'Oh yes, I just adore going to Edinburgh,' she

gushed. 'I had arranged to meet my old friend Mr John Gibson who had promised to give me a special tour of the city. [*For another intimate look at the activities of this wealthy philanderer, readers can consult Cremorne Gardens – RM*] As my family own shares in the North British Railway, I booked a suite at the new hotel the company has just constructed at the east end of Princes Street which I am sure you will agree is one of the finest thoroughfares in the world. Well, I was sipping tea in the hotel lounge and marvelling at the new clock tower that has been erected by the hotel. I said as much to Mr Gibson who joined me during this reverie, and he informed me that the tower was no less than one hundred and ninety feet high, and that the clock had been set at just under two minutes fast to enable passengers to catch their trains!

'We decided to break open a bottle of champagne in my suite and well, you all know what effect John Gibson has on women! He was dressed in a perfectly tailored grey tweed suit with a red silk handkerchief peeping out of the breast pocket. His merry blue eyes were full of bright mischief and, as ever, the sexual energy he generated was too tremendous to bear. I was helpless as he mentally undressed me with such style and elegance that, whilst I felt stripped both physically and emotionally, I was in no way offended. "Would you care to be fucked, Ann?" he asked me with the most tender consideration in his voice. "That would be rather jolly," I replied, and lay back to enjoy the sweetest of kisses whilst he unbuttoned my blouse and began to stroke my breasts. As we embraced I felt his sturdy Caledonian cock stiffen against my belly as I kicked off my shoes and helped John take off the rest of my clothes until I was naked except for my short linen shift.

'He shrugged out of his clothes and I slid my hand across his chest and then lowered it until I grasped his bare, swollen shaft. How hard and hot it was in my hand as John reciprocated by dipping his own hand between the inside of my thighs, stopping of course at my pussey to penetrate it with his experienced fingers, at first gently and then relentlessly as my cunney began to moisten under his skilled touch.

'The soft light made the ripples and hollows of John Gibson's body seem to glow. I knew then that I had to have his thick prick inside me as the musky smell of maleness filled my senses. He kissed me passionately, first my neck and throat, before moving down to my breasts. His tender mouth enveloped my engorged nipples, sucking gently as his tongue teased the erect red tips, making my breasts swell with excitement. Then I pulled his head down towards my silky bush and he began to lick and lap at my moist cunney, his tongue sliding through the smooth passageway to nibble playfully on my pulsating clitty. Very quickly I sensed that I was going to spend and I climaxed delightfully as he continued to kiss and suck my sopping crack.

'Then John carried me over to the bed and gently laid me down on the eiderdown. He gave his corpulent tool a quick rub and then placed himself in front of me, parting my thighs with his hands as I relished the idea of having his lovely prick lodging inside my cunt. Without further ado he pushed the red crown of his cock against my cunny lips which opened like magic to receive him. He began to thrust hard and fast, his round balls slapping my bum cheeks and his hands squeezing my breasts. Oh how we fucked away on that warm afternoon in Edinburgh! I shall never forget how with every thrust of his superb shaft my own hips thrust back, kissing his cock with my love channel. We rocked to and fro as I wriggled my arse to obtain even more of his gorgeous cock. I could feel its fat, gleaming head stretching my cunney which in some magical way expanded to receive it.

'Again and again he pounded his thick, veiny caber, faster and faster at a tremendous rate of knots which I could no longer even attempt to match. Oh, how I gloried in each powerful stroke as my love juice coated his cock, making it slide in even more freely. "Ah! Ah! Ah! I'm going to spend! Shoot your spunk inside me!" I cried out as my moment of truth swiftly approached. John's lean body went rigid as he shot a veritable torrent of gushing seed into my sopping crack before collapsing on top of me.

'Amazingly, his cock had not shrivelled up, however, but remained full and heavy looking. I clasped the monster and in a trice it shot up again, quivering with vigour in my hand. John turned me over and pulled my legs apart. "Push your arse out, please, as I want to fuck you from behind, doggie-style," he announced. Actually, this has never really been a particularly favourite position as far as I'm concerned, but John made me feel comfortable, stuffing a pillow underneath my tummy and tilting me in such a way that his cock entered easily from the rear. We both came again quite quickly and I decided that I needed to rest a while before beginning another round of fucking. So I ordered tea and Scottish shortbread biscuits to be brought up to the suite but, alas, dear John had to fulfil a previous engagement at half past six with Miss Minnie Morrison, whose fiancé had foolishly deserted her that evening for the pleasures of a day at Newcastle racecourse.

' "I can hardly disappoint her," he explained apologetically. "At present, her fiancé can only get his prick up once a week and I am the only other source for any bedtime frolics. However, I understand that she dallied to good effect with Mr John Walsh, the noted literary critic who had come up here for a Scottish Writers' Festival. But I can be at your service tomorrow morning at any time from ten o'clock. Let me take you on a tour of Auld Reekie [*the local colloquial name for Edinburgh – RM*] and after luncheon we can fuck the afternoon away, either here or perhaps more discreetly at my house in Chester Street." '

Ann Hennessey paused and the company sat in a stunned silence. 'Oh, dear,' she giggled. 'I have been a little too frank, haven't I?'

'Not at all, my dear, that was a most interesting description of a day in Edinburgh. By far the most interesting I have ever heard, I'm sure,' came the truthful reply from Professor Eames.

Colonel Grosvenor guffawed. 'Absolutely so. What a pity there were no magic lantern slides to illustrate it, Miss Hennessey, for I am sure I would have enjoyed seeing them as much as I liked listening to your dulcet tones.'

'No doubt you would, Percy,' said Mrs Wendover coldly, for she had just realised the connection between the over-free tale of Miss Hennessey's stay in Edinburgh and the empty whisky decanter that stood on the table beside the gallant Colonel. 'And that reminds me, Ann dear, do come into the study and let me show you the photographs I took at Hurstmonceux last week. Do you know I'd never been there before, even though we have lived in Sussex for five years now. Do you know the castle, Bob?'

Bob admitted he was unfamiliar with the place. 'It is a fairy castle, even more glamorous than Leeds or Bodlian, and is situated between Pevesney and Battle,' explained Mrs Wendover. 'It was built in 1440 and was one of the largest brick edifices of those times. The name comes from the de Herst and de Monceux Norman families who came over with William the Conqueror. It's well worth a visit though much still needs to be done to restore it to its former glory.'

[*The castle, now moated as it was in the War of the Roses, was restored in the early 1930s by Sir Paul Latham – RM*]

'Sarah, perhaps you would care to join us,' added Mrs Wendover with a plea of desperation as Miss Hennessey wobbled slightly as she walked across the room. 'Certainly, Aunt, I would be happy to accompany you,' said the helpful girl, and the three ladies left the room.

As the door shut behind them, Professor Eames exclaimed: 'By George! That was a pretty rum affair. What on earth made Miss Hennessey admit to such rude behaviour?'

'*In vino veritas*,' said Timothy Wendover heavily as he, too, had now noticed the empty whisky decanter. 'In wine there is truth as the Latin has it.' He whirled round to Colonel Grosvenor and said: 'Peter, that was a pretty rotten trick to play on a woman. It was you,

I take it, who spiked her tea.'

The Colonel spread out his hands. 'Guilty, your honour – but I plead mitigation. For Ann did the same thing to me a month or so back during a weekend at Sir Terence and Lady Whitley's place near Hastings.'

'Why on earth should she want to do that?'

Colonel Grosvenor shrugged. 'Well, it's a somewhat, ah, intimate story. May I rely on your discretion, gentlemen?' The company chorused its assurance and settled down in their chairs whilst Colonel Grosvenor recounted the following story:

'Both Ann and myself were invited for the weekend at the Whitley's and there were some ten or so other guests – including your Russian friend Sasha Labovitch, Timothy, incidentally. In fact before dinner I used him to attempt an escape from Miss Hennessey. You see, she has been asking me to fuck her for months now, but frankly, I don't think it would be a good idea. We're good friends and escort each other occasionally. Also, I don't mind telling you that she plays a damned good game of bridge. If I push the old pego in her juice box, I'll guarantee you that in no time at all we'll either be married or at daggers drawn.'

'Or both!' sighed Professor Eames who had been put under similar pressure by a lady in Leamington Spa a month or so before.

'Indeed, sir, as you say – or both! Well, to continue, I sent my carriage round to Miss Hennessey's and we made the journey together to Whitley Court. I was somewhat tired and Ann told me that I should not feel it impolite if I wished to take a little nap, and that she would take no offence. Nevertheless, I tried my best to stay awake, but in the end I dropped off and enjoyed a most pleasant forty winks. I was awakened in the most pleasant way you could possibly imagine. At first I thought I was dreaming when I felt the sensation of a soft hand taking hold of my bare cock. But when this hand began to pull on my shaft until it began to swell and throb under this ministration, I opened my eyes and By Gad! It was no dream! Ann had unbuttoned my flies whilst I had been asleep, taken out my cock and had begun to toss me off.'

'Hardly a complaint to take before the judiciary,' said Timothy Wendover with a little smile.

'Maybe not,' rejoined the Colonel, 'and I don't deny that she was an expert frigger, for as soon as she felt my rod tremble in her hand she swiftly leaned over and began to suck lustily upon it. She squeezed my balls and I spunked profusely into her mouth and she expertly swallowed all my frothy foam, uninhibitedly smacking her lips as she gulped down her drink. I was too astonished even to move, but she took out a pocket handkerchief and dabbed the remaining moisture off my cock before rolling my now limp staff back into my trousers and buttoning up my flies. "There now," she said brightly. "I'm sure we both feel more refreshed, don't we? Tonight we can continue our game as the Whitley's weekends are noted for their bedroom escapades, and no-one will say anything even if we are discovered together."

'Now, you'll think me ungrateful, but this little episode horrified me. There are some women with whom it is better to enjoy a purely platonic relationship, and I just knew that this was the situation between Ann and myself. Indeed, I had told her so but she would have none of it, saying that no-one misses a slice out of a cut loaf and it's true enough that my loaf has been sliced pretty thinly, don't you know.'

Bob Goggin stared at the Colonel and said: 'I hope you don't mind my making a comment, sir, but surely letting the lady suck your cock was a mistake. Surely she then expected you to fuck her that very same evening.'

'Precisely, my boy! You are absolutely correct, except that you are a better man than I am if you could wake up to find a pretty woman sucking your prick – and then summon the strength to tell her to desist!

'Anyhow, as I said, that evening before dinner I was enjoying a whisky-and-soda with Prince Labovitch who was gloomily telling me of his fears for his countrymen. "The problem is vodka, Percy. The Russian will happily die on top of a spirit cask whilst the foreigners remain sober." I said that a man needed a swig of vodka to be able to cope with the harsh life, and though the Prince agreed, he said that his people had much to learn from the Germans, the Tartars and even the Jews who live amongst them.

'This somewhat unhappy conversation was happily diverted by the ever-jovial Sir Terence Whitley himself. "Gentlemen, how good to see you," he said, clapping us on our backs. "Look here, Sasha, I know you've been a bit down since you spent a few weeks in Petrograd, but I think I can lift that cloud of Slavic depression for you. Percy, would you like to accompany the Prince upstairs and step into the fourth room on the right when you reach the top of the stairs. Anyhow, you won't miss it as I've asked for a small sign to be hung on the door which only you or I will understand."

'I had no idea at all what my dear old chum was blabbing on about. Still, nothing ventured, nothing gained, I thought to myself as I trudged upstairs with Sasha. Now, sure enough, on the fourth door on the right hung a sign in the Russian script. Well at least part of the riddle was solved for Sir Terence is one of the few Englishmen I know who can speak Russian fluently. He is also equally at home with German, Swedish and Finnish, incidentally, and if we ever have the time I must tell you about a night we spent together in Helsinki. But I digress. Sasha peered at the sign and laughed aloud. "What does it say?" I asked. He replied: "*Komnata za pola* – the room for sex. What do you think, Peter, should we go in?" '

'An unnecessary question, I would say, in such circumstances. It would have been bad form to upset your host by not at least sampling the hospitality he has obviously taken the trouble to procure for you,' observed Professor Eames.

'To be candid, I didn't need any such persuasion,' admitted Colonel Grosvenor, swallowing down the dregs of his drink and refilling his glass. 'Sasha knocked at the door and a sweet young female voice called out, "Come in!" I opened the door and we entered and what a delightful surprise greeted us – or perhaps we should not have been surprised considering what Sir Terence had written on the door! For lying on the bed, utterly naked except for the briefest pair of frilly white knickers, was perhaps the most voluptuous young lady it has ever been my privilege to view. And I speak, gentlemen, if I say so myself, as a man who has fucked all over the country for the last thirty-seven years!'

' "Don't be shy," said the ravishing, semi-naked

beauty in a throaty French accent. "Shut the door, *cheri*, and lock it behind you and perhaps we can have some fun." I hastened to obey her command and at first we made small talk. This lovely girl informed us that her name was Gigi and that she was from Cannes in the South of France where four years back she had been fucked by the then Prince of Wales, now of course His Gracious Majesty King Edward VII. "I was seventeen years old and had only been threaded by the lusty young cock of my nineteen-year-old boy-friend," she explained. "However, it was a great honour to have sucked the royal prick and the Prince gave me a charming little brooch as a memento of the occasion."

'Then, suddenly, Gigi clutched her left thigh with both hands. "What's the matter, m'dear?" I asked. Her face was screwed up in agony. "It is the cramp. *Zut, alors*, it is really very painful. Would you please massage it for me?" Well, I know little about massage (though I do recommend Madame d'Arcy's Massage and Herbal Baths in Mayfair to any gentleman who can afford their services) but I had no intention of passing up this opportunity. As soon as I touched her silky smooth thigh, my old todger sprang into life! I carefully caressed her soft, warm leg and after a few moments her cramp disappeared, though she was happy to let me continue to stroke the insides of her delicious thighs, right up to edges of her brief little knickers.

'She stared at my by now bulging crotch and said softly: "Ah, Colonel, perhaps you will allow me to repay the compliment." And before I could even nod my head, she tore open the buttons of my flies and her nimble fingers were wrapped around my bare cock, rubbing my shaft up to a huge erection whilst I reached down and fondled her breasts with my two frenzied hands. Meanwhile, Sasha had positioned himself on the other side of the bed and unbuttoned his trousers. He pulled them down along with his drawers and presented his engorged organ next to Gigi's cheek. Gigi looked round approvingly. "Very nice, but first come, first served," she said sweetly as she licked the first drops of pre-cum from my straining purple knob. Gradually she worked my eight-and-a-half-inch rod into her mouth, kissing the mushroom dome gently and stopping occasionally to lick my aching balls. I guessed that her pussey would be nice and juicy by now so, as she sucked on my cock and played with Sasha's thick prick with her left hand, I placed my hands on the top of her knickers and felt the quivering wetness of her cunney. Gigi groaned and gasped and jerked her hips upward which allowed me to pull off the silk garment with ease.

'The sight of Gigi's hairy mound was just too much for Sasha to bear and, with a hoarse cry, he jerked his hips and his veiny prick exploded a gush of creamy love juice splashing across the splendid girl's cheek and chin. Immediately she left off sucking my cock to gobble up as much of Sasha's spend as possible, licking and lapping and milking his cock of the very last drops of white froth.

'But neither Gigi nor I had yet come and were both ready for more. She opened her legs to give me fair view of her pouting, pink cunney lips that stood out in the dark hair of her thick muff and now before me lay her juicy, dripping honeypot. She gasped, pleading with me to put my cock in. So I spread her legs even wider and climbed on top of her. Ever so slowly I let my bursting knob slide between those welcoming lips and her warm crack totally enveloped my pulsating prick. She twisted and bucked so sensuously as I pumped away that our matted hairy triangles were both soaking in each other's juices as my cock slid in and out of those folds of lascivious glory. Then I began to tremble and shake like a leaf from head to toe until a huge climax flooded through me as my prick shot out thick wads of creamy spunk, crashing into her just as she too achieved her orgasm, and her juices mixed with mine to drench her cunt as we pounded away until we were both finally spent.

'Sasha's cock now stood up like an ivory shaft of love, but it took a few minutes before my own prick was ready for action. Sasha asked if he could fuck her bum and the sweet girl replied that she had no objection. So she bent over me and began to suck my shaft up back to its fullest length, tickling my balls with her busy hands whilst sticking out her fine, white-skinned bum cheeks ready for Sasha to board her. With a fine exclamation in Russian, he lubricated his swollen staff with cold cream from a pot that had been judiciously placed on the bedside table, and spread some more cream between Gigi's plump buttocks. Then in a trice he was upon her, his hard cock sliding between her wriggling bum cheeks until he found the tight, dark nether hole.

'Sasha is one of the most adept arse-fuckers of my acquaintance. He positioned his prick so cleverly to the mark that he managed to complete his insertion up to the roots of the hair, and was revelling in the delicious sensations and pressures to which Gigi's backside was treating him.

'Meanwhile, the lovely girl was continuing to suck my stiff prick as Sasha fucked her bottom in a perfect frenzy of lust as she wriggled her bum to extract the greatest pleasure from his exertions. All too soon I could feel the sperm boiling up in my balls, and Gigi must have felt my shaft pulse in her mouth for she squeezed my balls which made me spend straightaway, jetting a stream of spunk into her mouth, and she sucked and smacked her lips with gusto as Sasha sent a copious emission of love juice into her bum hole, spending so exhaustingly that he would have fallen backwards had he not clung to Gigi's neck.

'Frankly, Sasha and I would have preferred to stay upstairs with Gigi and share the sandwiches and champagne that our kind host had provided for her, but when we heard the sound of the dinner gong we knew we had to take our leave. However, we promised Gigi that we would visit her later that evening as soon as we could decently slip away. . . .'

Colonel Grosvenor paused and finished his drink. 'In fact Sir Terence asked me to fuck Lady Elstree when the ladies retired after dinner. "She has not been fucked since January when Sir Leon was sent to Delhi by his father to look after their Indian interests. Lady Elstree won't be able to leave for another five weeks and she desperately needs a sturdy tool between her legs before she makes the long journey."

'It would have been churlish to refuse such an entreaty, especially as Lady Elstree is a fine figure of a woman. So I asked Sasha to tender my apologies to Gigi but that I hoped I would see her again some day.

In fact, alas, I doubt if our paths will ever cross again for the last I heard of her was that she had married the eldest son of some French Marquis and was settling down to domestic life in his chateau just south of Lyons.'

'Still, I am sure you were comforted by Lady Elstree,' ventured Timothy Wendover with a strange gleam in his eye.

'Yes indeed, she was a fine fuck,' agreed the Colonel genially. 'But you sound as if you had prior knowledge of this fact.'

Timothy Wendover laughed. 'I'm afraid that Sir Terence misled you, albeit unknowingly. You see, Lady Elstree came to a house party here in April organised by my dear wife, and I can assure you that she was not coping with the unfortunate absence of Sir Leon by putting herself in a nunnery, so to speak.'

He was obviously going to spill the beans about another erotic episode about which Bob Goggin would have loved to hear, but the young man looked at his watch and announced that he had to be back at Arkley Hall that evening and would therefore have to leave almost immediately. At this point the ladies came back into the room, with Ann Hennessey looking much better for the little nap she had taken. 'Must you really leave, Bob?' said Sarah. 'I'm afraid so. But do write to me so that we won't lose touch. Now I must go as it's a good walk home and I don't want to be late,' said her lover with genuine regret.

'Don't worry, Bob, I'll drive you back,' said Graham Eames, heaving himself up out of his armchair. 'No, no, I insist. Frankly, I do so enjoy driving my motor car that it will really be my pleasure to take you back.'

Colonel Grosvenor looked sourly at the Professor. 'I hope you are not one of these lunatics who drive these wretched new machines at high speeds along our country lanes. Why, only last Thursday one such fool dashed past me on a narrow, winding road at what must have been twenty miles an hour. I shouted at the bounder to slow down but the fellow had the impudence to shout out that – pardon me, ladies – I should stick my head up my arse. Gad, if I ever see him in front of me on the bench, I'll throw the book at him.'

'Would you recognise him again, Percy?' asked Mrs Wendover.

'I didn't catch more than a glimpse as he was wearing goggles and a topcoat,' admitted the Colonel. 'But the coat was a distinctive grey and looked to be of foreign manufacture. I'm sure I would recognise it again.'

Bob Goggin somehow repressed an overwhelming desire to laugh out loud for the Colonel had described the very same coat that Graham Eames had been wearing that very same morning!

As they chugged down the winding roads back to Arkley Hall, Bob asked the good Professor whether he had been the guilty party who had invited Colonel Grosvenor to take up the almost impossible anatomical position mentioned.

'Oh yes,' chortled Graham Eames. 'I remember the incident quite clearly and I must thank you most sincerely for not mentioning the fact that I was indeed the guilty party. I don't make it a habit to shout imprecations to other users of the road, but I wasn't in the best of moods.'

'That sounds somewhat out of character. You seem an even-tempered chap to me,' said Bob mildly.

Professor Eames swung the motor car over to the edge of the road to avoid a cat which shot out from the hedgerow in pursuit of a field-mouse. 'Well, I'll tell you what made me so cross. I was one of a group of friends young Sir Andrew Stuck had invited down for a few days relaxation at his house near Alfriston. Do you know the area, Bob? It's a charming place that lies in what may best be described as a shallow saucer of the Downs and is an old-world village where one can enjoy peace and serenity far from the madding crowd. Anyhow, last Thursday the only guests remaining with Sir Andrew were myself and two foreign ladies, Miss Barbara Beckett from New York and an exquisite Japanese girl, Yoko Nomashita, from Tokyo.

'I slept late last Thursday and thought myself alone in the house. So I showered and went into the kitchen clad only in a bath towel draped around my waist. No-one was in so I thought I would make myself some breakfast. I took a bottle of milk from the ice-box and was about to put on the kettle when in strode Barbara Beckett. She was dressed only in a white tennis shirt and skirt and her long legs were uncovered almost up to the knee! "Hi, Graham, are you having a late breakfast? You lazy man, I've already been out for a two-mile run round the estate," she said with a friendly smile. "I'm dying for a drink, though. Oh, would you pour me a glass of milk?"

' "With pleasure," I replied and tipped some milk into a tumbler and gave it to her. "Just a moment," she said and went to the larder where, after rummaging round for a moment, she emerged with a big bottle of chocolate syrup. "I've been putting chocolate syrup in my milk for as long as I can remember," she said. I must have looked rather snooty about it for she added: "Come on now, Graham, try it first before you pass judgment." I squeezed a little on my hand and licked it off. It tasted far too sweet for my palate and said so. "Shucks, there's another way to enjoy chocolate syrup," she breathed softly, and proceeded to pour a little syrup along the length of my index finger. Then she took my finger and sucked it into her little rosebud of a mouth . . .

'Bob Goggin, my friend, the sensation was electric. The hairs on my arm stood up and I felt the first stirrings of my cock swelling up underneath the towel.

'Barbara giggled and said, "You know why chocolate syrup can be such fun?" I shook my head. "Because it takes so long to lick it off!" she replied as she squeezed the syrup over the rest of my fingers and licked it off in the most sensual fashion, her pink tongue lovingly stroking my fingers as she lapped up the dark, sweet liquid. "Would you care to return the compliment?" she asked, but when I picked up her hand she shook her mane of tumbling blonde curls and said, "No, no, not there, silly boy, just *here*," as she unbuttoned her shirt which revealed that she was wearing absolutely nothing at all underneath it!

'I gasped as I thrilled at the sight of her proud young bare breasts with their rosy, uptilted nipples and my hands trembled as I rubbed the gooey syrup all over her hard, stalky titties. My rampant cock was now pushing out from the cover of the towel and Barbara undid the simple knot that had kept it around my waist. I stepped forward, now completely naked, and as I flicked some syrup off her left tittie she poured the remainder of the syrup all over my prick. "Quick, lie down on the towel," she whispered, and after I had lapped up all the sweet liquid from her titties, she wriggled around and took my knob in her mouth which made me quite dizzy with ecstasy.

'She began by licking all the syrup from the knob in quick little strokes, but what joy as she rubbed her mouth along my meaty shaft and began licking all around my balls. She then took my helmet into her mouth and let it slide back down her throat, sucking lustily on her chocolate-covered cock. The effect was mind-shattering, and all too soon I could feel the sperm boiling up in my ballsack. I shot a huge jet of spunk into her mouth and she eagerly swallowed all my cream along with the last traces of the syrup. "M'm, that tasted really good," she smiled, smacking her lips. "I find that jism is a little too salty for my taste, but mixed with syrup – why, there is just not a drink in the world that is so refreshing."

'I was not inclined to argue, for my prick was still fairly hard and all I wanted to do was to fuck this sweet girl. I unbuttoned her skirt and she pulled down her own knickers to expose a lovely hairy muff of silky blonde hair. I ran my fingers through this golden bush as our mouths met in a passionate kiss. But just as my todger was stiffening back up to its full height, we heard the back door open. As quick as a flash we scrambled up and I pulled Barbara into the larder, leaving the door slightly ajar. How embarrassing if we were discovered by a kitchen maid, I thought, for what on earth could we say to our genial host, Sir Andrew, if word of our little tryst reached his ears?'

'It would be a rather difficult situation to explain away,' said Bob Goggin sympathetically.

'Quite,' continued his companion. 'Such a shocking example to the working classes, if nothing else. However, it turned out that we had been interrupted, not by any servants, but by Sir Andrew himself and Yoko, the petite Japanese girl. They were both barefoot and dressed in loose white tunics. I was puzzled at first but then I recalled that at luncheon the previous day, the conversation somehow turned to military skills, and our host remarked that he was most interested in Eastern martial arts. Yoko had replied that she had studied Tang Soo Do [*actually, a Korean variant of karate – RM*] and that she would be happy to give Andrew a demonstration the next morning.

'So it appeared that her invitation had been accepted, for Andrew was saying: "Ah, Yoko, that was bloody marvellous – I now feel as fit as a fiddle and ready for just about anything the world can throw at me!" The tiny Japanese girl smiled enigmatically and said: "Are you really, Andrew? I must confess that for me, an hour or so of tang soo do leaves me feeling very landy."

' "Landy?" repeated Andrew in some puzzlement. "Oh, wait a mo', you mean randy! Does it now – well, let us see just how landy, I mean randy, you really are, my little pearl of the Orient." I could hardly envy Andrew as I had just had my prick sucked by the delightful Barbara, but I must tell you, Bob, that Yoko was a very, very attractive girl. She was tiny, with porcelain skin and, when she slipped off her martial arts costume and stood naked in front of me, my cock saluted her small but beautifully proportioned breasts and the lovely mounds of her delectable little arse. Indeed, Andrew's eyes gleamed as she turned round and wiggled those delicious rondeurs suggestively in front of the handsome young sportsman. "I say, Yoko," he said hoarsely. "God knows how this bath towel comes to be in the kitchen, but it gives me a good idea.'

'And with those words he too whipped off his costume and sat down cross-legged on the towel with his thick cock jutting up between his legs like a flagpole. Yoko let her tongue run across her lips and she knelt down in front of Andrew, but facing away from him so he was given a fantastic view of those gorgeously rounded bum cheeks. He massaged those exquisite buttocks with his large hands and then Yoko lifted herself up and reached back for Andrew's sturdy prick. She took hold of the ivory-coloured shaft and slowly lowered herself on to it, and Barbara and myself were treated to the sight of his knob disappearing between those rounded globes as, inexorably, Andrew's thick, veiny shaft was sucked up inside her juicy cunney. Yoko then began an extraordinarily sensual up-and-down motion that became more and more frenzied with each downward push until even Andrew's balls seemed to be swallowed up inside her surprisingly elastic pussey.

'He closed his eyes and groaned, his body shaking all over, as Yoko rode his cock like a stallion, opening and closing, clenching and unclenching her cunt and then with a growl, Andrew's hips bucked upwards as he discharged a copious emission of love juice inside her love channel. This was sex with an ardour and vehemence I had not seen since Lord Didsbury's famous orgy last year in Manchester to which I'd had the honour of being invited – but that's another story.'

Bob Goggin stroked his chin. 'Well, Graham, that all sounds terribly exciting, but what I don't quite understand is why, when you left Sir Andrew Stuck's home later that morning, you were in such a foul mood that you mouthed curses at Colonel Grosvenor.'

The Professor chuckled and said: 'To be honest, I suppose that I had little about which to grumble. After all, Barbara's sucking off was amongst the best I have ever experienced. But the truth of the matter was that I was still feeling pretty randy myself after watching Andrew fuck Yoko. My cock was standing to attention and I was feeling Barbara's delicious strawberry titties. Now Andrew and Yoko had gone immediately to bathe and all I could think about was taking their place on the towel when, damn it, we heard the voices of Mrs Burtonshawe the cook and Betty the housemaid outside. So we were forced to flee upstairs where I hoped Barbara and I would consummate our union in my bed. Alas, in our haste to avoid detection, the poor girl slipped as we reached the top stair, twisting her ankle so painfully that she could hardly walk the few remaining paces to her room.

'Fortunately, she had recovered somewhat by mid-morning, which was as well because Andrew had ordered a carriage for eleven-thirty to take the girls and their luggage to the station where they caught a fast train back to London. So I never managed to fuck Barbara and that missed opportunity made me so frustrated that I felt really foul as I drove away from Stuck Lodge shortly afterwards. I was motoring at some speed, probably as fast as twenty-five miles an hour, when I passed this chap whose horse reared as my car whizzed by. I only had a glimpse of the fellow but I thought it might have been Colonel Grosvenor whom I had met previously at the Wendovers.

'Although I was driving at speed, I didn't use my horn and I think it is up to the equestrians to train their animals so they will not take fright at the approach of a motor vehicle. For mark my words well, the motor will be the common mode of transport in the twentieth century and the horse riders will just have to accept this unpalatable fact. Still, having said that I was wrong to let my personal feelings affect my driving. However emotional one may feel, one should always respect the fact that your car is a potential lethal weapon that can kill and maim not only others but yourself.'

Bob nodded as they cruised through the dusty but empty lanes until they reached Arkley Hall. At Bob's request, Professor Eames stopped outside the main gates and Bob thanked the older man for making his day off so packed with incident. 'Mind, my sketchpad is hardly full of masterworks,' he joked. 'Plenty of time for that – meanwhile, enjoy yourself as much as you can,' advised the academic.

'Good-bye Bob, I do hope our paths will cross in the future.'

The young gardener hurried down the driveway to the rear entrance of Arkley Hall. The butler must have seen him coming for Mr Heavan was standing by the open door as Bob turned the corner from the front of the house.

'Hello, young Goggin, I was wondering when you would be back,' said the old retainer with a sly grin. 'What lucky girl enjoyed your favours today, eh?'

'Oh, nothing like that, I'm afraid,' fibbed Bob. 'I spent the day walking round the lovely countryside and making a few sketches.'

The butler snorted his disbelief but Bob would not be drawn further and he made his way up to his room. He threw open the door and was about to chuck his bag on the floor when, to his great surprise, he saw that he was not alone! For fast asleep on his bed was none other than the pretty housemaid Selina who, as you will remember, dear reader, had been splendidly bum-fucked by Sir Paul Arkley just before the arrival of his luncheon guest.

Bob looked down at the girl with some amusement. He gently shook her shoulder and she woke up with a start. 'You must have been working very hard, Selina,' said Bob with a friendly grin. 'It was quite a day,' agreed the cheeky young miss. 'I'm sorry I used your bed for a quick nap, Bob, but I had just changed the sheets for you and the bed looked so inviting that I thought I would just take forty winks.'

Selina stretched her arms out and yawned. 'Tell you what, though, it wasn't exactly the housework that tired me out today,' she sighed.

'Don't tell me Sir Paul finally had his wicked way with you?' teased Bob. 'Oh, it's alright, I won't tell, but it's as plain as a pikestaff that he fancies you.'

'No more than Miss Penny only has eyes for you!' flashed back the saucy girl. 'Mind, I'm not denying that I let Sir Paul pop his cock up my bum this morning. No, what really left me exhausted happened just after tea-time. I was in my room, as I'm free between half past four and seven o'clock, and I was reading this horny story in one of Sir Paul's magazines that he keeps hidden away and thinks we don't know about. So there I was, reading this exciting tale of lust and I just couldn't put it down, especially when the hero, the Duke of Hertfordshire bursts into Lady Susan's bedroom, rips off her satin nightgown leaving her naked and trembling on the bed and, after tearing off his own clothes, jumps on top of her and she takes hold of his thick prick and presses the knob between the lips of her juicy, wet cunney . . .

'Well, without thinking I had allowed my hand to slip inside my blouse and, lowering my chemise, I soon found my nipple, which was quickly aroused to hardness as I played with it between my middle and index fingers. I really was hardly aware that I was playing with myself, wriggling away in my chair, but I was enjoying myself and my pussey was already beginning to moisten. I continued to read on, quite glued to the page where by now the Duke was kissing Lady Susan's large red titties and making his way down to her neat little blonde triangle of crisp hair that covered her cunt.

'I shivered and undid the buttons of my skirt and then pushed my hand into my knickers. My fingers strayed towards my pussey and first one, then two fingers were sliding in and out of my hot, wet cunney. Oooh, I felt so randy as I read happily on, slowly and luxuriantly dipping my fingers in and out of my love channel, rubbing my thumb against my clitty in a series of tapping movements which always drives me on to a good spend.

'Oh, Bob, I was just on my way to paradise when I almost jumped out of my skin. I don't know what gave the game away. Maybe he sighed or groaned, or something, but suddenly I became aware that I was no longer alone. I looked up and saw the face of Lewis

Brackenshaw, the odd-job man from the village, leaning in the doorway looking at me with a heavy-lidded, lust-laden expression. I gasped, pulling my hand away from my pussey and trying desperately to compose myself.

' "Please don't stop, Selina," he said hoarsely. "I've seen so much already it would be cruel not to let me see you finish yourself off."

'I'd never played with myself in front of a man before and part of me felt extremely shy and embarrassed – yet there was something weirdly exciting about knowing that a man was watching me and that his prick was hardening as he saw me perform. So, slowly I began to undress, opening my blouse and exposing one bare breast, letting it jut out proudly to his excited gaze. Then I spread my legs apart and pulled my knickers completely off so he could see my glistening wet cunney.

'I began to massage myself slowly, taking my clitty and pressing its pink, shell-like firmness, then I began to finger-fuck myself, my eyes closed in a delicious mixture of shyness and pleasure. I squeezed my legs together, sending streaks of delight shooting all over my body. Oooh, just thinking about it is making my pussey dampen again!

'Anyway, when I looked at Lewis again I gave a little yelp – for there he was, standing there with his trousers down, furiously rubbing his big stiff cock and each time he slid his hand up and down the shaft it made a juicy, sexy noise from the love juice that had already leaked out in his excitement. Lewis was blessed with a thick, veiny shaft that bobbed up in front of him like a sword. His foreskin had been pushed right back as his purple crown had grown so large and I just couldn't resist taking this gorgeous prick in my hand and popping the shiny knob in my mouth. His whole body shuddered as he moved closer to me as, lingering on the rock-hard hot flesh with my lips, I took his hairy ballsack in my other hand and gently scraped it with my fingernails. This sent Lewis wild and his prick bucked uncontrollably inside my mouth as I sucked in as much of his shaft as I could.

'Actually, this made his tool swell even more and my jaw began to hurt with the strain, so I brought him off quickly by grabbing his bum cheeks in my hands and pulling him even closer. I massaged the underside of his pole with my tongue, moving my head up and down as Lewis jerked his cock in and out of my mouth until he suddenly went rigid. With a cry, he then spurted jets of warm, sticky spunk which I swallowed and swallowed until every last drop of juice had been milked from that hard, throbbing prick.

'Oh, Bob, I do so love sucking cocks. I would like nothing better than to suck away for hours, but I've yet to meet the man who can hold back for more than five minutes once my tongue is curled around his knob. I do so enjoy caressing the bare helmet and lapping out the sperm. It has such a nice tangy taste, too, and I always spend myself when the boy begins to squirt out his spunk between my lips.'

This randy confession had sent Bob's own prick shooting upwards inside his trousers and he wriggled uncomfortably as he said: 'Fair enough, Selina, but I don't see why just one sucking off should have tired you out so much that you fell asleep on my bed.'

'Ah, if matters had ended there, you would have a

point. But of course after he had recovered, Lewis begged to be allowed to fuck me. I explained that unfortunately, it was a time of the month that he couldn't spunk into my cunt unless he had a Frenchie [*a condom – RM*], and though he promised he wouldn't spend inside me, I'd known of too many accidents playing Vatican roulette [*coitus interruptus – RM*]. So he asked if he could go up the back way, but Sir Paul had already been up my arse and, as I told Lewis frankly, one fuck a day in that position is sufficient for me as otherwise I find sitting down uncomfortable afterwards.

'So we settled for a mutual sucking off. I positioned him on his knees in front of me between my legs and I opened them as wide as possible so that he would have full view of my pouting cunney lips. I then took his hand and placed it in my silky, wet clump of cunney hair. His long fingers splayed my outer lips and the knuckles of his other hand ran down the length of my crack. I gently pushed his finger in to penetrate my squishy slit and my hips rose to meet it. Oh, how I really wanted his delicious cock there, but resisting the temptation I slipped round his glistening wet shaft and jammed down the foreskin, delicately fingering the swollen purple dome and, as he lay down beside me, I bent over to lap up his pre-spend juice that was already oozing out of the funny little "eye" on his knob.

'I moved up and over Lewis so that my cunney was now over his face and he immediately buried his face in my soaking bush, licking my cunney in so passionate a fashion that my whole pussey was soon dripping juice onto his lips and chin. My own lips were now busy and I ran the tip of my tongue all around his knob before I crammed as much of his shaft as I could into my mouth. I wrapped one hand around the throbbing, veiny shaft as I ran my teeth up and down it, pausing only to suck the gleaming red helmet and flick my tongue over its slitted end whilst my left hand cradled his big balls through their crinkly covering of pink skin.

'It was all so exciting that we soon climaxed together and my own juices streamed out over his face as he shot a hot stream of creamy spunk so fiercely that the first jet hit the back of my throat. Indeed, he spent so copiously that I could not swallow all his sperm and some of the white froth dripped out from my mouth into the rough black hairs around his cock.

'Even Lewis was sated this time and we lay together for some fifteen minutes or so. I thought this was the end of the affair, but it turned out to be no more than an interlude! For this randy boy gave his cock a friendly tug and, to my astonishment, the shaft began to swell up again until it was as erect as a Guardsman at attention.

'Would I ever be able to tame this monster? This time I decided to toss him off, so as we exchanged a burning kiss, our tongues entwined in each other's mouths and I slowly fondled his twitching shaft, pulling my hand up and down to his obvious delight. "Is that nice, Lewis?" I asked, temporarily disengaging our lips from the delicious kiss. "Oh, yes, yes, that's marvellous. Just rub up and down a little harder, darling, and put your other hand on my balls. Move your hands further back, still further, ah yes, that's it, just there."

' "Is that better?" I enquired.

' "Yes, oh, yes, ah, that's paradise," he groaned as

I increased the pace of my firm yet gentle handling of his swollen staff. I rubbed away, faster and faster until, with a sudden spurt, a great fountain of hot, creamy froth spurted out from the top of his knob like the eruption of a miniature volcano. His shaft throbbed in my hand as great globs of white spunk burst out, most of which I managed to catch between my lips as I swooped downwards to gobble furiously on his thrusting tool.

'Now it was as well that neither Lewis nor I had time to continue with these high jinks, although his amazing prick was still hard enough to manage the fuck for which my yearning cunney was aching! As he dressed, I complimented him upon the staying power of his cock. "I cannot claim any credit," he said modestly. "It is simply a God-given gift for which I am truly thankful.'

' "Ah, but you keep yourself in good trim and I would wager that you drink only moderately," I remarked.

' "That's true enough, and I don't smoke, either. My Uncle Timothy told me on my fifteenth birthday that, despite what the village schoolmaster or the parson might tell us, tossing off never did a boy any harm at all. [*An enlightened view in times when medical opinion held that masturbation led to illness or even insanity! – RM*] 'But keep away from tobacco,' he warned me. 'You won't be able to enjoy your fucking if you can't control your breathing. And anyhow, in my experience of thirty-five years of pointing my prick at pussies, I've yet to meet a girl who likes the smell of stale tobacco on your tongue." '

'And with those words and a nice farewell kiss, my

odd-job man left me feeling tired yet frustrated,' sighed Selina, her head drooping down quite piteously.

Bob shrugged his shoulders. 'Well, there's always a next time,' he pointed out. 'Lewis is round here about once a week and where there's a will there's a way.'

Selina smiled prettily and nodded. 'That may well be, Bob, but for some reason I thought today was the seventeenth when in fact it's the nineteenth, so it would have been quite alright to have Lewis's cock in my cunney after all!'

'Oh dear, what a shame,' said Bob politely. 'Never mind though, he'll be round again next week.'

'I can't wait that long! I want a big fat prick in my pussey now,' said Selina boldly, reaching out to stroke Bob's cock through the thin material of his trousers. 'Come on, now, I won't tell Miss Penny if you won't tell Sir Paul.'

I can't be unfaithful for a second time today, thought Bob, struggling to stop his shaft swelling up under Selina's crafty ministrations. As if reading his thoughts Selina whispered: 'Don't worry, Bob, I promise I'll never tell and you know what they say – a slice from a cut loaf is never missed.'

Still the young gardener hesitated until Selina used her free hand to unbutton her blouse whilst continuing to stroke his cock. Then the sight of her voluptuous bare breasts simply overwhelmed the poor chap. Their bodies crushed together and they undressed each other in a mad frenzy of lust. Bob's mouth moved from her rich red lips to devour her huge nipples that stood out like buds about to burst as Selina stroked his rigid rod with her fingers. Bob responded by caressing her hips, her firm bum cheeks and then gently brushed her silky pussey hair, and she parted her legs slightly so that he could feel the wetness and so know she was ready to be fucked. The delectable girl lay back and opened her legs wide, coaxing Bob to kneel in front of her and taking hold of his pulsating white prick, then slipped the head of the swollen shaft between her pouting pussey lips.

'Oooh, Bob, you are a big-cocked boy! Fuck me, fuck me, fuck me,' she whispered and Bob thrust forward, sliding every inch of his cock inside her hot, wet love channel until his balls banged against her thighs. A tidal wave of exquisite sensation washed over them both as his throbbing tool stretched the walls of her cunt to their limits. Her hands grabbed Bob's buttocks as their movements became faster and faster until he felt the sweet feeling of an impending orgasm. Thoughtfully, he slowed the pace of his thrusts and waited until Selina's moans grew higher and higher and he judged that she, too, was ready to spend. Then he speeded up the rhythm, plunging his shaft in and out of her soft, wet crack until she arched up from the bed, holding herself there before falling back as Bob shot a tremendous jet of jism inside her as they shuddered into a glorious, simultaneous climax.

Both Selina and Bob would have liked to have enjoyed a further fuck, but the sound of the gong rang out to summon the staff to supper in the servants' hall. So they dressed quickly and ran downstairs where the rest of the staff were already seated at the long table. 'Where have you two been?' demanded Mr Heavan from his place at the head of the table. 'Sorry we're late,' said Selina brightly. 'I was just helping Bob unpack his bag and he was showing me his sketches.'

The butler's eyes narrowed, but he could hardly accuse the pair of anything improper so he stayed silent. The meal in the servants' hall was eaten in a somewhat strained atmosphere with the other members of staff wondering why Mr Heavan was in such a grumpy mood. He could have informed them that he had lusted unsuccessfully after Selina for some time now, but that the saucy minx had totally rebuffed his advances, threatening to report his behaviour to Lady Arkley herself. And, of course, once he discovered that none other than the master of the house, Sir Paul Arkley, had been dipping his prick into Selina's succulent slit, he knew that it was most unlikely that he would ever have his way with the nubile young chambermaid.

So later that night, Mr Heavan retired to his room and lay on his bed, his tormented brain still obstinately refusing to blank out the image of a nude Selina being fucked by the lucky Bob Goggin. He heard the sound of the hip bath in the bathroom above him being filled, which led to a new sensual vision flashing across his mind about the fair Selina.

Mr Heavan's cock lifted itself from his thigh and swelled upwards as he was assailed by lusty thoughts of Selina standing naked by the tub, her gorgeous breasts, arse and cunney fully displayed, and then he saw her step delicately into the bath which was full of hot soapy water. He cupped his cock in his hand and slowly rubbed the swollen shaft as he imagined Selina sponging her silky pussey hair and pressing her fingers against her cunney lips for a few moments before soaping her breasts, making the large red nipples hard and enlarged until she slid right down the bath so that her legs peeked out of the lower end. Now he could see her wet cunney lips outlined through the soap bubbles before she stood up, wriggling her soapy bum with the hairs and pussey lips showing through between her legs. As he fantasised about the delicious girl tickling her wet pussey with her fingers, the butler rubbed his prick with added fervour and, in a trice, his spunk bubbled out onto his hand, rivuleting through his fingers and dripping onto his belly.

'Somehow there must be a way to make Selina agree to a fuck, or at least a sucking off. Otherwise I'll go completely barmy from frigging myself all the time thinking about her,' he muttered to himself. But how could she be cajoled into his bed?

To be fair to the butler, the horrid idea of physically forcing the girl never for a moment crossed his mind. Such nefarious deeds were performed only by the wicked or the inadequate. For what sane, red-blooded man could contemplate, let alone enjoy fucking a girl against her will? The art of persuasion was all, though Mr Heavan played the sweet game with no holds barred. He would tease and tantalise, use every trick known and then some, and more often than not he was rewarded with, at the very least, a quick kiss on the lips, whilst many a time he would thrill to the feel of luscious young breasts, the delicious feel of soft feminine hand on his rock-hard cock, and sometimes there would be no objection to his stealthy hand sliding up under a skirt to pat a damp pair of knickers.

But we must leave Mr Heavan now as he ponders on which way forward he must go to further his desires.

CHAPTER FIVE

Once again, dear reader, we invite you to suspend the march of time and force back the hands of the clock to just after half past three in the afternoon on this grand day for the mating of cocks and cunnies. For even though the twenty-four hours in question has already seen, perhaps, more than its fair share of fucking, an honest scribe is bound to record without fear of favour the complete history of all relevant events without excision. So let us return to the quiet surroundings of Arkley Hall where the eponymous master of the house, Sir Paul, has just waved a fond farewell to his guest, Señor Ribalta, who is now bound for his appointment with the Ambassador at the Spanish Embassy in London.

Both gentlemen had enjoyed the sumptuous repast provided by Sir Paul's famous cook, the redoubtable Mrs Angela Bickler, whose expertise in culinary matters had even reached the ears and, indeed, quite recently the belly of no less a personage than His Royal Highness King Edward VII himself, God bless him! Indeed, only a solid trencherman like His Majesty could even think of partaking of afternoon tea, and the consumption of Mrs Bickler's noted Upside Down

Cake, after wading through one of the cook's splendid luncheons.

Nevertheless, although somewhat tired from his hefty meal, this in no way prevented Sir Paul Arkley from licking his lips when the ever-randy baronet espied for the first time the new assistant parlourmaid, a pretty young girl from the nearby village whom his dear lady wife had engaged only the week before. This new addition to the household was being shown round the library by none other than Selina, whose mere presence would (as on this occasion) stiffen his cock-shaft against the cool material of his fine, Irish linen undershorts, three pairs of which were sent over every Christmas by his sister Edith who was domiciled with her husband, Captain O'Regan, in Dublin.

The new girl was certainly a real find, mused Sir Paul as he looked her over from his comfortable chair. She was genuinely pretty in the fashion beloved by artists for illustrations on boxes of chocolate, with large, dark eyes, a small *retroussé* nose and rich, generous lips. Her sweet face was set off by her long natural tresses of dark brown curly hair. Her figure, too, was pleasing with ample bosoms straining out of her white blouse, a narrow waist – and lovely long legs under the black maid's skirt, I'll be bound, thought Sir Paul, licking his lips again in hopeful anticipation.

Now, as aforesaid, these chronicles must faithfully reflect all happenings, so alas, it must be recorded that Selina's account of her day given to Bob Goggin was, shall it be noted, somewhat economical with the truth! For as one may have already guessed, Selina was privy to some further hanky-panky with Sir Paul Arkley that she had neglected to mention to Bob when she related how frustrated the day had been for her, as she had been labouring under the mistaken belief that she was unable that day to entertain Mr Pego in her itchy pussey. But let us return to the library . . .

'Ah, Selina,' said Sir Paul, stroking his moustache. 'I don't think I have yet met your new assistant.'

Selina looked up innocently. 'Haven't you, sir? Why, this is Norma Sprandall from the village who is going to help me keep the house as Lady Arkley would wish it.'

'Good afternoon, Norma,' said Sir Paul courteously. 'I hope you enjoy your work here and I am sure that Selina will take good care of you.'

'Oh, we're great friends already, sir,' said Selina. 'Why, Norma is sleeping in my room for now. If she's a good girl, she'll move into Mary's room when she leaves next month.'

'So you are sharing with Selina?' said Sir Paul, now even more interested in his new servant. 'I'm sure she will make you feel at home.'

'Thank you, sir, she has certainly done all that I could hope to expect – and more,' said the girl as she curtsied to her new employer.

Sir Paul smiled as he noticed that she looked back boldly at him, seemingly not in the least abashed by meeting the all-powerful master of Arkley Hall.

'By Gad, here's a fine filly,' murmured Sir Paul as he nodded back an acknowledgement, taking hold of Selina's elbow and guiding her across the room to where he could speak to her in private.

'This new girl,' began Sir Paul. 'I like the cut of her jib.'

Selina giggled. 'I bet you do, and you like the shape of her titties as well, that's for sure.'

'Well, yes, though I am sure yours are just as smooth, firm and rounded. Anyhow, you have nothing to worry about, Selina. I assure you that our little games will continue, never fear.'

'But perhaps with new rules to take account of an extra player?' she queried, with a suggestive little smile. 'It should not be too difficult to arrange.'

Sir Paul rubbed his hands together and returned her smile. 'Well, well, well, so you think she would not be averse to joining in a threesome frolic?'

'I don't see why not – as long as she is suitably rewarded for her time. I'm sorry if this disappoints you, but Norma is not totally inexperienced, even though she is not eighteen until November. But she and I took part in a fine whoresome foursome, with Stanley the milkman and Ronnie the grocer's boy, on the village green a couple of weeks ago.'

'Really? So she has taken several pricks in hand, then?'

'And in her mouth, in her cunney and in her bum,' laughed Selina gaily. 'Of course, she hasn't yet enjoyed popping your big cock in her pussey and she has still to learn about some of the finer points of fucking, but I know she would be very grateful if you would be kind enough to demonstrate these to her.'

Sir Paul needed no further bidding. He told Selina to tell her new assistant that both would find five pound notes under their pillows that evening if they would be good enough to meet him in his bedroom in twenty minutes' time.

'Ah, there is just one tiny problem,' murmured Selina. 'You remember that I told you this morning that I cannot entertain your cock in my cunney today.

So I'm game so long as you promise not to try and make me break my resolve.'

'That's understood,' said Sir Paul hastily. 'I would never force my way in any pussey if my attentions were not welcomed. Gad, Selina, I'm an Old Etonian, after all.'

'That's no guarantee,' said Selina darkly. 'But as the only other Old Etonians I knew were both expelled for "the usual reason", I'll take your word that you'll just let me take you in hand.'

'Or in the mouth or up the bum?'

'Naturally.'

The rules of the game having been laid out, it now only required the players to prepare themselves for the fray. Sir Paul and Selina retired upstairs whilst Norma was dispatched to the kitchen to bring out a bottle of champagne from the ice-box. By the time the young girl arrived in the beautifully decorated bedroom, the priapic Sir Paul had already almost undressed and was sitting on the bed clad only in his underpants, with the thick, veiny shaft of his cock standing up high out of the opening of his pants. Selina had already taken off all her clothes except her knickers and was fondling Sir Paul's throbbing staff as the baronet ran his hands lasciviously across her ample breasts, rubbing the red nipples up to erectness against her palms.

'Do come and join in, Norma,' Selina said invitingly as the girl appeared to hesitate.

'Yes, yes, no need to be bashful, m'dear,' said Sir Paul encouragingly before turning to Selina and adding, 'Stop wanking my cock, there's a love, or I'll come too quickly.'

Norma sat down on the edge of the bed and slowly undressed, and it was hard to tell whether it was Sir Paul or Selina who were the more excited when the exquisite girl stood up in all her glorious nudity. Her pretty face was now complemented by long, silky locks of dark brown hair that fell to her shoulders, and her firm, proud breasts were topped by large, dark red aureoles which were capped by two berry-like nipples, so delectable that both Sir Paul and Selina could hardly restrain themselves from each taking a tittie in their mouths. Her snow-white tummy led down to a slim waist from which she was blessed with legs that were a dream of slender elegance. Furthermore, between the creamy columns of her thighs, there lay a forest of curly black hair through which her cunney lips could just be seen peeping through. When Norma turned round and the voluptuous pair viewed the splendid rounded orbs of her arse, Sir Paul breathed: 'What a magnificent bum! And such lovely breasts! Oh, I can hardly wait to slip my prick inside that juicy pussey! Look how stiff you've made my cock!

'Now, Selina, I am going to leave you for a moment and stay on the other side of the bed, because otherwise I shall certainly spend in seconds. Meanwhile, you and Norma can show me what naughty girls get up to when their boyfriends are away.'

Norma giggled at this as she lay down next to Selina and the two lewd girls began kissing and cuddling each other, their legs entwining and their bodies pressed up as closely as possible against each other's soft flesh.

'Shall I be the gentleman?' said Selina.

'Yes, please,' gasped the other trembling girl, twisting round to lie on her back, her legs spread wide as she exchanged a passionate French kiss with Selina whose hands were now busy tweaking Norma's long nipples, which had risen up to greet Selina's clever fingers. She clung to Selina and moaned with desire as the parlourmaid's ardent lips now roamed over her breasts, and her nubile body writhed with the sweet pleasure of it all when Selina began to caress her inner thighs, letting her long fingers stray and linger in the dampening bush of hair at the pit of her belly.

'Is that nice, Norma?' enquired Selina, nibbling gently on the younger girl's ear.

'Mmmmmm!' came back the choking affirmative reply. Expertly, Selina raised her thumb and with each forward twitching of her hips, Norma could feel it touch the tip of her swelling little clitty. The thrilling contact of her cunney upon her hand was so exciting that Norma began to groan petulantly and work her bottom faster while Selina increased the circling motion of her thumb. She lay shimmering with pleasure, swimming in a delightful sensation that warmed her entire body until a deep quivering shook her frame and, all of a sudden, she spurted on Selina's fingers which now drove in and out of her sopping cunt as the two girls exchanged a further burning kiss, sucking their tongues inside each other's mouths.

Sir Paul saw all this and simply could not forbear from taking hold of his cock which was now swollen to its highest extent. He rubbed his throbbing shaft furiously as he kneeled down beside the girls and, in seconds, he ejaculated a stream frothy white spunk all over the panting tribades.

Selina smeared the warm sticky juice all over her

breasts with a little moan. 'Oh, how I'd love to be fucked!' she cried out.

'Only too happy to oblige if you and this delicious young girl will suck my prick up for me,' panted Sir Paul.

Selina scowled. 'Don't start all that – you know I can't fuck today.'

'Don't worry, Selina dear,' cooed Norma. 'Look what I brought up with the champagne.' And with a flourish she produced a superbly carved, smooth wooden dildo. 'This was modelled on the prick of David Nash, the painter who I met in the village last month whilst he was working on what he called a country landscape.'

'Very appropriate,' said Sir Paul heavily. 'And was yours the cunt he landscaped?'

'He wanted to, that's for sure, but the vicar happened to be passing so there wasn't an opportunity. Still, he gave me this dildo as a souvenir of our meeting. He said that it was modelled for him as a birthday present from his favourite model.'

'Never mind all that now,' cried out Selina. 'Will somebody *please* attend to my aching pussey?'

'Allow me, please,' said Sir Paul throatily as he gently prised the dildo from Norma's hand. The randy *roué* kissed Selina and immediately she slipped her tongue inside his mouth. He met it halfway with his own, stroking it softly against her and then licking around the outside of her mouth, tasting the sweet flavour of her scent – which the naughty girl had purloined from Lady Arkley's dressing table just before she took off her clothes.

Sir Paul grunted with satisfaction as he pressed her

hands against her plump breasts and felt the nipples stiffen as he stroked them. Selina could feel a warm wetness already gathering between her thighs as she raised her bottom slightly so that Sir Paul could lay his hand underneath it and tweak her cunney upwards with his fingers. He wasted little time with preliminaries as he probed around her pussey with one hand whilst rubbing and cupping her breasts with the other. Selina trembled all over as the ripe, red lips of her cunt opened magically under his fingertips. The skin of her pussey was wonderfully soft and wet, and though he had done this several times before, Sir Paul always marvelled at the sleek wetness of her crack and how smoothly his forefinger could work in and out.

Then he replaced his finger with the smooth, rounded head of the dildo and Selina gasped as he pressed it between her yielding cunney lips. 'Oooh, that's lovely! Oooh, it's almost as good as a real prick! Finish me off with it, if you don't mind.'

Obediently, Sir Paul slid in the dildo almost to the hilt and brought it out again, the wood now glistening with Selina's love juice. He worked diligently, slipping the imitation cock in and out, increasing the pace of the rhythm as the girl twisted and bucked as she enjoyed the sensation to the utmost.

Meanwhile, Norma had not been idle. When Sir Paul first began to play with Selina's pussey she, too, idly passed her hands between her thighs and as the baronet began to administer the dildo to Selina, Norma took hold of his big throbbing shaft in one hand and rubbed it up and down as with the other she continued to frig herself, dipping two fingers in and out of her hungry slit.

'Together – let's all come together!' gasped Sir Paul as he felt the familiar feeling of sperm bubbling up in his balls. The three of them heaved as one, and with a 'Har-ah' Selina shuddered, her hips squirming with the bliss of final rapture whilst Sir Paul trembled on the brink of a second spend. At this point, though she had already reached a self-induced little spend, Norma took her hand away from her master's throbbing tool. 'Please don't spunk yet, sir,' she urged. 'Selina might not be able to fuck your cock in her cunney, but I most certainly can!'

Gallantly, Sir Paul transferred his hand from Selina's soaking cunt to Norma's equally liquid, oily cavern. His cock was as stiff as a poker and, if anything, over-ready for action. But ever a gentleman, Sir Paul first engaged in a little foreplay to ensure that Norma's juicy crack was one hundred per cent ready to receive his rigid rod.

He was down on his knees in a trice, gluing his lips to the lovely little cunney, sucking and kissing madly to the infinite delight of the seventeen-year-old girl whose few previous lovers had not been as skilled as Sir Paul in the art of eating pussey. She wriggled deliciously and it was now impossible to hold back. He scrambled back up on his knees and brought the head of his straining shaft to the charge and, with one fell swoop – to Norma's high squeal of delight – fairly crammed his fat prick right through her love-channel into the depths of her clinging cunney until his balls banged hard against her bottom cheeks.

They lay still for a few seconds whilst her pulsating pussey throbbed and squeezed his cock so delightfully that he almost swooned away with pleasure. Then she heaved her arse and he responded by a shove of his own and they commenced a most exciting fuck. Sir Paul's veiny pole fairly gleamed with Norma's juices as he worked it in and out of her sheath, her cunney lips clinging to it at each outward stroke of withdrawal as if it was determined not to lose such a delightful partner.

Norma was the first to spend and she jerked like a wild animal as her arms flailed around, her balled fists banging against the mattress. As she shook all over in a rapid series of drawn-out spasms, her cunney squeezed Sir Paul's shaft even tighter, and this made the sperm surge out of his cock, sending him into delerium of orgiastic ecstasy as he pumped a copious emission of white, creamy froth into her wet, warm cleft.

This third libation left Sir Paul *hors de combat* and he collapsed totally and utterly exhausted, lying face down on the well-sprung mattress. The girls were still ready for further fun and games, however, and Norma sat up on her hands and knees and pushed the cheeks of her entrancing young bum outwards, holding them in her hands so that the puckered brown rosette of her nether orifice was staring Selina in the face.

'Ah ha, you would like to be fucked via the trademen's entrance,' gasped Sir Paul, clutching his shrunken shaft which he simply could not coax up to a third stand, despite his frenzied handling.

Selina giggled. 'Well, tools rush in where angels fear to tread, as I heard Mr Oscar Wilde say when Mr Beavan and I caught him buggering a page boy at your last Christmas ball, sir. But I'm afraid that poor Norma will have to make do with a dildo.' And with that, she smeared some pomade on the godemiche before carefully parting Norma's firm buttocks and sliding the head of the dildo between them. Norma gave out a cry of pleasure and twitched her bottom lasciviously as Selina gently pushed the wooden cock forwards. Her rounded bum cheeks jounced and jiggled as Selina pushed relentlessly on until Norma cried out: 'That's deep enough! Now fuck me!' Selina began to slide the dildo in and out of the wrinkled little opening and, at first, Norma wriggled uncomfortably, but then her sphincter muscle relaxed and Selina manipulated the dildo with ease, plunging in and out of the now widened rim as Norma jerked her supple hips to the rhythm of Selina's frigging of her arse.

Sir Paul gallantly reached out to slide a hand up to finger-fuck the sweet girl to double her pleasure, and very soon the love juices were pouring out from her as she built up to a fine climax, screaming out: 'Faster, faster, you two, I want more up my bum and more in my cunney! Hoo-oo-AH!' With a frantic shudder, Norma achieved a delicious spend as she fell face downwards on the bed next to Sir Paul. Selina still had the dildo inside the girl and she extracted it with an audible plop as Norma's backside gave one final wriggle.

'Oh, how naughty!' panted Selina. 'Well, sir, we can stay just a few minutes longer and then Norma and I have to finish our chores. You won't forget out little presents, will you?'

'Certainly not, my dears,' said Sir Paul with a hint of indignation. 'You know that I have never welshed on any of our arrangements, and I don't intend to start doing so now, especially after such a glorious fuck.

'I only wish I could get my cock stiff again for a final fling,' he added, looking down sadly at his limp prick.

'I'll see what I can do, sir,' said Norma, taking hold of Sir Paul's shaft which hung thickly, with his helmet almost fully absorbed back into his foreskin. She leaned over and tongued the tip of his knob before taking it between her lips and cramming his turgid member inside her mouth. But alas, despite all her efforts, Sir Paul just could not rise to the occasion.

The Master of Arkley Hall took his still-soft shaft out of the girl's mouth. 'Oh well, Norma, thank you for trying but I think we'll have to wait till tomorrow night,' he said philosophically wisely realising that to carry on, vainly willing his prick to rise, might be injurious to his general health.

There is no doubt that Sir Paul was right to call a halt there and then to the proceedings. Even the randiest reprobates, such as the famed Mr Alan Brooke of Mayfair (whom we shall soon meet again), would probably have been unable to present a stiff cock after Sir Paul's programme this day that comprised a morning bum-fuck, a rich luncheon prepared by Mrs Bickler, and the lewd goings-on we have just witnessed. Indeed, as Mr Brooke, perhaps the most vigorous and frenetic fucker in London, was known to say when his cock failed to rise to the occasion: 'If at first you don't succeed, try and try again – and then you must simply give up for an hour or so. It's amazing how a nice little nap can change the condition of an exhausted prick.'

Small comfort this, however, for the crestfallen Sir Paul who would have gladly donated five hundred guineas to a charity of their choice to any man or woman who could have produced a magic elixir which would have stiffened his cock! Especially as Selina cooed: 'Who says we are the weaker sex, Norma? Why, most girls I know can continue fucking for hours. It's always the lack of stiff pricks that signals the end of the sport.'

'Quite true,' admitted the younger girl, slipping an arm around Selina's waist as they gathered their clothes together. 'Come on now, I challenge you to run naked up to our room. Are you game? There's no-one around here at this time of day.'

Never one to resist a challenge, Selina accepted the dare. They gave Sir Paul a goodbye kiss, planting their lips first on his cheeks and then on his hairy ballsack before skipping lightly out of the room.

Now Norma was quite correct in her assumption that no-one should have seen the two girls dash naked up the stairs to their attic bedroom. But as luck would have it, Mr Heavan had decided to lumber up to Mrs Bickler's quarters to ask her advice about which bottles should be decanted that evening for dinner, as in addition to her culinary prowess, the cook was noted for her wide knowledge of the finest French wines.

And what a surprise awaited him as he slowly climbed the stairs – for as he turned to take the final few steps, the naked girls pattered across the landing before his very eyes before disappearing into Selina's bedroom.

The butler rubbed his eyes in disbelief. Was he seeing two erotic ghosts? It couldn't be the effects of drink. Mr Heavan was capable of imbibing substantial quantities of cognac from the Arkley Hall cellar, but in all truth he had not touched a drop of Sir Paul's special 1882 Napoleon V.S.O.P. which had been sent to the Arkleys the previous Christmas by the Belgian *Chargé d'Affaires* in London, Colonel Aspis, who like Sir Paul was an *aficionado* of the wild *salles privées* of the West End of London. [*In several underground magazines of the 1890s such as* The Oyster, Cremorne Gardens *and* The Jenny Everleigh Diaries, *Colonel Aspis is often mentioned* en passant. *He was an honorary steward at the Jim Jam Club, Great Windmill Street and a committee member of the ultra exclusive Cock and Crop circle, both of which were often patronised by The Prince of Wales – RM*]

Mr Heavan climbed the final stairs to the top landing as quietly as possible and stood outside Selina's bedroom, listening to the high-pitched giggles of the two 'ghosts' inside. He bent down and tried to peer through the keyhole, but the aperture was obscured as, just for once, Selina had locked her door. 'Where are my knickers?' he heard Norma ask, and he knew then that his eyes had not deceived him and that for some reason (as yet unknown), the two girls had taken off all their clothes and had gone back to the room to dress.

'It must be the master up to his old tricks again,' he muttered. 'It's just not fair. He can fuck from morning till night with as many girls as his cock can handle, whilst I'm lucky if I get as much as a sniff of pussey.'

The very thought of Sir Paul slicing his sinewy shaft between the proud, firm bum cheeks of young Norma was enough to send Mr Heavan's cock stiffening upwards. The butler relieved himself by unbuttoning his fly and letting his not inconsiderably sized truncheon out into the open. He grasped it in his hand

and began to work it up and down until, with a satisfied grunt, he sent a stream of spunk flying across the landing. 'Damn and blast,' he thought to himself, for having neglected to wrap his prick round with a handkerchief. He was now faced with the task of explaining away the wet dribble of jism that ran down Selina's bedroom door and onto the pink carpet.

At this juncture Selina opened the door and the girls swept right by him. 'Afternoon, Mr Heavan. Keeping well, are you?' asked Norma with a touch of cheekiness in her voice. The butler blushed and nodded a brief acknowledgement. He stood rooted to the spot as the girls made their way downstairs, chattering and laughing, and Mr Heavan could swear he heard the words 'suck, fuck and cock' interspersed in their conversation. Would he ever have his wicked way with one of the staff?

Meanwhile, Sir Paul Arkley was enjoying a nice little post-fucking snooze. Although he was dreaming of Norma's cherry nipples, when he finally awoke, he looked down with a crestfallen expression for, despite the erotic content of his dream, his usually tumescent tool had remained obstinately soft and flabby and was lying at rest over his thigh.

Sir Paul frowned and gave his shaft a little shake – to no avail. What should I do? he thought, and fortunately he remembered the instruction given to members of the Jim Jam Club at their last meeting. The committee had invited the noted sexologist, Doctor David Zwaig of the University of Bohemia, currently a Visiting Professor at University College, London to prepare a lecture on poorly standing pricks, and though Sir Paul had thankfully rarely been afflicted with this problem, he had listened closely to the words of Doctor Zwaig. 'The first rule is never to panic,' the good doctor had stressed. 'Before intercourse, the main reason may be simply nervousness if the lady has not previously been fucked by you before, or because you have eaten too much or passed the port once too often – or, indeed, because you are worried that her husband might come home early and catch you *in flagrante delicto*.

'After the fucking the same reasons could well apply for, alas, none of us is getting any younger and no man in the world is living who can fuck at fifty as he could at eighteen! My personal recommendation is a short sleep, and if one's partner is not readily available to attempt manual or oral stimulation, in an emergency one could always try out a remedy passed on to me by Count Gewirtz of Galicia, and old friend who I think is known to many members of the Jim Jam Club.

[*Count Gewirtz was certainly known by Sir Paul Arkley, who eagerly accepted the invitation to a monumental orgy at the Count's Mayfair mansion at which the Prince of Wales was present – for a full account see* Cremorne Gardens – *RM*]

'A few years back, one of the Count's horses, Silver Geschaft, which should have been in contention for the Derby, always missed out because of a laziness in starting to run. When the Count questioned Captain Monty Smythe-Edgware, who looks after the Count's stables at Lambourn, he was told of an old French method of stimulation which was to jam a phial of mustard up the horse's backside. Well, you may laugh, gentlemen, but the horse went on to win the Cambridgeshire and several other races – so long as at the line-up, the stable-boy inserted the necessary little packet.'

'I don't really believe this malarkey,' muttered Sir Paul, 'but I suppose it must be worth a try.' He rang down to the kitchen and told the kitchenmaid to bring up a pot of mustard and leave it outside his door. He could always have asked her to smear it on his prick, but Sir Paul did not really fancy the girl and – to give credit where credit is due – did not wish simply to take advantage of his position. Also, to be frank, Gertie was not the prettiest of her species and Sir Paul had little trouble in behaving in a chivalrous manner towards her. We will record his gentlemanly attitude, however, and place it in the credit side of his personal ledger.

Be that as it may, Sir Paul gathered up the tray left outside his door and looked quizzically at the little silver pot of mustard that had been so promptly delivered to his door by the obliging Mrs Bickler.

Despite his concern, he couldn't resist smiling as he suddenly thought about what the estimable Mrs B. might have made of his strange request, and what perhaps she might comment upon the matter. Indeed, his imagination had correctly prophecied the actuality, for at that very moment the plump cook was saying to the butler: 'You won't believe this, Mr Heavan, but Sir Paul has asked me to send up a pot of mustard to him. No sandwiches nor any food, but just a pot of mustard. What on earth can he want it for?'

'He can stick it up his arse for all I care,' said the butler gloomily, still in the throes of contemplating the unpalatable fact that, despite all the sweet young pussey apparently on offer in Arkley Hall, he seemed unable to find any progress further than a solitary five knuckle shuffle. He would have been cheered, perhaps, to know that his reply was more accurate than he could ever have guessed but of course, what happened in Sir Paul's bedroom never reached his ears.

Mrs Bickler shrugged and carried on with her work. She guessed what was troubling the butler, but though she sympathised, she had no way of helping him solve his problem.

For although Mr Bickler had run off nine years beforehand with the eldest daughter of Lord and Lady Beigel, the cook had been successfully wooed by Sergeant Plancey of the local constabulary.

It was known both upstairs and downstairs that for the last five years they had enjoyed a very comfortable arrangement by which Mrs Bickler spent all her free time in the Sergeant's charming cottage. This suited her perfectly as he could wield his truncheon to far better effect than her former lover – who was last seen travelling fourth class on a one-way ticket to Buenos Aires, having been waylaid in a public bar by a group of desperados hired by Lady Beigel. So everyone except, perhaps, the unfortunate Mr Bickler was quite content with the cook's slightly unorthodox arrangements.

In the meantime, Sir Paul was gingerly daubing his fingers with mustard as prescribed by the good Doctor Zwaig. He lay flat on his back on the bed and smeared the yellow paste all over his shaft. As he did so, his cock quivered and, as he continued to rub, began to swell up until his foreskin snapped back and his purple knob popped out proudly from its covering. 'By Jove, it works!' he gasped, and continued to frig his now fully erect prick for a moment until he suddenly stopped and said aloud: 'It would be madness to waste this,' Then, as if by magic, there was a tap on the door. 'Who's there?' he called out. 'Selina, sir.' 'Come in quickly, please,' and added wittily. 'Something's just come up that I think you should know about.'

The insatiable girl was delighted to see his stiff-standing shaft as she entered the room. 'I somehow thought you might recover, but why is your cock as yellow as a Chinaman's? What's wrong with you? Have you been told to put some medical ointment on it?'

'Don't worry, silly girl. It's only mustard,' he said testily.

Selina giggled. 'Mustard? I've seen it all now. Remember I told you how Sir Denis Le Baigue liked to smother his prick in cream and have me lick it all off. Or that nice old Reverend Hammond who used to dip his balls in brandy and have me lap up the liquor as it dripped down from his ballsack. But I don't fancy mustard, except with a nice ham sandwich!'

'All right, all right, don't make a meal of it,' said Sir Paul, and he too burst out into a peal of laughter as he realised his inadvertent slip of the tongue.

'You can explain it all later,' said Selina wickedly, grabbing hold of his pulsating penis. 'Well, it's lucky that I guessed you'd be game for another ride as I didn't put on my knickers! Let's see if I can make you spunk again.'

She quickly undressed and took the knob of his prick in her mouth, washing the soft-skinned dome with her saliva. Then, placing the swollen shaft between her big breasts, she whispered in Sir Paul's ear: 'Fuck my tits, sir, you know how that turns me on. Oooh, that's nice, you'll make me spend if you do that!'

Sir Paul was happy to oblige as Selina clasped her rounded globes and squeezed them round his throbbing shaft. He rocked his hips back and forth as he slid his tool between the snug cushions of Selina's full breasts. She threw back her head and her white teeth glistened as her lips parted and her eyes closed in ecstasy. 'Yes, yes, yes, yes, yes, YES!' she screamed as she fingered her pussey with one hand and fondled Sir Paul's hairy ballsack with the other.

As she came, the baronet whipped out his shaft from the delicious cushion and spurted a stream of hot spunk splashing across her titties. He pumped his prick with his hand, squirting wads of sperm over Selina's heaving breasts. He rocked back on his knees as he emptied his balls, the final sprays shooting out onto Selina's chin. She rubbed the love juice all around her red aureoles and erect little strawberry nipples that stood out like bullets.

When she had licked up as much of the precious liquid as she could, Selina looked up at Sir Paul mischievously and said: 'I hope Mrs Bickler has lots and lots of mustard in the larder.'

'So do I,' he rejoined. 'It certainly did the trick as far as I was concerned. What an effective if unusual remedy.'

Whilst not grudging this happy pair their frolic, dear reader, it is perhaps a shame that a report about their fuck took some time to reach the ears of Doctor David Zwaig, whose learned advice had apparently worked wonders. For in truth, he had only mentioned the mustard treatment as a joke. Nevertheless, when he was finally informed about it by Count Gewirtz – for

Sir Paul gleéfully recounted the incident at the Jim Jam Club six months later – the good Doctor was delighted that his treatment had turned out, as he was later to say, so 'sucksexful'!

Yet Sir Paul remained unsatisfied and, as he stroked his still erect cockshaft, he made a mental note to write a letter of thanks to Doctor Zwaig though, unknown to him, the sexologist was soon to move to France. His mind then turned to matters more erotic as he continued to rub his massive tool up to bursting point. Thoughts of his recent trip to Edinburgh crossed his mind. When in the company of his old friend, John Gibson, the wealthy Scottish dilettante, he had enjoyed the favours of Sophie, a French student at the university in Scotland's capital city, who the kind Mr Gibson had taken under his wing – and into his bed! But, as ever being the generous host, the Caledonian cocksman had insisted that Sir Paul watch him perform a bedroom reel with Sophie after which he, Sir Paul, would be cordially invited to join in the proceedings.

Sir Paul's hand travelled up and down his shaft as he recalled that glorious afternoon. John Gibson had just shown the value of a kilt, there being no damned buttons or trouser legs out of which to struggle before throwing yourself down on the bed between the smooth thighs of the gorgeous Sophie. Gad! The frisky French filly had nevertheless waited patiently until he had struggled out of his clothes and, when at last he found himself on top of the delicious girl, her hands slipped down immediately to clasp his bum cheeks as she eagerly lifted her hips to welcome his thrusting cock which slid squelchily in and out of her sopping crack, already so wet with her own juices and those of Mr

Gibson who had already deluged her love channel with a copious effusion of his essence.

Sir Paul groaned as he thought of the exquisite grip of Sophie's velvet cunney walls, as the clever girl sinuously moved her hips as his heavy balls smacked against her inner thighs. The memory proved too delicious for his tingling tool which pulsed under the pressure of his insistent frigging. Suddenly, a torrent of white sticky sperm flooded out of his cock and covered his hand as the delightful sensation of orgasm cascaded throughout his body. Sir Paul sighed as he wiped his hands on a hand towel that he kept under the pillow for this very purpose, and decided then and there that he must work out an excuse to visit Mr Gibson again as soon as possible, especially as Sophie would be returning home to Paris before Christmas.

The problem, though, was how to get away without the encumbrance of his dear lady wife, who almost always insisted on accompanying him on any trip north of the border. For Lady Arkley was a firm believer in the old Welsh saying that when a man's away, his cock will stray – especially as far as Sir Paul was concerned! So she had insisted on accompanying him on his last visit to Edinburgh, but luckily she had spent that afternoon taking tea with her maiden aunt who lived in Stirling. Sir Paul had managed to miss the tea party by pleading a bad headache. He had cashed that particular cheque, so to speak, so what excuse could he think of now? An eternal optimist, Sir Paul knew that in time he would think of a foolproof plan.

Let us now leave Sir Paul secure in the arms of Morpheus, dear reader, and look at happenings at Newman

Woods, which are situated just over a mile away from the Arkley Hall grounds. Who do we see idling along the path there towards the village but Lewis, the odd-job man who plugged Selina's bottom-hole well enough just before, but whose stalwart staff now positively ached for a taste of soft, squelchy pussey, for we must remember that Selina felt it necessary to deny him this ultimate delight.

His thoughts turned to his long-standing girl friend, Tessa, who worked as a milkmaid for Farmer Clee. A twang of conscience pricked the young man who had just enjoyed the pleasures of the flesh with another girl, but he shrugged it off with a mutter about a slice off a cut loaf never being missed.

With that comforting thought in mind, he scrunched his way along the leaf-strewn track and suddenly heard the sweet sound of a laughing feminine voice wafting on the breeze. Lewis paused and listened carefully, thinking at first he must have simply heard an early nightingale calling from the woods. But no, there it was again, although now the first voice was joined by another masculine one. He could not quite make out any of the spoken words, but the girl's voice sounded suspiciously like his own Tessa's – but what on earth was she doing in the woods with a man at this time of day?

Lewis walked stealthily towards the voices, making as little noise as possible. It soon became obvious just what was going on, and his handsome face had darkened with a raw anger by the time he reached the edge of a small clearing. There, as he had expected, Tessa lay on a mossy bank of leaves and grass, entwined in the arms of none other than the curate, an earnest young man named Marcus Thatcher, who somewhat nervously was attempting to undo the buttons on Tessa's low-cut blouse which barely covered the white swell of her bosoms.

'Here, let me show you how to do it,' she cried. 'Why, I never knew anyone so clumsy before. Anyone would think this is the first time you have tried to unbutton a lady's garment.'

The young man blushed to the roots of his hair. 'Well, actually, I must confess that it *is* the first time, Tessa.'

'Really?' she squealed happily. 'Does this then mean you've never ever – ' She had no need to finish her sentence as Marcus's head hung low. 'Oh now, don't worry, dear,' said Tessa brightly. 'We all have to begin sometime and you're just a late starter, that's all.

Lie back and relax and I'll get you going, that's for sure. That is, if you really want to fuck me,' she added, pushing him down upon the mossy hillock.

'Oh Tessa, I want to make love to you more than anything else in the whole world,' he answered, his voice cracking with emotion. She smiled mysteriously and smoothed her hand over the bulge that had formed in Marcus's lap, and slowly unbuckled his braces. Then her practised hands opened the buttons of his fly and released his stiff cock which Lewis noticed, with barely suppressed irritation, was as thick and perhaps of even greater length than his own well-endowed equipment.

Tessa now began to massage Marcus's swollen shaft, drawing back his foreskin which made the purple helmet swell and bound in her hand. He gasped as she suddenly bent down and planted a loving wet kiss on his uncapped knob. 'Goodness me, what are you doing?' he whispered. 'My, my, don't you know about sucking off? Oh, Marcus, what a lovely surprise you have coming to you!' she replied with an infectious giggle. 'Just lie back and I'll show you what I mean.'

Marcus could hardly believe his eyes as Tessa knelt down to make herself more comfortable before giving his twitching helmet another quick little moistening lick. She then opened her mouth wide and took at least three inches of his throbbing tool into her mouth. As Lewis, watching this lewd scene knew full well, Tessa was an excellent exponent of this delicious art, and Marcus was soon in the seventh heaven of delight as her moist mouth worked its way along the length of his succulent shaft, her hand grasping the base of his cock as she pumped her head up and down, keeping her lips taut, kissing and sucking until suddenly she pulled her lips away to look at the pre-spend juices which were now oozing out of the tiny 'eye' at the top of his knob. She knew that he would be unable to hold on for much longer so she clamped her lips back over his prick and slurped noisily over the mushroom dome as she gently squeezed his balls. With a hoarse cry Marcus shot a tremendous stream of foamy spunk into her mouth, its force sending the precious cream to the back of her throat. Greedily, she rubbed his pulsating pole frenziedly as she sucked in and swallowed his powerful jets of love juice, milking his cock of every last drop until she felt his rock-hard member soften in her mouth to a semi-stiffness. She looked up at him wide-eyed, her mouth slowly disengaging itself from its sweetmeat.

'How did you enjoy that, your reverendship? I'm sure you really enjoyed that first lesson. It beats tossing yourself off, doesn't it now?' she asked in her blunt country way.

'Oh yes, Tessa, it was wonderful. I don't see how, er, actual intercourse can be better than that.'

'Ah, you just wait a moment and let me undress,' chuckled Tessa, standing up and turning her back to him. After kicking off her shoes she quickly shrugged off the blouse from her shoulders and slipped out of her skirt. She stood naked except for her white cotton knickers, which she rolled down with a tantalising slowness, revealing the perfect rounded globes of her bottom to the astonished curate who could still hardly believe what this sunny September afternoon was offering him.

She turned round to face him, and Marcus's heart began to pound as he drank in the erotic beauty of Tessa's pretty face, her proud, jutting red-tipped breasts and the soft triangle of blonde furry hair that nestled between her legs.

'Now it's your turn,' she prompted and needing little further bidding, he tore off his clothes, flinging his jacket and trousers aside, tearing off his shirt with such force that he ripped off two buttons which would never be recovered.

Tessa reached down and took hold of his throbbing prick in her hands. It had risen up smartly again to its full height and it was now time for Marcus to make his first-ever journey through the soft, slippery folds of Tessa's love channel to Elysium. The delightful girl put her hands on his shoulders and made Marcus kneel before her. With a smile of satisfaction she followed suit and then lay down in front of him, spreading her thighs open as she took hold of his hot, velvety-skinned shaft in order to guide him to his first blissful experience of fucking.

Marcus trembled uncontrollably as the tip of his cock touched the soft folds of Tessa's cunt. The dear girl wondered at first why he did not plunge his prick directly into her wet, waiting cunney. Then, in a flash, she understood how nervous he still was and so, clasping his tight little bum cheeks, she pulled him inside her. The sweet stimulation of her cunney muscles sent shivers of exquisite delight racing through Marcus's body as he began to jerk his shaft in and out of heaven's gate. The pace of their fucking increased and, though this was not only Marcus's initiation into the grand old sport but also the first time Tessa had entertained his meaty todger, somehow it seemed so natural that it was as though they had performed this act many times before. Their breathing was in unison, deeper now as a sheen of sweat oiled their writhing bodies. His pulsing penis tingled with excitement from the firm pressure of Tessa's inner walls and they fitted together so snugly, as Marcus was later to confess to his old friend, the Reverend Porlocke, it was as though a benign Providence had designed each for the pleasure of the other.

Tessa lifted up her legs even more and crossed them behind his waist, pressing him down still further inside her, though she was careful not to grasp too tightly and inhibit his natural rhythm. They speeded up and it was just as well that Marcus had previously spunked or he would never have been able to keep going until the end of the ride to glory. Tessa enjoyed the virgin cock that slewed so lustily in and out of her dripping crack, as each renewed level in tempo took the pair inexorably towards the final climax. Now it was Tessa's turn to tremble as she felt the first delicious tinglings of an approaching spend, so she reached down to squeeze Marcus's balls. This had the desired effect as a strangulated cry came from his throat and his prick released a veritable tidal wave of jism that flooded uncontrollably from his twitching shaft. Tessa screamed out her joy and she matched every surge as she, too, discharged her love juices as tide met tide in the whirlpool of their joint orgasms.

Yet though they both panted and shuddered as their heightened senses began to descend from the very peaks, there was no sudden collapse or final exhausted thrustings as smoothly they slowed to a halt, Marcus's cock still lodged in Tessa's now-satisfied slit.

'You're still hard,' said Tessa with wonder in her voice. 'Stay inside me, I can still feel you.' Tenderly, they hugged each other until with a last quiver of emotion, his prick began to lose its stiffness and he finally withdrew his shaft. Tessa kissed him, a look of total fulfilment spreading over her pretty face. She whispered: 'Well done, Marcus! You are a natural cocksman and I envy the girl with whom you will finally settle. Please don't ever forget, though, that it was Tessa Brownlow who gave you your first taste of pussey.'

Marcus rolled off the girl's curvaceous body and he sat up, saying: 'I'll never forget your kindness, Tessa. But the way you speak leads me to think that we will never enjoy the pleasure of a mutual fuck again. This makes me very sad – do tell me I am wrong.'

'No, I'm afraid you are quite correct. I think we would both find that a second bite of the cherry would not taste so sweet,' replied the milkmaid who was wise beyond her years. 'Besides the fact that Lewis the odd-job man and me have an understanding, you'd begin to get a conscience about screwing me. After all, what do you think about every Sunday in Church?'

He blushed and said: 'Your rebuke is well justified. However, this little secret romance will remain indelibly fixed in my memory, Tessa.' She nodded and tossed him his underpants. 'Get dressed, Marcus, and you be off. We had better make our separate ways home.'

Once he had dressed, the curate kissed her goodbye and walked briskly away, leaving Tessa, still naked, sitting with her arms around her knees on their bed of leaves. Now Lewis decided to break cover and strode purposefully into the clearing. Surprisingly enough, Tessa looked at him with an unhurried sigh: 'Hello, Lewis, I wondered when you were going to come out from behind that bush.'

'You knew I was there?' he said in astonishment.

'Oh yes,' Tessa said calmly. 'I saw your face peeping out whilst I was sucking off the curate.'

'Did you now,' he said sourly. 'And did you think that was a nice thing to do when, as you told Marcus, we had an understanding.'

She looked coolly at him. 'Nice enough when the boy you have an understanding with is busy fucking a parlourmaid up at Arkley Hall!'

Lewis's jaw dropped in amazement. Tessa gave a short laugh and continued: 'Oh Lewis, don't look so surprised. Don't you know by now that you can't sneeze in this village without someone offering you a handkerchief.'

'I deserved that, as Marcus just said,' he replied after a brief shamefaced pause.

'Yes, you did,' said Tessa, whose pussey was beginning to itch again. 'But you can make amends here and now by taking off all your clothes and sitting next to me.'

He looked up bright-eyed with a new-found happiness. 'You forgive me, then?' Tessa's eyes twinkled as she nodded her assent. Within a minute or even less Lewis was sitting next to her, caressing her marvellously firm breasts that jutted out so magnificently with their cherry-topped titties which were so sensitive to his touch, springing up to erection in his hands.

'I've been naughty as well, Lewis,' Tessa confessed timidly. 'I think I might have sucked Marcus's cock even if I hadn't found out about you and Selina.

'Mind you, I wouldn't have let him fuck me afterwards,' she added hastily.

'So you've been naughty?' echoed Lewis softly. 'Well now, you know what happens to naughty girls, don't you?'

There was a slight pause.

'You do know, don't you?' he repeated.

'They get their bottoms slapped,' she answered with a giggle as she scrambled to her knees and draped herself over Lewis's knees.

'That's right – now open your legs a little wider 'cos I want to make sure that your pussey feels the back of my hand, too.'

Tessa felt his cock rise stiffly against her tummy as with one hand Lewis fondled her hanging breasts, and with the other smoothed over the smooth white skin of her peach-shaped arse cheeks. Then he brought both hands to run them over her perfect backside, opening the cheeks to reveal her wrinkled little brown rosette and then pushing them tightly together again before beginning her chastisement with a few light, rapid slaps which made her wriggle deliciously and made his shaft rock-hard, despite being crushed between their two bellies.

'That's nice, I like this, but not too hard now,' she gasped. 'Ow! Ouch! Not too hard!'

Lewis ignored her plea and quickened the pace of his slaps, although he did not really hit her reddening cheeks any more forcefully. 'Ow! Ow! Ow!' she yelped until Lewis said: 'Quiet now, you've been a bad girl and you must be punished like all naughty girls. Besides, I love to see your arse cheeks jiggle and change colour as I slap them. Why, they are getting quite rosy now!'

However, after she pleaded with him to stop, he gave her one last whack on her gorgeous rump before he let her stand up and rub her poor bum. His cock was now almost bursting as he looked down upon his veiny shaft with its uncapped red helmet which twitched away as if it possessed a life of its own.

Tessa sank to her knees in front of him and took his shaft lovingly in her hands. 'Would you like me to suck you off?' she enquired.

Was there a red-blooded man in the whole wide world who could resist such an erotic invitation? Of course not! 'Yes please,' said Lewis politely as she lightly kissed the swollen knob and licked her way round the rim.

Lewis held her head tightly in his hands as she sucked in the majestic crown of his cock, enclosing her lips around it as tightly as she could. She worked her tongue all around the smooth dome, washing the soft, hot skin as she eased her lips forward, taking in more and more cock as her hands circled the thick base of his staff. She worked the loose skin up and down his big pole and began to bob her head up and down, aided by the push on the back of her head by Lewis's strong hands. She almost choked on his throbbing tool and Lewis immediately pulled out a couple of inches of his swollen shaft. 'I'm so sorry,' he muttered. 'I got carried away.'

Tessa smiled and went back to work with a will, licking and lapping his glistening prick, gobbling noisily on his vibrating organ until Lewis cried out hoarsely that he was about to spend. She braced herself as the frothy spunk spurted into her mouth and she tried hard to swallow all of his creamy emission, but try as she could, some sperm dribbled from her mouth as she milked his prick beautifully, caressing his ballsack to extract every last morsel of nectar from his heavy testicles.

Lewis wanted to continue, but even for a girl with such a voracious sexual appetite as Tessa, enough was enough and she said: 'Let's save your spunk for later on, Lewis, or have you forgotten that Farmer Clee is giving all his hands supper at the Bell Inn tonight to celebrate the engagement of his daughter to General Platts-Lane's son?'

'Do you mean that twit Harold Platts-Lane who you told me offered you a sovereign if you would show him your titties?'

'That's the boy, and I sent him away with a flea in his ear, I can tell you. I'm proud of my titties but I'll show them to whom I choose.'

Lewis agreed and felt proud that his lady-love had stood her ground against the silly young fool who could apparently only get a girl to bare her breasts by offering her money. 'Have you time for a beer?' he asked, changing the subject as they entered the village.

'Won't you be guzzling enough tonight? I don't want you getting brewer's droop,' retorted Tessa.

'I'm thirsty now,' said Lewis simply and began to sing an old drinking song:

'O, good beer, I love you,
In you I put my luck.
I'd sooner go to bed with a belly-full
Than I'd go to bed for a fuck!
Though on you I spends my money
And go without good clothes,
Yet, O, good beer, I love you,
So down my throat you goes!'

'I see, Lewis Brackenshaw, you prefer swilling a pint of ale to slipping your cock in my cunney. Well, if that's the way you feel perhaps I should look out for another,' cried out Tessa in mock severity.

'No, no, don't do that – I'll sign the temperance pledge if you want, so long as you always keep your dear little pussey lips open for me,' he said hastily.

Tessa kissed him again and said: 'That won't be necessary, darling, for you know what they say, a little of what you fancy does you good!'

And on that note we will take our leave of the lovers as they walked on past the churchyard, pausing only to record the quaint inscription on the stone put up to the memory of Colonel Horace Bent, the village squire between 1752 and 1788:

Vixi, Peccavi, Poenitui,
Naturae, Cessi, Resurgam.

[I lived, I sinned, I repented; I have paid the debt to Nature, I will rise again – RM]

Back at Arkley Hall, Bob had changed his clothes and was washing his cock and balls in the sink as he was quite a fastidious young man and, though partial to the tangy aroma of pussey, preferred to clean himself up after a good fuck. He dried himself and went to his linen cupboard for some fresh underpants when he heard sounds coming from the adjoining room which belonged to Charles, the Arkley's chauffeur. Now the wooden dividing wall between the two rooms had been rather carelessly thrown up by a local builder. There was no back to Bob's wardrobe and for the first time he noticed that there was a small but distinct hole in the wall, big enough certainly for him to peer into and see what was afoot next door.

Although he had long suspected Charles of wanting to fuck Selina, it was an open secret downstairs at Arkley Hall that the chauffeur was regularly servicing Henrietta, the beautiful daughter of General Platts-Lane, whose stupid son Harold, it will be recalled had tried to buy the favours of Tessa the milkmaid.

This clod's sister, though, was as different in both brain and beauty to her brother as chalk is to cheese. Henrietta was only seventeen years old but had been much admired by scions of the local gentry for some time.

She was one of Tennyson's rosebud garden of girls, a truly exquisite beauty with gold-dusted light-brown hair which she wore long and loose. Her pale skin set off her rosy red lips and perfect white teeth and when she went out walking, young men who passed her would be almost overawed by her breathtaking loveliness. Indeed, it was this shyness, afflicting the young men her choleric father might have found suitable for his daughter, which had led Henrietta into the arms of the admittedly handsome Charles. He had boldly courted the girl whenever Sir Paul and Lady Arkley had visited the General and Mrs Platts-Lane (who in her day had also turned many heads and had been rumoured to have been one of the first mistresses of the Prince of Wales).

Bob could hardly banish lascivious thoughts from his brain as he saw that this gorgeous creature was taking off all her clothes in front of Charles, who had already undressed and was helping Henrietta step out of her skirt, his thick cock standing stiffly upwards out of a mass of dark hair, his uncapped knob pressing against his flat belly, high above his navel. Bob's own prick also swelled up to a tremendous erection as the divine girl wriggled out of her knickers and showed to full advantage her superbly formed uptilted breasts, each crowned with a tiny button of a pink nipple, her slender waist and the glossy thatch of brown hair at the base of her belly.

Then, when she sat down on Charles's bed and opened her legs, Bob almost swooned at the sight of the most delightful cunt he had ever seen. From the silky brown moss, her serrated cunney lips were slightly parted and from them, projecting at least two or even three inches, a fleshy clitoris almost as big as a man's thumb.

With a lascivious smile, she parted the lips of this

glorious cunney with her long, tapering fingers and Bob's hand flew to his bare cock as he imagined passing the tip of his tongue around those most sensitive feminine parts, taking the delicious morsel in his mouth and rolling it around in his mouth, savouring the pungent aroma whilst playfully attacking it with his teeth.

Delightful as this fantasy was for young Bob, the actuality was even more pleasurable for the lucky Charles who Henrietta encouraged to take all the liberties he desired with her, kissing and sucking her pretty titties, handling her bum cheeks and frigging her erect clitty whilst she stroked his big cock with skilful fingers. He climbed on top of her as she lay back, but when he moved to insert his knob against her cunney lips, she pulled his shaft forwards between her rounded breasts. Nothing loath, Charles tit-fucked the trembling girl, rubbing his shaft between those exquisitely formed spheres while she cupped his balls in one hand and played with her pussey with the other, dipping her fingers in and out of her sticky honeypot.

'Oooh, oooh, oooh, oooh!' she panted as she quickly achieved a spend. 'Oooh, that's really divvy, Charles. I must suck your cock now and make you come in my mouth! You know how I love to swallow your sperm.'

Again, the chauffeur was more than happy to fall in with her wishes and he rolled off her and lay on his back, his massive truncheon curving upwards in a lewd salute to the girl as she curled her fingers around the hot, rock-hard rammer. Poor Bob could no longer contain himself when she dipped down her mass of curls and began to lick Charles's enormous, red-mushroomed helmet and sent a fountain of jism splashing against the wall as he frigged furiously away.

Meanwhile, Henrietta was clearly a girl who thoroughly enjoyed cocksucking. She began by tonguing Charles's shaft, licking and lapping in long, lingering strokes until she reached his bursting ruby crown which she greeted with a series of hot, liquid kisses which pushed him to the very edge. Her magic tongue circled his knob, savouring its spongy texture, and he moaned in sweet agony as her teeth scraped the sensitive skin of his helmet. Carefully, she drew him in between her lips, sucking slowly as she took as much of his staff as she could in her mouth, sending waves of pleasure throughout his entire body. She quickened the movements of her mouth and let her right hand snake down to frig again at her still sopping cunt.

'I'm coming, Hennie!' he gasped, and she craned her neck forward and somehow managed to force the entire length of his prick into her throat, her lips almost touching his balls. With a cry, Charles shot off his love cream into her mouth as he was transported to the highest pinnacle of pleasure. He pumped a copious emission of spunk between her lips and she greedily milked his twitching shaft of jism until he withdrew his wet, shrunken shaft. Charles slumped back exhausted on the bed, and the thought flashed through Bob's brain that the chauffeur was obviously a one-fuck man, and he wondered whether Henrietta would be interested in a fresh cock for so far her pussey had not yet been pierced, except for her own frenetic frigging.

Indeed, by the time he had slipped on a dressing gown and padded out to the landing, Bob's cock had already swollen up to a prime state of erection.

He knocked on Charles's door and he heard a flurry

of activity in the bedroom. 'Don't worry, it's only Bob Goggin from next door,' he whispered through the keyhole. Charles opened the door an inch or two and muttered: 'What is it? You've, er, caught us, I mean, me at a bad time right now.'

Bob grinned. 'I wouldn't say that and I don't think Henrietta would either. Come on, be a good sport and let me join in the party.' He pushed past an astonished Charles who stood transfixed, trying to fathom out how the hell Bob could possibly have known what was taking place in his room. But Henrietta was quite unflustered by the unexpected appearance of the young gardener's assistant, for the fact of the matter was that she had seen him at work several times that summer, almost always on hot days when he had stripped to the waist. Although only seventeen, Henrietta was already a connoisseur of the male body and she much admired Bob's neat, trim frame.

'Hello there, Bob Goggin,' she said softly, sensually smoothing her hands down the sides of her thighs. 'How on earth did you know I was here?'

'I cannot lie to you. I heard you and Charles through the thin partition wall that divides our rooms,' he confessed, which was truthful as far as it went, but he failed to add that he had been able to see as well as hear the hi-jinks between Henrietta and his fellow member of staff.

Henrietta laughed and said: 'I think you'd like to join in our fun and games, wouldn't you? Come and stand next to the bed. No, Bob, don't bother yourself to answer, for your dressing gown cord has opened and, unless I'm very much mistaken, I can see what looks like a nice meaty stiff prick standing up high between your legs.'

'Come on, take off your robe and let me have a better look at it. Charles, don't be jealous, you've had your fill and you mustn't begrudge me mine. You can look whilst we fuck if you like; Bob won't mind, will you?' she added, leaning forward to rub her palm against the tender underside of his shaft. 'M'mm, that's a nicely formed tool. Well, don't stand there like a lemon, let's put you and your cock to work.'

Bob shucked off his dressing gown and Henrietta pulled him down beside her. Their mutual desire drew them together as she covered his neck with kisses. Bob responded passionately, working his tongue down from her shoulders to her cherry nipples which rose to meet him. Henrietta worked her fingers down through his chest hairs, half tickling a trail to his inner thighs and to his rampant cock, its gleaming helmet bobbing urgently in her grasp.

The happy pair were now joined by Charles whose limp prick had now made a full recovery and had grown back to its formidable stiffness. As Bob was concentrating on Henrietta's right nipple, Charles moved his head to suckle on the moist red hardness of her left tittie, and her senses reeled with the delight of having both breasts sucked at the same time. The nibbling of their tongues sent wave after wave of pleasure coursing through her entire frame as she tingled with anticipation as to what other new joys she might now experience.

A hand stroked her thighs and she wondered whose it was as she parted her legs. A tongue now flicked around her silky pubic bush whilst a second slid wetly between the folds of sensitive skin, lapping eagerly at her cunt.

'Oooh, that is nice! What a gorgeous double tonguing! Ah-re, I am going to spend! Ah! Oh, I must! Oh, there! Aaah!'

With that she clamped her legs around the two heads that continued to pay homage to her delicious pussey as she spurted a warm, trickling tribute in a fine, salty rain over their tongues.

Henrietta was now more than ready for action. 'Have you any pomade, Charles? Yes? Then prod my arse whilst Bob fucks my cunney,' she commanded as she wriggled free, pulling Bob upwards towards her.

She then turned him over on his back and glued her lips to his, holding her hands firmly upon his shoulders as she reached down for his iron-hard cock and eased his knob into her juicy crack. Bob thrust upwards to bury his shaft fully within her throbbing sheath and as Henrietta rode up and down on Bob's pulsing pole, he grapsed her luscious arse cheeks, parting the fully rounded globes to expose the tiny wrinkled rosette between them.

Clambering up behind her, Charles lathered his prick with pomade and immediately found the mark, sliding his thick length between the open bum hole. With only a short cry of discomfort, Henrietta accommodated both cocks, her ecstatic buttocks gyrating wildly as the two boys jointly rammed their tools in and out of the respective orifices. At one stage they both pushed in together and each felt his own sheath rubbing against the other, separated as they were only by the thin divisional membrane that ran between them.

The three writhed uninhibitedly in paroxyms of pleasure until, screaming with excitement, they simultaneously reached the summit of the mountain of love and Henrietta thrilled to the lustful sensation of sperm shooting up her cunney and bum-hole at the same time! Charles withdrew his now flaccid prick and sat back on his haunches and Henrietta thrust down to receive one final spatter of spunk from Bob's twitching cock which now also was beginning to lose its hardness.

As this naughty scene was played out, poor Mr Heavan was sipping a cup of tea with Mrs Bickler at the kitchen table, still unable to rid himself of the strange intuition that there was a great deal of fucking going on in and around Arkley Hall – if only he knew where to find it!

CHAPTER SIX

Tempus fugit, gentle reader, and for this concluding episode we must once more shift dear old Father Time – not backwards as before but forwards to around a quarter past eleven o'clock. We fly across the southern shires from Sussex to the heart of London's West End and specifically to the pavement outside the Garrick Theatre where, it will be recalled, the cheeky cocksman Alan Brooke had persuaded Lady Arkley to allow him to escort her daughters Katie and Penny to a little party, whilst she goes on to spend the rest of the evening at a reception graced by the presence of no less a personage than Her Majesty Queen Alexandra.

The stratagem of the cool cocksman had been craftily planned for he knew that a meeting with the Queen was a bait that Lady Arkley simply could not resist. So without further ado, let us rejoin Katie, Penny and Alan in their carriage on their way to Jackson's Mews, Mayfair where Gwendolen Bracknell was entertaining a few friends for supper and a somewhat *recherché* evening entertainment.

Lady Arkley was somewhat doubtful about leaving her daughters with Alan Brooke, but thought they would be in good hands mixing with the *creme de la creme*. However, although Gwendolen was the daughter of Lady Augusta Bracknell, one of the stalwarts of London Society, unbeknown to her Mama, young Gwen was a junior member of the ultra-fast South Hampstead set, a loose group of epicurean debauchees who devoted their days and nights to sampling all manner of joys – and especially the pleasures of the flesh. . . .

Now, as Alan Brooke knew from their wild joust earlier that evening, Penny Arkley was extremely fond of fucking and he rightly judged that Katie, her extremely attractive elder sister, was equally keen on cock. Still, he thought, it would do no harm to test the water before they arrived at Gwen Bracknell's. Certainly, the gallant gentleman had no desire to offend any lady who did not share his boisterous life of lustiness. If Katie did not wish to partake in an uninhibited party, he would arrange for Grahame the coachman to take her home directly.

As it turned out, there was no need for this as Katie was a good sport and, like her sister, was a chip off the old block and enjoyed all the many variants of *l'arte de faire l'amour. [The girls followed in the footsteps of their father, Sir Paul Arkley, whose participation in an orgy given for the then Prince of Wales by Count Gewirtz of Galicia, is documented in* Cremorne Gardens, *Headline Books, London, 1990 – RM]*

'Do you read much, Katie?' enquired the wily young blade, deliberately pulling the conversation around to country matters. 'I have just been reading *The Lustful Turk*, an erotic classic of some eighty years ago which I have found most stimulating.'

Katie sensed that she was being tested and decided

that she would see if she could hoist the disingenuous Mr Brooke upon his own petard. 'I've never read it myself, although I know it is a bestseller at Hotten's.' [*John Hotten's Bookshop was a small establishment in Piccadilly where the owner kept a large selection of explicit books and photographs for an upper-crust clientele who protected him from any police harassment. When this protection could no longer be afforded, Mr Hotten prudently left the country for the Continent with a considerable fortune – RM]*.

She added: 'I find that more modern works of gallant literature like the diaries of Jenny Everleigh or Rosie d'Argosse are more to my taste.'

Alan Brooke was impressed. 'You are not easily shocked then. This is just as well, for I feel I must warn you that Gwen Bracknell's parties do get rather wild sometimes, and I wouldn't want to upset either of you in any way – '

'You would only upset us by not inviting us,' interrupted Penny with a gleam in her eye. 'As long as there are some good-looking, clean gentlemen on hand for us to look over.'

'I think I can safely promise that you two pretty girls will have the pick of the bunch,' he laughed.

'Actually, talking of randy reading, I must introduce you to the explorer Jonathan Crawford who I know will be joining us tonight. He has just published in *The Oyster* some fascinating sketches he made in a Turkish harem. He managed to gain entry to the establishment by posing as a eunuch and when he was discovered he was very fortunate not to actually leave in that happy condition. Only a payment of a hundred pieces of silver saved his manhood from being cut off in its prime.

'However, whilst there, he observed in intimate detail all the arcane rituals and enjoyments of the harem and these are shown to good effect in his portfolio of drawings. I must admit that in his sketches there was such a proliferation of pussey, so many girls doing quite extraordinary things to other girls, that I became quite aroused.'

Penny giggled. 'Did you now, Alan? Well, I do hope that Rosalind Lambeth was on hand to relieve your feelings.'

'Good God! How do you know about me and Mrs Lambeth?'

'We receive all the news down in sleepy Sussex,' answered Katie. 'Papa is a member of the Jim Jam Club and we sometimes cannot help overhearing all the gossip from London.'

He now looked at the girls in a new light and he murmured: 'I can see I shall have to watch my step in future.'

They arrived then at Jackson's Mews in good heart for the party. Gwendolen Bracknell welcomed the girls warmly and immediately introduced them to the other members of the gathering. A friendly, hospitable girl, tall but most attractive with a superb figure. Several artists had expressed a desire to paint her in the nude and it was rumoured that the great Whistler had in fact secured her as a model posing *au naturel. [Like so many of its kind, this rumour was in all probability false, for I have found no such portrait in any catalogue of Whistler's work – RM].*

As promised, amongst the men was the aforementioned explorer, Jonathan Crawford – a handsome, tall fellow who captured Katie Arkley's heart almost from the first seconds of meeting. Other gentlemen included Professor Antony Hammond, a second cousin of the Duke of Cambridge who was a fine-looking man with a dark, well-brushed beard and who appeared to be squiring Gwen Bracknell; the aptly named Mr Paul Maycock, the poet and critic, a good-looking young man in his early twenties, light-skinned and blue-eyed with a shock of brown hair which he wore far too long, even for the extremes of fashion, although his debonair sophistication was of great appeal to Penny; and Sir Gerald Newman, the wealthy business tycoon and philanthropist who, in his own words, was always game for a good fuck whether it be in Belgravia or Bethnal Green.

The girls included the Honourable Miss Celia Debden-Hunte, a slender, fair creature with soft blue eyes; Lady Laura Gantshill, a merry young spark with chestnut hair and a pair of plump breasts whose charms she accentuated by wearing a low cut dress that barely covered her thrusting nipples and, indeed, their outline could be easily distinguished against the light material which just kept her from exposing her delights to all and sundry; and finally Jemima Loughton, perhaps the prettiest of them all, blessed with jet black hair, a nose cast in the Roman mould and two captivating dimples which appeared when her full, red lips broke out in a laugh that also exposed her two rows of perfect white teeth.

'Surely we may spoil the fun as there is one girl too many here,' murmured Penny to Alan Brooke.

'Not a bit of it,' replied the randy rascal. 'Wait until things liven up and you'll see that each and every member of this jolly gathering will have a part to play.'

Whilst Penny digested this cryptic reply, Katie was listening with admiration to Paul Maycock who had just been encouraged to recite to us. At first he declined but then said with a great flourish: 'My dear Miss Debden-Hunte, I dedicate these lines that have just come into my head to you.' Gwen called for silence whilst he declaimed:

'Come dear love and dwell with me,
Under the shade of the old oak tree,
No one will more happy be,
Than I if I am blessed with thee.

Flowers bloom in that sweet spot,
Unknown fragrance fills your mossy grot,
Come, Celia, to our secret spot,
Kind girl, entwine in love's old knot.

At first the room fell silent until Sir Gerald Newman guffawed loudly. 'Ha, ha, ha! That's a good one, Paul. Write it down so I can recite it tomorrow night at the Duchess of Bristol's literary soirée.' The other guests remained puzzled and even Penny, usually so quick-witted, could honestly see little merit in the little piece of doggerel. If they had seen the words laid out, of course, it would have been a different matter.

But then her sister suddenly realised the rude joke played upon them by the poet and she whispered the secret to Penny, who giggled appreciatively. 'Gerry, don't tell anyone – let them work it out for themselves,' admonished Paul Maycock, slipping his arm around Penny's unresisting waist. But the party had started some time before and alcohol is good for preserving practically everything but secrets. The business tycoon soon released the information, especially and indeed immediately after Laura Gantshill murmured in his ear that if he told them the secret, she would let him feel her glorious breasts, and that if he promised to be a good boy, she might even suck his cock before the evening was out.

'No-one can ever accuse you of driving a hard bargain, Laura,' said the thick-set captain of industry afterwards, running his hands all over her rounded beauties, sliding his hand under the silk of her dress to caress her big, red nipples.

'Bring them out so we can all look at Laura's titties,' called out Alan Brooke, who could see the beginnings of some real fun and games in this situation.

'Yes, come on, Gerry, don't keep them all for yourself,' added Professor Hammond. 'If you don't want to suck them, I'm sure that any and every person present of both sexes will be only too pleased to oblige.'

'Thank you very much,' protested Laura, though from the tone of her voice it was easy to tell that she was by no means upset at the Professor's remarks. 'But Gerry Newman has first refusal and if he is half the man I've heard he is from Mrs Holland, I don't think I'll be able to offer my nips to anyone else for some time!'

Oh ho, thought Alan Brooke, we're about to start the best business of the evening. He could see that Penny was somewhat taken with the dashing Paul Maycock – but he had already fucked Penny that afternoon and, though he had no objection whatsoever to ejaculating his spunk inside her cunney again, the randy rascal's eyes and cock were as irresistibly attracted to the lovely Jemima Loughton as metal to a magnet.

So Alan Brooke moved across the room to stand next to the gorgeous Jemima and he said, quietly: 'I think we are about to start the proceedings of the evening in earnest now.' She looked up at him and smiled. 'I do hope so,' she replied calmly. 'Gwen assured me that you would be present, Alan, and that though you have been dallying with Miss Arkley, you would not think it too forward if I asked you to allow me the pleasure of placing your prick in my pussey before the night is over.'

The sturdy cocksman's eyes brightened. 'Gwendolen is rarely wrong in matters of etiquette. I assure you, the pleasure would also be mine. Shall we retire to a bedroom?'

'In a moment, if you don't mind, for I should rather like to see Laura Gantshill being threaded by Sir Gerry Newman. Celia tells me that he fucks with real style. Watching them will whet my appetite very nicely,' she said happily, reaching down beside her to give his balls a friendly little squeeze.

As if to prove the truth of this remark, the subject of her comment was now entwined with Laura on a mattress which Professor Hammond and Gwen Bracknell had dragged into the centre of the room. The lusty lover had already uncovered Laura's plump round breasts and was fondling these bare beauties in his hands, flicking and teasing the dark red nipples up to little peaks. She responded avidly, tearing open his shirt and massaging his hairy chest. They broke apart for a moment and the sensible girl held out a restraining hand. 'Gerry, let us undress properly. My Papa paid fifty guineas for this dress from Madame Zelda of Bond Street. It would be a shocking waste to damage it in some way.'

'Quite right, my dear, how thoughtful of you to concern yourself about the family at such a time. Your concern does you the greatest credit,' said her partner, whose fortune had been made, as he often said, by watching the pennies and letting the pounds take care of themselves. So the couple stripped themselves completely of clothing and stood stark naked in front of the other guests.

Professor Hammond put a record on the gramophone and the sounds of *The Blue Danube* filled the room. 'Would you care to dance?' asked Sir Gerald. Laura curtsied and the nude pair danced around the room, and Laura's superb breasts jiggled and jounced delightfully as they waltzed gaily round before sliding down onto the mattress. The others crowded round to watch, but Alan Brooke protested that they needed a little more room. 'Let's all sit down and make ourselves comfortable. For a start, let's all take off our clothes,' he cried.

'What a good idea,' said Jonathan Crawford, who had said little so far but had formed a silent, though mutual, admiration for Penny. 'Miss Arkley, may I help you with the buttons on the back of your dress?' Paul Maycock and Alan Brooke immediately offered the same service to Jemima and Katie whilst Gwen and Jemima availed themselves of the dextrous hands of Professor Hammond.

Naturally, Gerry and Laura had already begun their journey to paradise whilst the company were disrobing.

The tycoon's hands were clutching the girl's peach-like buttocks as she took his rock-hard prick into her grasp. However, his shaft was so thick that she needed both hands to encompass its massive girth. 'Gerry, you really are a big boy,' she said admiringly. 'M'mm,' he replied, slipping his hand between her arse cheeks, 'and your cunney is so lovely and tight and wet!' She was now so worked up that she demanded to begin the game by riding a St George on his enormous cock. Gerry lay down on the mattress and Gwendolen thoughtfully brought a pillow so that he would be comfortable. 'I'm going to really enjoy this!' enthused Laura, clambering on top of his somewhat paunchy belly. She took hold of his rigid rod and slipped its fat red knot between her cunney lips, easing her weight over it until she was completely engorged.

'Oh Gerry, what happiness!' she groaned, driving herself up and down and kissing him frantically all the while.

'What a penis, more like,' said Gwen Bracknell wittily, but everyone was too busy watching Laura take her pleasure to laugh at her clever little joke.

Gerry cupped her divine breasts in his hands, weighing them as they fell into his palms as Laura bobbed up and down, her love channel squeezing deliciously on his slippery shaft as her cunney muscles contracted and relaxed in an ecstatic rhythm. Now Laura rocked forwards and backwards on his throbbing cock, and when she rubbed herself across the tip of his knob, he gasped out that he could no longer hold back the semen that was boiling up inside his balls. As the orgasm approached she drove down hard, spearing herself on his glistening prick as an enormous torrent of spunk burst out, drenching her pussey as Laura, too, achieved the bliss of a shuddering spend.

'Look, Gerry's cock is still pretty stiff,' commented Professor Hammond, struggling to keep any note of envy out of his voice. 'Surely he cannot continue so quickly. Someone else should surely take his place. Perhaps we should call for a volunteer. I'd be quite happy to oblige if called upon to do so.'

'Not bloody likely,' snarled Gerry, who was busying himself with stroking Laura's lovely white, quivering bum cheeks for the dear girl was now offering herself doggie-style, her arse stuck out saucily and her head buried in the pillow so kindly provided by Gwendolen, who proved herself to be a perfect hostess by now giving Gerry Newman a little bottle of baby oil. 'Thank you so much, that's just what we need,' he enthused, carefully pouring out the liquid between Laura's buttocks so that it dripped over her bottom-hole and lower down all over her pussey. He slipped the flat of his hand between her bum cheeks and gently rubbed in the oil. 'Oh, Gerry, that feels fantastic,' she cried, reaching back to feel for his swelling cock. 'Now please pop in your todger and take me from behind.'

This was an invitation not to be refused! Gerry pulled Laura's long white legs further apart until he had full view of the pouting pink lips of her dripping crack. She gave a final rub to his now fully erect tool before helping to guide it safely to the waiting lips of her sopping cunney. She dropped her arm and left it to her love to effect a safe lodgement, and with one vigorous thrust he buried his gleaming shaft to the hilt, his heavy balls flopping against her heaving, rounded buttocks. At least two of the watching girls sighed, wishing themselves to be in Laura's place as Gerry sluiced his sticky pole in and out of her squelchy slit at an ever quickening pace – but then suddenly he stopped and stayed absolutely still, gasping for breath, with his pulsing prick fully embedded in her juicy sheath.

Laura poked her head round and was about to enquire as to whether he was capable of continuing this frenetic fuck. But before she could speak, he began to pump his piston in and out, penetrating her cunney and tickling her clitty with lightning force and speed. He somehow managed to keep up this amazing pace for perhaps as long as a full minute, and Laura writhed sensuously as she achieved a delightful spend. As soon as he felt her reach the summit, Gerry stopped and held still until the orgasm ceased. He fucked her yet again in this manner, and then once more, but this time he was ready to climax, and with an almighty groan his body stiffened and he flooded her pussey with boiling sperm as they cried out in joint ecstasy before collapsing together in a heap, their glistening bodies bathed in perspiration.

'What a splendid way to finish,' said Jonathan Crawford, whose arm was already round the unresisting shoulders of Katie. 'Gerry Newman is certainly in very good condition for a man of his age.'

Katie's long blonde tresses shook as she nodded her agreement. 'Yes, and what I liked is that he tried so hard to keep his sperm in his balls until his partner was about to spend. I know it's not always possible, but I have no time for selfish men who care only for their own pleasure and don't even think about whether their girls enjoy themselves or not.'

'I don't blame you at all,' said the tall adventurer, his hands moving down to explore Katie's creamy breasts which, though not of the size of Laura Gantshill's, were superbly fashioned with large red aureoles and stalky strawberry nipples that Jonathan positively ached to suck. His cock began to rise and Katie took hold of the swelling truncheon as their faces came together and their lips fastened in a passionate kiss.

Jonathan caressed her silky golden pussey hair but she gasped: 'No, Jonathan, not in front of my sister and all these people.' Courteously, he pulled back his hand and said: 'I quite understand, Katie, but perhaps we could retire to the privacy of a bedroom.' She smiled gratefully and the couple slipped away to tumble onto the fresh white sheets of the bed Gwen Bracknell had set up in the spare room.

Within the privacy of the bedroom, Katie felt far more relaxed and, being a wise lover as well as a gentleman, Jonathan Crawford made no attempt to force any unwanted attentions upon her. If he were to progress, he knew he would be far better advised to further matters along at a speed with which his girl was comfortable, rather than to simply attempt to force her to submit to his desires. For even though they were both naked, Jonathan knew full well that more pussey was won by fair means than foul and that in any case, a truly memorable fuck was far more likely with two fully consenting partners. Of course, there was no harm whatsoever in keeping up the momentum by some sensual petting – so he snuggled Katie's golden-haired head onto his chest and they settled themselves down on the bed, Katie placing one of her hands not upon his heavy, semi-erect cock but nearby upon his upper thigh.

'So you have just come back from Africa, Jonathan. Was it a very dangerous trip?' asked Katie.

'It was interesting rather than dangerous,' he replied, cuddling up even closer and running his hands through Katie's hair. 'I was acting as a guide to the famous ornithologist, Mark Norrie, who is studying the lives of the greenshank birds.'

'The greenshank?' echoed Katie. 'Surely these are wading birds to be found in Scotland.'

'Ah, but you see, my employer was looking for evidence that the birds migrated to Africa, which is how we came to find ourselves in Kenya, and we soon discovered that as he had believed our feathered friends did indeed make an annual long trek from the cold climes of Bonnie Scotland.'

'So you returned home post-haste with the news?'

'Not exactly, Katie, for although Mr Norrie took the first boat home, I decided to stay on and study the life of the Fukawi tribe.'

'Goodness, Jonathan, are these a tribe of fierce cannibals ready to cook you for dinner?'

The good-looking adventurer laughed. 'No, no, no, far from it, they are a very peaceful people who live deep in the heart of the jungle where they wander around. Indeed, that is why the Fukawi are so called, for as often as not they get lost in the dense growth of the tropical forests and then they begin to shout: "We're the Fukawi!" '

'I don't believe that for a minute!' giggled Katie, and being unable to keep a straight face, Jonathan joined in the merriment. 'You're quite right not to – but you'd be surprised at how many people take the story seriously!'

This humorous little chat eased any remaining inhibitions and still giggling, their two faces moved slowly together until, closing their eyes, their lips met in a passionate kiss, the moisture spreading into their mouths as if they were eating a fruit which melted and dissolved. The big man then moved his mouth down to her thrusting nipple, running his tongue around the sensitive encircling aureole before, cupping her breast in a surprisingly gentle hand, he took the swollen nipple between his lips and playfully teased it with his tongue.

Now fired, Katie reached to grasp Jonathan's hard, throbbing cock and she massaged the hot, smooth shaft as his hand glided across her blonde pubic bush and spread the lips of her cunney, opening her for what was to come . . .

'Katie, darling, your little pussey is sopping wet – are you ready to take my cock?' he asked her tenderly.

'Oh yes, Jonathan, yes, slide your staff inside me!'

He grinned and rolled the sweet girl over onto her back, his hands slipping to grasp her glorious bum cheeks as he lowered himself on top of her. The tip of his prick just touched her pouting cunney lips and she repeated her lascivious demand to be fucked. Slowly but surely he inserted the domed knob of his cock inside her love channel and he pushed forward, inch by inch, until all his nine inches were embedded inside her pulsating pussey. Katie rotated her arse around the fulcrum of his plunging prick and she whimpered in appreciation as, without hesitation, he withdrew three inches of meaty shaft and then pushed forward again. He continued this delicious process until the length of his shaft was glistening with the lubrication of Katie's ambrosial juices.

Now he increased the pace, his balls banging against her bottom with each lunging thrust. 'I'm fucking you, Katie,' he panted, his voice husky with lust, as he added his fingers to tweak her clitty and pounded his tool in and out of her squelchy crack. Her body quivered as a wildfire of sensation ran through her being. She twisted and turned until her form stiffened under him and she screamed out: 'I'm coming! I'm coming! Quick, flood my cunt with spunk! Now!'

His cock vibrated as it slid in and out of her slit faster and faster until, with a hoarse cry, he jetted an enormous torrent of frothy white sperm inside her womb which mingled with the flood of her own piquant love juice that overflowed out from her cunney and trickled down her thighs.

Katie sighed with delight as they dissolved into the mutual glow that accompanies such a spend and she said: 'What a delight it is to share such a marvellous first fuck with a dear, new-found friend.'

They snuggled up together and Katie said: 'I really felt you explode in me just now, Jonathan. Has it been a long time since you enjoyed the pleasure of sexual intercourse?'

'You noticed a certain extra release of tension when I spent? I wouldn't be at all surprised. You see, Katie, my last girlfriend, Jennifer – and being a gentleman I cannot, of course, mention her full name, especially as she may be known to you – has developed a strange penchant for frigging and, to be frank, kept taking me to the front door but never actually let me cross the threshold. To be fair, we have only been going out together for a few weeks, but we have kissed and petted almost to the point of no return and I had every reason to believe that when we would have the chance to be alone together we would enjoy the greatest joy our beneficient Creator has provided for us.'

'This sounds like a good tale. Do tell me more.'

'Well, for example last Tuesday, I called round to her house in the afternoon knowing full well that her parents were not at home. Jennifer welcomed me warmly and, after tea, we managed to avoid the prying eyes of the servants and found ourselves in her bedroom.

'Once there we kissed and cuddled and she encouraged me to unbutton her blouse. My fingers teased her hard stalky titties as she tore off my shirt and soon we were rolling, entwined on her bed. By now my cock was fairly bursting as she rubbed her bare breasts against my chest, nipple to nipple. Her skirt was already undone and was easy to pull off and I moved my hand down to her pale blue knickers which were already stained with her wetness. I slid them down over her bottom and she kicked them off, opening her legs so that I could begin to stroke her pussey lips. She moaned with unalloyed delight as I slipped a finger into her moistness and then began to finger-fuck her with one, and then two fingers, but then, just as I was about to substitute my cock for my fingers, she took my hand away and whispered: 'Watch me, Jonathan, you'll like this, I promise you.' And she made me get off the bed and stand by her so that she could look at me whilst she played with her clitty by herself!

'Now Jennifer is a stunningly attractive girl, and it was a most erotic sight to see her writhing in ecstasy as she manipulated her clitty with one hand and played with her titties with the other. When she approached her climax, she threw back her head and her pussey arched upwards as she panted and squealed lewdly which drove me insane with unslaked desire. My hand grabbed my stiffstanding shaft and I frantically rubbed my straining staff. Her eyes gleamed and she gasped: 'Yes, yes, Jonathan, shoot your sperm all over me!' My hand moved like greased lightning and carefully aiming my knob, I exploded a jet of creamy spunk all over her breasts. 'Aaah!' she breathed, rubbing the warm jism over her titties as more and more spilled out of my cock in glorious spasms as I squeezed out every last drop from my pulsing prick.

'Now, once we had recovered, I thought it almost a formality that our bodies would naturally join together.'

'This shows that you must take nothing for granted, Jonathan,' said a girl's voice, interrupting this sorry tale. Katie and Jonathan looked up to see who had entered the bedroom and the explorer grinned as he made out the tall, shapely form of their lovely hostess who was standing at the foot of the bed.

'Hello, there, Gwen. I hope you do not mind Katie and I using your bed for a private fuck,' he said.

'Not at all, Jonathan, please be my guest. I could not help overhearing your sad story about Jennifer's reluctance to entertain your cock in her cunney. I am afraid that such behaviour gives girls a bad name. We rightly demand that you boys respect our wishes as to whether or not we wish to be fucked, or indeed, just how far we wish to take matters, stopping short of actual intercourse. However, I deplore prick-teasing, as the common vernacular has it, of promising more than a girl really wishes to deliver. It leads to frustration and bad feeling all round. Flirtatiousness is one thing, but sexual teasing can often end up in tears.'

Gwen looked down at the naked pair and added: 'You do look very comfortable in my bed. Would you mind very much if I joined you?'

'Not at all, please do,' they chorused and after slipping off her only covering of a silk chemise, the supple, lithe body of Gwen Bracknell soon found itself between Katie and Jonathan, being caressed and cuddled by them both. Gwen may have possessed a somewhat boyish figure, but her small breasts were nicely rounded and her cherry-red nipples were already like erect little stalks as Katie passed her hand across them. Jonathan admired her firm, tight bum cheeks as she turned over to return Katie's caresses, and he managed to part the two girls for a moment to take his place in a quite delicious three-way kiss as the trio pressed their lips together and wriggled their tongues around in each other's mouths in a most lascivious fashion.

Jonathan cleared his throat and somewhat sheepishly asked: 'Gwen, my love, I have the strongest fancy to see you kiss Katie's pussey. Would you humour me and honour her by going down and eating her cunney? Katie, I trust you will have no objection?'

'I'd love to suck you off,' enthused Gwen as she stroked Katie's snowy white tummy. 'You have such a pretty blonde bush of cunney hair and such sweet cunt lips that look so inviting.'

'Will you allow Gwen to pleasure you?' Jonathan asked Katie eagerly. 'She is, I am reliably informed, amongst the best pussey-eaters in England.'

'Of course,' said Katie gaily, pulling Gwen towards her. 'I am sure that I will treasure the experience.'

Jonathan quickly pressed Gwen's head down upon Katie's beautiful breasts and the lovely girl sighed with delight as Gwen moved her tongue from one tittie to the other, twirling her tongue around the upright red nipples. Each nipple rose, engorged and hungry for more, and a little mew of pleasure escaped from Katie's lips.

All at once Katie was aware of a sudden wetness between her legs and she closed her eyes, lost and drowning happily in the flood of sensual delight that swept over her. Emboldened by the girl's response, Gwen threw her arms around Katie's soft, trembling body as she continued to tease her nipples, nibbling and sucking them up to new heights. Then she let her pink tongue travel the full length of her velvety skin, lingering briefly at her navel before sliding down to between her thighs and burying it in the silky golden thatch around her cunney lips. Katie's skin was so soft and smelled so clean that Gwen felt her own pussey beginning to moisten, a process helped by the ever-helpful Jonathan Crawford who reached out to press his hand between Gwen's long legs.

Gwen was now almost too far down the road to paradise to even notice Jonathan's fingers playing with her clitty as she nuzzled her lips around Katie's blonde bush. Her hands clamped around the girl's rounded bum cheeks as her tongue flashed unerringly around the dampness, until Katie lifted her arse to enable Gwen to slide her tongue between the pouting cunney lips, licking between the grooves of her clitty in long, amorous strokes. With a groan of ecstasy, Gwen lost herself in this delicious cunt, licking and lapping greedily at the tangy juices which flowed from this honeypot.

Gwen's tongue was revelling in Katie's sopping muff, from which her clitty was now protruding a full inch from between the rolled cunney lips. Gwen took the clitty in her mouth, rolling her tongue all round it as Katie quivered all over and jerked her body on the bed. Gwen continued her sweet massaging of Katie's clitty, sucking delicately at it, which brought her to the very verge of coming. Then the fiery tribade withdrew her lips and tongue and ran a finger slowly down the length of Katie's cunney lips.

'See, the parting of the ways,' she said with a wicked grin.

Katie begged to be finished off and Gwen, remembering her manners, apologised for leaving her partner unsatisfied. Her hands cupped Katie's breasts and she spread out her fingers to encompass the soft, twin orbs. Then she dipped her head back between Katie's legs and buried her face in the silky blonde triangle, her mouth gently pressing against the yielding cunney lips as she probed Katie's utmost parameters of desire with her clever tonguing.

'Let Katie eat your pussey, Gwen, as that way you can both achieve satisfaction,' cried Jonathan Crawford whose massively thick truncheon was now swelling up again to a bursting, rock-hard stiffness.

Without moving her mouth from Katie's warm wetness, Gwen wriggled her body around, her lips still glued to her partner's cunney until she lay right across the younger girl and her own finely developed clitty, which stood out like a miniature cock from between her cunney lips, was directly above Katie's mouth. She lowered herself down and the two girls were soon frantically engaged in a frenzied *soixante neuf* as Katie's lips nuzzled round the dark curly hair that surrounded Gwen's pouting pussey lips.

They thrashed around passionately in this lewd, tribadistic coupling and Jonathan found this so exciting that he was determined to join in the party. He positioned himself behind Gwen and he parted Gwen's bum cheeks so that he was able to slip the ruby knob of his cock between them. He nudged his way forward to the wrinkled little brown rosette of her bum hole, but Gwen lifted her head and gasped out: 'No, no, Jonathan, don't fuck my arse, I would far rather you placed your prick in my cunt.'

On hearing this request, Katie lay back to enjoy the sight of Jonathan's tool plunging into Gwen's wet, welcoming slit from behind, and Katie licked his hairy balls as they bounced against Gwen's arse.

'Aaah! Aaah! A-h-r-e! Further in, Jonathan, further in! Empty your balls, you fine fucker!' shrieked Gwen. Her bottom responded to every shove as the explorer drove home, his lusty cock excited to raging peaks of lust as the friction of her cunney made every nerve thrill, not only in his pulsing penis, but throughout his entire body. With a hoarse groan, he pumped a stream of hot spunk into her waiting crack. Gwen gurgled with joy as the frothy white cream flooded into her cunney and Katie, too, shuddered with joy as a wave of ecstasy rushed through her.

This lascivious threesome continued to desport themselves in Gwen's spare bedroom. Both Gwen and Katie sucked off their lover, nibbling and lapping at his stiff, pulsating prick until Gwen could bear it no longer and brought his mushroomed red crown to her salivating lips and washed the soft dome with her tongue, tasting his salty 'pre-cum' juice. She then grabbed his sizeable shaft in both hands and hungrily stuffed it into her mouth as far as she could, and Jonathan pumped deeper and deeper down her throat.

'I would love to be fucked again by Jonathan's big cock,' declared Katie with a sigh. Gwen pulled his prick from out of her mouth but, alas, the damage had been done! His shaft was already trembling and it was obvious that the hot, white love juice was inexorably making its way from his balls, and nothing could delay its progress. Gwen was about to complete her work when the first jet of creamy sperm came hurtling out of his cock. The first jet splashed against her left cheek, but she hastily clamped her lips back on the wildly jerking shaft so that she could gobble up the remaining jets of salty spunk. As his spurting knob rested upon her tongue, she swallowed swiftly to keep pace with him and then, as his spend passed its peak, she took his whole shaft back inside her mouth and sucked it for all she was worth to extract the very last drops of cream from his twitching tool.

They lay silent for a spell until Gwen remarked: 'Ah, Jonathan, I did enjoy sucking your thick prick. I could happily play with it for hours, but of course all you men are the same – you all squirt your sperm in just a few short minutes. None of you can make it last long enough as far as I am concerned. Oh for a prick that could last for ten minutes.'

'My boyfriend, Walter Stanton, can keeping going for as long as twenty minutes while I suck his cock,' said Katie shyly.

'You are very lucky,' commented Gwen. 'He must have an amazing amount of self-control. If you ever tire of him, please do not hesitate to pass my name to him. A hard man is good to find. Look after him, Katie.'

Jonathan felt that he should not let these slurs on the male sex pass by unanswered. 'It's all very well for you to grumble,' he said, 'but what about those chaps whose girlfriends won't do anything but lie back and think of England when they're in bed together?'

'This can be a pretty difficult problem to solve,' said Gwen thoughtfully. 'I do know that there are some girls, for example, who cannot bring themselves to suck their boyfriends' cocks. Or if they do, they try not to swallow the love juice, which I find quite extraordinary as I adore both sucking and swallowing! There is nothing that can beat spunk for tasting so clean and tangy.'

'And there is the additional benefit of being able to have fun in bed without the worry of getting oneself in the family way,' added Katie. 'I think a lot of help should be given to girls who are kept in ignorance, or who are sternly warned against the joys of fellatio.'

Gwen nodded her head in agreement. 'Yes, you are absolutely right. I am constantly amazed to find out how many of my acquaintances have been kept unaware of the pleasure to be had from sucking a thick prick – or indeed from having their pussies licked out by their lovers.'

'I must admit that many men are also ignorant of the delights of eating pussey,' admitted Jonathan. 'In my travels I have found that only the Continentals are skilled at this art. The French, as you might expect, are probably best at lapping, but the Italians and Spaniards run them a close second.'

'To be fair, some Englishmen have learned from their European brethren. Why, Alan Brooke is called upon to perform cunnilingus in all the best houses in Belgravia. But then, he is an exception to the general rule.'

'Perhaps the answer is to make such educational books as *Fucking For Beginners* by Sir Michael Bailey and *A Lady of Quality* more readily available?' suggested Katie.

'Jolly good idea,' said Jonathan, whose mighty cock was now stirring into life under the kind ministrations of Gwen's tongue. Katie joined her in attempting to coax his shaft back to action, but they could only bring it up to a heavy-looking semi-erect state. 'Give me another ten minutes or so, girls, and I'll be ready and eager,' grunted the explorer. 'Meanwhile, let me play with your pussies as you have both obviously recovered more quickly than I from the last little game.'

Katie and Gwen needed no further encouragement. They rolled over on their backs and both girls invitingly opened their legs to beckon Jonathan over. He chose Katie's cunney for his first port of call and lay his head between her quivering thighs. The handsome explorer worked his lips down into the cleft that was half hidden by the silky covering of blonde hair, and he sniffed appreciatively at the delicate aroma that drifted towards his nose. He slid an arm underneath her and pulled her gorgeous bottom up to provide a little elevation as he placed his lips over her lovely crack and sucked it into his mouth, where the tip of his tongue began to wash it from all directions. He found the base of her clitty and twirled his tongue around it. Katie crossed her legs over his head, moaning her approval as he continued to work his tongue up and down across her clitty, licking and lapping as she ground her cunney against his mouth.

However, so as not to disappoint Gwen, Jonathan let his left arm run across to her belly where his hand soon moved down to stroke her dark, mossy thatch. Once he had found her pouting pussey lips he rubbed them lewdly with his thumb before slipping one and then two fingers into the damp slit, and Gwen's whole body began to vibrate when his naughty finger found her clitty. He began rubbing it at a steadily increasing pace that had her almost swooning with delight and it would have been a foolish man to wager which girl was going to spend first – Katie, from the wet friction of Jonathan's tongue or Gwen, from the manipulation of Jonathan's fingers. In the end it was Katie who spent first, her tangy juices pouring out over Jonathan's face, although Gwen followed less than a minute afterwards, her libation soaking Jonathan's fingers as she too achieved a delightful climax.

Meanwhile, in the living room, the party was now in full swing. All inhibitions had been cast aside and the guests were all engaged in various refinements of *l'arte de faire l'amour*. In the centre of the room Professor Antony Hammond was standing with his eyes closed, his head thrown back in ecstasy, as the Honourable Celia Debden-Hunte sucked lustily on his ironhard stiff-stander. The lucky man groaned as he let her tongue encircle the red crown of his cock, which was already oozing drops of moisture. Then she drew his shaft in between her rich, generous lips, sucking as hard as she could as he instinctively pushed his cock in and out of her mouth as her warm hands toyed with his heavy, hanging balls.

As she continued her licking she unpinned her hair, releasing the glorious dark cascades that spilled over her shoulders and tickled Antony Hammond's thrusting shaft unmercifully. Very soon it became abundantly clear that the Professor was about to spend and Jemima called out: 'Now, Celia, do remember your Nanny's insistence that every mouthful should be well chewed before it is swallowed.'

This brought forth peals of laughter, but nothing would deter Celia's sensual progress as her lips pursued their insistent way down the Professor's giant prick. She gently squeezed his ballsack and was rewarded by the hot waves of spunk that burst out of his knob into her greedily receiving mouth. Swallowing hard, she speedily drained his cock of its copious emission, nibbling daintily at the reddish crown until the last milky drops had been finally coaxed out of his now softening member.

'For this relief, much thanks,' he murmured. 'However, I fear that I am temporarily *hors de combat* and you will require a fresh cock to satisfy your cunt, which must now be aching to be satisfied. I see that Alan Brooke's tremendous tool is ready for action. Would you care to fuck her, kind sir?'

This question remained unanswered, for before Alan Brooke could accept or decline this kind offer, the ring of the electric doorbell interrupted proceedings.

'I'll answer it as Gwen's otherwise engaged,' said Professor Hammond, and the company waited to see who was at the door. Hopefully it would not be an enraged parent who could, upon seeing the naked state of all present, hardly remain unaware of the nature of Gwendolen Bracknell's little party.

There was a brief silence as they heard the door close and the new arrival murmur some words to Antony Hammond. After they heard a loud chuckle emanate from the hall, a collective sigh of relief ran through the living room – the newcomer was obviously unshocked by the Professor's bare body, so all should be well.

The door was flung open and the guests cheered as they were given view of the new arrival, who was none other than Richard Gewirtz, the good-looking younger son of the revered Count Gewirtz of Galicia, and almost as noted a sexual athlete as his famed father. Now for his part, the scion of the Gewirtz dynasty looked on with interest at the pretty unclothed girls who welcomed him. But the others, too, looked on Richard with equal amusement for this handsome rake was dressed in trousers that appeared to be far too large for him. Also, the jacket he was wearing was similarly ill-fitting and, indeed, was not even from the same suit.

'Well, well, Richard,' drawled Alan Brooke. 'I must congratulate you on inventing a highly comical new form of fancy dress.'

Richard grinned. 'Thank you for the compliment, but all dress is fancy dress is it not, except when, like all of you here, we are in a state of total nudity.'

'Ha, ha, ha! You are right at that, but if you want to stay you must tell us how you came to be wearing such odd garments,' laughed Celia, who had long harboured thoughts of being fucked by this attractive continental gentleman.

'Certainly, Celia, as it would be unfair to my tailor if you believed that I would willingly be seen in such peculiar clothes. Ah yes, a glass of champagne, thank you Jemima. Look, I'll tell all whilst I take off these dreadful clothes. Perhaps Gwendolen will give them away to some deserving pauper tomorrow, as I'll stay the night and send my man round in the morning with a fresh set of togs.

'Anyhow, the reason why I appear before you dressed like a drunkard is rather embarrassing. As most of you know, there is a married lady living not a million miles away from here whom I have been visiting twice a week as her husband does not or is incapable of performing his marital duties.'

'Gosh, who's that?' asked Jemima eagerly.

'Now, now, Jemima, no names, no pack drill. No gentleman would disclose the name of his amorata – to do so would be the action of the blackguard. Mind, if he later finds out that he has caught an infectious disease from the lady, it is his bounden duty to inform all his friends!

[At the notorious Prick and Pussey Social Club in Great Titchfield Street, which flourished in the early years of the twentieth century, a list of both ladies and gentlemen who had transmitted sexual infections was pinned to the wall of the members lounge by the Secretary – RM]

'However, to return to my story. I had planned to be here earlier but my motor car broke down in Walshaw Street, which happens to be just around the corner from Maggie's – oops! Oh well, hopefully none of you will know to whom I am alluding.

'Anyhow, as I was driving myself I opened the bonnet to see what was wrong. Alas, I am no mechanic and unfortunately I made my hands and cuffs rather dirty. So I decided to call at Maggie's and use the telephone to call my chauffeur, who would come round and effect the necessary repairs, or have the vehicle towed to the nearest garage. The other reason why I broke my journey at Maggie's was that, unknown of course to her husband, I kept a change of clothing in her cupboards!'

'You really are your father's son,' said Paul Maycock admiringly. 'I recall Count Gewirtz telling me only a few months ago that he always kept spare shirts, underclothing and twenty-five sovereigns [*pounds – RM*] in his lovers' homes to cover any emergency situation that might possibly arise.'

'So I'm following in father's footsteps.'

'Yes, you're following your dear old dad. But pray forgive me for diverting your riveting narrative.'

'Certainly, Paul, but only on the condition that you introduce me to that beautiful lady whose hand you are holding,' smiled the son of perhaps the greatest European fuckmaster of our time.

Paul Maycock laughed and with a low bow said: 'Certainly, I had no idea that you had not met before now. Miss Penny Arkley, may I present Richard Gewirtz. Mr Gewirtz, Miss Arkley.'

'I am delighted to meet you, Miss Arkley. Perhaps we will be able to get better acquainted later when I have finished this extraordinary story.

'So there I am, safe and snug at Maggie's, with the telephone in one hand and a whisky and soda in the other. Luckily, my man, Harold, was at home and he has a spare set of keys for my motor. I then called Grahame at Prestoncrest Carriages to arrange for a vehicle to be at my disposal for the rest of the evening, and then went upstairs to change my shirt. Now Maggie had followed me upstairs and I guessed that I might be required to pay in some way for my telephone call and drink. "Now, now, Richard, what's the hurry? I'm sure the party won't miss you for an hour or so. My husband is at his club and won't be back until ten at the earliest."

' "How can you be so sure? David might return earlier than you think," I said with a deep breath as she stroked my bare shoulder. Maggie is really a most attractive woman. She is only in her late twenties and, if I were married to her, I would resign my membership of every club *privé* in London, for I would be too busy fucking her night and day to look elsewhere. Not that David, her husband, was inserting his ramrod elsewhere. All he seems to live for is billiards and bridge. However, there is no accounting for taste.

'At first I protested that a hurried fuck was never as good as leisurely lovemaking, but my defences were immediately lowered the instant she brought her face close to mind and brought her mouth upwards to fasten on my own. She thrust her tongue slightly between my lips and I captured it firmly between my teeth and abandoned myself to my sweet fate.

'I would defy any red-blooded man to have walked away from the situation. Maggie is a ravishingly attractive woman, a sprightly beauty with rosy cheeks, large black eyes and sensual red lips, too full and frank perhaps for classic beauty. Her figure is sheer perfection with large bosoms, a slender waist and long legs that never fail to excite me. And sure enough when she shrugged off her dress, my prick swelled up as soon as she displayed those proud ripe breasts, so firm that the hardened nipples which sat in big red aureoles jutted upwards towards my yearning mouth.

'Her titties acted as magnets, and I buried my face in the swell of these snowy orbs before settling down to nip each juicy nipple, sucking one and then the other into my mouth and nipping them gently with my teeth, which gives us a most delightful mutual feeling. I travelled slowly down her trembling body, caressing those wonderful breasts with my hands until my lips were inches away from her lightly covered cunney. Automatically Maggie opened her legs to make the wet, swollen lips and clitty more accessible and my tongue moved, eager, delving, probing, sliding from the top of her slit to her bum hole, my tongue licking and lapping her fragrantly feminine juices.'

Celia sighed and shut her eyes, the better to imagine this lewd scenario. Instinctively she began to stroke her own pussey with one hand whilst reaching out for a cock to rub with the other. The lucky recipient of her ministrations was Paul Maycock, who at first looked down in surprise at the soft feminine hand that was clasping his thick erect shaft, but then settled back like Celia to enjoy the conclusion of Richard Gewirtz's story.

Richard polished off the rest of his champagne and continued: 'Blissfully I inhaled the aroma that arose from her wet pussey and thrust my tongue forcefully inside her crack, making her moan with delight as I circled round her clitty with long, loving strokes.

' "Oooh, oooh, that's very nice. But I want your big fat cock, Richard," she gasped, lifting my head away from her honeypot. "Give it to me! Push it in me now!" Scrambling up, I replaced my tongue with my rigid rod which I slid into her as far as it would go. "Ah, that's lovely, push in and out so I can feel your strong, hard prick moving inside me!" As I pushed I shifted my position slightly – first to one side and then to the other – so that my cock embedded in her cunney and she put her arms around my neck and clamped her legs around my hips. I thrust deeper and deeper inside her but between thrusts I paused, leaving only the tip of my knob tantalising her cunney lips, before plunging in again with regular but forceful movements, and each time my cock slid into her she let out a groan and dug her fingernails lightly into my shoulders.

'Her body began to jerk as an impending orgasm welled up inside her and she screamed out: "Yes! Yes! Yes! I'm coming, Richard, you fat-cocked fucker!! A-h-r-e, what a gorgeous spend!" I could no longer hold off and spurted my spunk, her cunney walls nipping and clipping my shaft as I expelled a fountain of thick, gruelly sperm inside her sticky wetness.'

'Sounds all very nice so far, but this doesn't explain how you come to be wearing such odd clothes,' observed Sir Gerry Newman, whose erect shaft was now pressing between the peach-like cheeks of Lady Laura Gantshill's delicious arse.

'Ah, well now, I'm just coming to that. You see, just as we lay back, recovering from this grand fuck, we heard the sound of the front door being opened and closed downstairs! We jumped up and I whispered: "Who the hell can this be? The servants have the night off so we either have a burglar on the premises or your husband has returned home early."

' "I hope it's a burglar," she hissed. "There's a revolver in the top drawer of my dressing table. But I fear that in all probability we have David to contend with." And sure enough, just as she spoke a voice called out: "Darling, I'm home – where are you?"

'I looked wildly around for somewhere to hide as we heard his footsteps getting louder and louder as he climbed the stairs to the bedroom. Where could I hide myself? Suddenly I saw that Maggie's wardrobe was open and I dived inside, pulling the door behind me but leaving it slightly ajar so that I could see what was happening in the room.

'I had only a few seconds to wait as Maggie hastily flung my own clothes under the bed. David came in and said: "Hello, old thing, how are you? Gosh, you're ready for bed so early? Are you well?"

' "I'm just a wee bit tired, dearest, but tell me, is all well with you? I didn't expect you home so soon."

' "No, to be honest, nor did I. Trouble was that most of the other fellows at the club shot off to the Jim Jam tonight to see some extraordinary performance called the Victor Pudendum, or some such business *[this Soho Club was famous for its notorious lived sex shows – RM]*, so I came home."

'Maggie somehow suppressed the urge to giggle, but she cast a look to the wardrobe where I was squeezed in between her dresses. "Quite right too," she cooed. "Why go all the way to Soho when you can have your own little show right here. Why don't you take off your clothes, darling, and then switch off the lights and we can have our own little performance right here in Walshaw Mews."

'David's eyes gleamed and he undressed with the utmost alacrity, which surprised me, for Maggie had always maintained that he did not care all that much for bed, and was not nearly as fond of fucking as her. But he did not appear to be slow in coming forward as Maggie cast herself down naked on the bed, her legs wide apart, showing her pink cunney lips to great effect. "Come on, David, stick your prong in me. I'm never too tired for that!"

'His cock waggling in anticipation, David climbed upon her rich curves immediately. A satisfied grunt from both signalled that he had reached his goal without any problem, and momentarily I envied him as I saw his meaty shaft slide sweetly in between the velvet lips of his wife's pussey, wetted, though luckily he did not know, only minutes before by my own libation of love juice.

'And there the couple lay enlaced and still for a moment, until Maggie panted: "Come on now, David, bugger the billiards, give me a good fucking instead! Yes, that's right, keep thrusting! Faster, faster, I know you have spunk boiling up in your balls for me! Work your hips and make me spend! Ah yes, that's great, ooh, listen to the squelch of our juices."

'His rampant cock pumped up and down and I could tell by their shudderings that they were fast approaching the point of no return. When David started to spend, Maggie squealed with pleasure as he jetted great blobs of hot creamy spunk into her cunney, which quivered from the little darts of fire inside her. David then withdrew his glistening shaft and sank back on his haunches, as his spendings melted away to a tiny drop of white liquid on the top of his knob, which was still heavy looking and almost fully erect. "Suck me off, please, Maggie," he asked hoarsely, and he leaned forward to bring the tip of his helmet to her mouth. Her reply was to kiss the ruby, uncovered dome and suck gently on his thick prick. I saw her tongue run up and down the shaft which made it swell up to its previous rock-hard fullness. David was now transported back to paradise and, at this point, as she lustily sucked on her sweetmeat, I quietly opened the door, slipped on my shoes and socks and dressed myself in the set of gentleman's clothes which were hanging up in Maggie's wardrobe.

'Maggie saw me creep out of the room and even gave me a cheery wave of the hand as she concentrated on sucking David's cock, which he was moving in and out of her wet mouth. I was so relieved not to have been discovered that it was only when I reached the front door that I realised that the clothes I had hastily slipped on were not mine at all! I looked inside the jacket and, sewn on the inside pocket, was the name of the tailor, *C Labovitch, St Christopher's Place*. Now I patronise Soames and Jolyon of Savile Row so I knew I was not suffering from some trick of the imagination. There was no time, though, to ponder the matter further as I heard a yell coming from the bedroom and I guessed that David had shot his load and might come downstairs to bring back a bottle of champagne to celebrate, for as most of you know, he is a noted imbiber!

'It was whilst I was walking briskly over here that the truth of the matter dawned upon me,' he added, swinging round to face Sir Gerry Newman who put up his hands in mock surrender and said: 'Why are you looking at me? I promise you that I hardly know the lady concerned.'

Richard smiled. 'No, I know you don't, but your writer friend Nicholas Clee is now very friendly with her. If you recall, he dined at your house last month when you gave a party to mark Lord Baum's appointment as chairman of the Al Fresco Fayre in Aid of Distressed Unfortunates. I was there along with Maggie and David and I noticed at the time that Mr Clee paid close attention to the lady, whilst David was polishing off a bottle of your '69 Napoleon brandy. Also, he is taller than me and finally, I clearly recall that the conversation did at one point touch upon the lack of good, reasonably inexpensive tailors in London, and he mentioned the fact that he had decided to try out this new chap, Labovitch, who has just opened up in Mayfair.'

He paused and then added: 'The case rests, your worship. Obviously I had not been alone in paying my respects so to speak. At first I was hurt and surprised at being deceived, but really, when you think logically about it – '

'What's sauce for the goose is sauce for the gander,' cut in Gwen Bracknell, who had come in with Jonathan and Penny from the bedroom and had heard the latter part of Richard Gewirtz's fascinating story.

'Quite right, Gwendolen,' said Jemima Loughton, joining in the attack on male chauvinism. 'I have never understood why it is that a man who boasts of a substantial number of notches on his cock is a rollicking, roistering man about town whilst a lady who entertains more than one prick at a time is looked down upon as a loose woman. It is all too unfair for words.'

'I quite agree with you, Jemima, and I am sure that I speak for all the other gentlemen present,' said Richard Gewirtz with a tone of utter sincerity in his voice. 'You speak of the prevailing hypocritical standards of society and not, I assure you, of the liberated progressive minds and bodies of your dear friends.'

'Hear, hear!' chorused the company, and to show her gratitude, the exquisitely pretty Jemima stepped forward and kissed the storyteller, who had now stripped down to his drawers, full on the lips. This reward from the beautifully, naked girl swept all the past trauma of the evening from Richard Gewirtz's mind. Oblivious now to everything except the gorgeous girl nestling in his lap, Richard returned her kiss with burning passion. His hands roamed all over her lovely body and he wrapped his arm around her waist which was so slender that it made her ripe young breasts appear even more prominent, with their tempting, taut rosy nipples set in the large red circles of their aureoles.

Also uncaring of the presence of their friends, Jemima slid her hand inside his undershorts and brought out his stiff, throbbing shaft with its massive purple helmet. Like most high-born continental men, Richard had been circumcised in infancy and Jemima ran her hand down the smooth trunk of his tool, unburdened by any barrier of loose foreskin. 'Ah, Richard, such a splendid shaft. I cannot think of anything I want more than to ride upon this great big poker.'

'Your wish is my command,' he replied, gently raising himself to his feet so that she could pull down his drawers.

'M'm, such heavy balls, too. Will you shoot a fountain of sticky cream inside me?' she cooed, sitting astride the broad, powerfully built frame of this scion of Central European aristocracy who was now lying on his back on the carpet by the fireplace. Richard put up his hands to mould her glorious breasts, and she reached down to insert her forefinger in her cunney, diddling her clitty in gentle circles, making Richard's cock quiver in excited anticipation. Slowly she lowered her moist cunney onto the tip of his mushroom-like knob and, inch by inch, her oily channel took in all of his iron column of cock until she was sitting lightly on top of his thighs.

Holding her pouting cunney lips open, she eased herself into a fully comfortable position and then began to ride up and down the stiff shaft, and Richard met her thrusts with his own, jamming his thick prick upwards as she pushed joyously down on his stiff-stander. Jemima wriggled delightedly, and from the closed eyes and expression of sheer bliss on Richard's face, the assembled company were left in no doubt whatsoever that Jemima's clever cunney muscles were working their special magic, nipping and clipping his cockshaft as it pulsed in and out of her love channel.

Jemima's rounded little bum cheeks were now raised up and these caught the attention of Professor Antony Hammond whose long, stiff tool twitched uncontrollably against his belly. 'May I have the honour of fucking your bottom, Jemima?' he said, bending over the trembling girl. 'That would be very nice indeed,' gasped Jemima, still extracting great enjoyment from Richard

Gewirtz's stalwart staff that was sliding slickly in and out of her cunt.

The Professor joyfully straightened up and took his position behind Jemima, kneeling with his legs on the outside of Richard's legs. Alan Brooke came forward and, ever the gentleman, dipped the Professor's prick in a glass of champagne before taking hold of his affair and placing it carefully between her gorgeous white, dimpled spheres, where the veiny shaft pulsed urgently, waiting with impatience to slide forward into Jemima's bottom.

'Thank you, I'll take over from here,' murmured the Professor, grasping his prick and inserting the tip of his knob in the puckered, brown rosette. As his cock was notable for length rather than breadth, it was well suited for bum-fucking and he was able to sheath himself in fully whilst snaking a hand round her slender waist. Indeed he was able to playfully manipulate her clitty as he dived his hand down into the crisp dark triangle of her pussey hair. The two men could feel each other's cocks slewing in and out, separated only by the thin divisional membrane between Jemima's cunney and arsehole. This very thought excited them all so much that they came very quickly – first Richard who sent a stream of spunk whooshing up Jemima's cunt, then Jemima who exploded into one of the most intense spends she had ever experienced, and finally Professor Hammond who shot a copious emission of gushing jism that flooded the girl's back passage, and he continued to work his prick back and forth until, with a 'pop', he uncorked it from her now well lubricated bum hole.

'That's what I call a really good fuck,' said Paul

Maycock enthusiastically, leading a spontaneous round of applause which rippled round the room. 'Don't you agree, Penny?'

Penny considered the question before answering. 'I was excited by the erotic performance, but I suppose I must be an old-fashioned girl at heart. My boyfriend Bob Goggin and I have tried making love standing up, with me on top, sitting in a chair, my bending over doggy-fashion and others. But frankly, Paul, I honestly prefer the straightforward, simple method of lying on my back in a soft warm bed on a springy mattress, feeling his prick slide between my cunney lips and the weight of his body pressing down on me. Generally speaking, no deviation offers me any greater pleasure.'

Sir Gerry Newman chipped in. 'I don't see anything strange in that, my dear. The so-called "missionary" position is my number one favourite, too.'

'You don't count, Gerry, as you would fuck in any fashion with anybody in a skirt between the ages of fifteen and fifty,' exclaimed Alan Brooke.

'Except a Scotsman,' said Celia.

'Don't be too sure,' added Paul Maycock darkly.

The randy baronet joined in the laughter. 'Now, now, now, I have often been called a hard bugger over the years, but I assure you that the epithet was perjorative rather than descriptive.'

'Why is it known as the missionary position?' wondered Penny Arkley.

'Oh, that's an easy question to answer,' explained Professor Hammond. 'It is because the missionaries in Africa and the South Pacific were horrified at the fact that these naughty brown and black people were actually enjoying sexual intercourse in many varied ways. So, as well as bundling the poor natives into unnecessary clothes, they also foisted their version of joyless religion upon the benighted heathen. And they taught that man-on-top, woman-underneath was the only permitted way to fuck.

'Mind, I would also agree that this position is the most pleasant for fucking. But variety is the spice of life, you know, and you would be surprised at the ingenuity of some couples to find new ways to perform.'

Lady Laura Gantshill nodded her head in agreement. 'My regular boyfriend, the Polish pianist Konrad Kochnaski, is fabulous between the sheets. He continually likes us to experiment with new positions and the latest is for me to keep one leg on the bed after he has stuffed his great sausage into my pussey, and then lift the other as high as I can. Having studied ballet I can lift my leg well above his shoulder so that I am practically doing the splits.'

'Really,' said Gwen Bracknell with interest. 'I must try this some time, although it sounds rather uncomfortable.'

'Oh, no, not in the slightest. It enables Konrad to make the very deepest penetration and as you know, Gwen, he has a most enormous penis. This makes me reach my climax more quickly and I know that he also derives great enjoyment when we make love in this way.'

'The right time of day is important,' chirruped Jemima, whose proud breasts were now being fondled by Alan Brooke. 'We mostly fuck at night when we are tired, or in the mornings when we are still waking up from a deep sleep. But I think I best enjoy being fucked in the afternoons, especially in summer. Just lying on the bed after luncheon waiting for my lover to come and satisfy me always makes my pussey damp. When he arrives and closes the curtains against the bright sun, I am always more than ready for him.'

'We've had a glorious summer, so you must have spent a great deal of time in bed!' laughed Penny Arkley.

'Yes, I suppose I have enjoyed my fucking this year more than at any time before. To be fair though, my regular beau has been the literary agent, Loring Sayers, a dear man so extraordinarily skilled in *l'arte de faire l'amour*.

'Indeed,' added Jemima with a shy little blush. 'We are to announce our engagement at Christmas, and then of course both of us will retire from gatherings such as these and will remain faithful to each other.'

'Many congratulations,' said Alan Brooke. 'I take it that between now and the announcement of your betrothal you are using the time to enjoy as many pricks as possible, whilst your intended is on a parallel course regarding an assortment of pussies.'

'Precisely so – it is my firm belief that if we satisfy our wilder curiosities before marriage, this will help cement the matrimonial bonds. Generally speaking I do not approve of adultery, unless, of course, a husband or wife is causelessly withholding from the pleasures of the marriage bed. In that case, gentlemen like Richard Gewirtz here are performing a valuable function in servicing lonely, unfulfilled women.'

'Well, we must make hay whilst the sun shines if we are to lose you after Christmas,' declared Lady Laura

Gantshill firmly. 'Come, sit upon my knees and allow me offer my own, very personal felicitations upon the occasion of your forthcomng nuptials.'

Jemima moved across the room and joined Lady Laura, who was sitting next to Alan Brooke on the sofa. The two girls kissed lusciously, their lips pressed together and their tongues waggling in each other's mouths as their hands busied themselves, nipping, pinching and caressing titties, bottoms and cunnies until Laura pushed Jemima down so that the gorgeous girl lay on her back with her legs wide apart, to allow Laura to lick and lap at her splendid cunney.

'What a perfect pussey,' sighed Laura, gently running he hand over the glossy covering of curly black hair. She bent forward to kiss the mount of love and the serrated vermilion lips of her cunney from which popped out quite three inches a stiff, fleshy clitoris, as big as a thumb. Laura opened the lips further with her fingers and passed her tongue lasciviously around the most sensitive parts, rolling this marvellous clitty in her mouth and playfully nipping it with her teeth. Jemima wriggled deliciously as with a cry of: 'Oooh! Aaah! You are making me come, darling!' she spent profusely all over Laura's mouth and chin.

The girls now changed places and Jemima lay on top of Laura. With her clever fingers she opened Laura's crack as wide as possible and then, directing her clitty, she somehow managed to stuff it between Laura's cunney lips, holding them tightly together with her hand. This novel fucking was tremendously exciting for both the pretty girls and, of course, for Alan Brooke, who was now sitting on the arm of the sofa, his huge penis standing as high and erect as a guardsman on parade. He moved between Jemima's legs and, as her cunney slipped out of Laura's, the great cocksman pulled her pert bottom cheeks up to enable him to insert his prick inside her from behind. As his shaft slid in and out of her sopping cunt, she kissed and sucked on Laura's big breasts whilst she pushed her thigh against her dripping pussey. Alan, meanwhile, was cupping Jemima's titties in his hands as he manfully kept his lusty tool sliding rhythmically in and out of her juicy love channel, despite Jemima's writhings, for now she had moved her arm round to attack Laura's pussey from behind, her fingers sliding squelchily in and out of the sticky wetness.

The threesome tossed and turned, and Gwendolen Bracknell was momentarily concerned that they might fall off the couch and injure themselves on the glass occasional table that stood perilously near. But all was well as Alan Brooke shot a fierce stream of frothy white spunk into Jemima's cunney, and this very soon led to the two girls reaching delightful climaxes, their love liquids running freely down their thighs which, combined with Alan Brooke's copious emission, left a huge puddle of juice on the sofa.

'Oh dear, that will be difficult to explain away,' said Jonathan Crawford gloomily as the participants decided to refresh themselves with some more champagne.

'Don't worry, that sofa has had more sperm spilled on it than you could ever imagine. My maid uses a bottle of special preparation on it which was given to her by Sir Percy Grosvenor's butler – you probably know that Sir Peter is very fond of fucking immediately after he has dined, and often does not wait until he and his amorata are in bed. Anyhow, this cleaning fluid removes spunk stains as if by magic, so please feel free to fuck anywhere and everywhere in this house,' said Gwen hospitably.

Indeed it was Penny and Gwen herself who were next to use the couch for a threesome fuck. The good looking Paul Maycock was their not unwilling 'victim', and he certainly offered no resistance when Gwen lay alongside him to suck and nibble at his extraordinarily thick cock, and Penny positioned herself across his face so that he was able to bury his head between her soft warm thighs and lap at her damp, pouting pussey lips with his tongue. At the same time he reached up to cup her gorgeous titties and flick at her erect nipples with his fingertips as she squirmed lewdly, pressing her pussey even harder upon his mouth. By this time Gwen's tongue was lashing around Paul's pulsating prick, noisily gobbling his stout veiny shaft, her head bobbing up and down as she brought him up to a delicious spend. 'Here it comes, Gwen, brace yourself!' he cried, and she gratefully swallowed the outpouring of white gruelly cream that poured liberally from his knob, enjoying to the full the clean, salty taste of his spunk.

Richard Gewirtz's circumcised cock was now sticking up impressively against his flat belly, as he now politely asked Celia Debden-Hunte if she would care to be fucked.

'Certainly,' said the blonde girl, rising to her feet. 'Although you must surely be exhausted after all your previous exertions earlier this evening.'

'Ah, *quando viene il desiderio, non è mai troppo*,' responded the handsome European youth. 'An old

Italian saying, Celia, that when desire comes, it is never excessive.'

Celia giggled and took his twitching truncheon in her hand, enjoying the feel of its hot, smooth skin against her fingers. 'This is truly a magnificent cock,' she said admiringly. 'I just hope that you are able to use it with all the finesse of your father who, though I only speak from hearsay, is one of the finest fuckers in all Europe.'

'I'll do my level best,' Richard promised, and without further ado he covered her mouth with a burning kiss and slid his hand between her legs, rubbing the silky blonde cunney hair against his palm. They made their way to the sofa, recently vacated by the lascivious trio of Gwen, Penny and Alan, and Celia began to moan with pleasure as Richard tenderly opened the yielding lips of her crack, sliding a finger gently in and out of her dainty quim that was already moistening to a delicious degree of wetness. As he frigged her first with one, then two, and then three fingers, she took hold of his huge cock and rhythmically stroked his straining shaft.

She leaned over to wash his purplish round knob with her tongue and licked his prick from the tip of the crown all the way down to his hairy ballsack and back again. She then looked up and whispered: 'Please fuck me now,' and so Richard lifted himself on his knees between her long legs, hooking them over his shoulders so that her lovely bottom was lifted into the air, and a low gurgle of anticipation escaped her lips as he cupped her arse cheeks and she took hold of his throbbing tool and guided it between her glistening pink pussey lips. He slipped his full nine-inch staff inside her welcoming cunney up to the hilt until their pubic hairs were mingled and for a moment he lay still, allowing her to enjoy the sensation of having her cunney crammed with this swollen shaft.

Then, slowly but surely, he began to pump in and out of her sopping slit, leaving only the tip of his helmet inside her as he pulled back, but pushing in with a will so that every last fraction of cock slid back inside her cunt. Celia had the knack of contracting her cunney so that it grasped Richard's cock like a most delicate hand frigging his shaft, and she wriggled away happily as he now increased the pace of his fucking, pumping his pulsating prick in and out of her sopping cunney. Her cunney muscles clasped his cock and they gloried in the lubricity of a grand fuck as her juices dripped against his balls as they banged against her bum. Cupped now in his broad palms, Celia's firm bottom cheeks rotated savagely as his lusty rammer raised the friction in her cunt to new heights. Her kisses rained upon his neck as she reached climax after climax as his throbbing tool reamed the furthest depths of the sodden slit.

'I can't take much more,' panted Celia. 'Just spunk into me whenever you like, you big-cocked boy!'

Richard plunged down hard, crushing her luscious breasts as in one last short burst he ran the final furlong in this delicious course. The boiling spunk rose from his balls and, with surging force, it spurted deep inside her love channel and in a magnificent spend that shot copious floods of creamy white froth into her juicy dark warmth.

Even for Richard Gewirtz, this urgent, powerful fuck exhausted his proud prick and he withdrew his limp member, coated with their love juices from Celia's cunt.

Professor Antony Hammond leaned over them and commented: 'I think you would both score ten out of ten for that performance at one of the Jim Jam Club's Victor Pudendum shows, where couples fuck for the entertainment of the patrons as well as themselves.'

'Thank you very much for the compliment,' said Richard modestly. 'But Celia did climax before me and so we didn't manage to achieve a simultaneous spend.'

The Professor snorted. 'So what? There is absolutely no point working towards simultaneous spends. In fact, jolly as they are when they happen naturally, if you allow the thought that you must come just at the same time as your partner, you can take away a great deal of joy from the love-making. As my old friend Sir Michael Bailey has written in his excellent little tome, *Fucking For Beginners*, climaxing at different times allows one partner to concentrate on exciting the other, which is far more important.'

Katie Arkley caught the end of this little homily as she munched on a leg of chicken taken from the laden table at the end of the room. Her tousled blonde tresses shook as she nodded her agreement and exclaimed. 'I do wish you would repeat that speech to my boyfriend Walter Stanton [*see* Cremorne Gardens, *Headline Books, London, for an account of Walter and Katie's erotic adventures – RM*]. He's so worried if we don't come together and I sometimes fib and say I've spent just to keep him happy.'

'Do tell us more, Katie. I've had this problem myself with one or two lovers,' said Celia, propping herself up on her elbow.

Katie said, 'Well, to be honest, this happened on the last time we made love about three weeks ago. We were snuggled up in bed in his room at the Rawalpindi Club and we were more than ready to begin fucking. Walter had rolled me over on my back and had firmly pressed his helmet against my pussey lips which were quite swollen with desire. He thrust his strong shaft straight in without the slightest difficulty and his balls slapped against my bum as I wrapped my legs around his back and clawed his shoulders with my nails.

'By now we were rolling around the bed and I found myself on top of his lean, muscled body. I reached down and found his huge, rock-hard cock and I impaled myself on the helmet of this magnificent monster. His chest and shoulders were glistening with sweat as I rode him like a jockey rides a thoroughbred colt at Newmarket Races. My cunney was on fire as his trembling prick twitched in a manner that I knew was heralding a spending.

'Sure enough, I felt his body go rigid and then he arched his back upwards and shot out his spunk with such intensity that I could almost imagine it splashing off the rear wall of my cunt. Indeed, so abundant was his emission that my thighs were well lathered with sticky white cream which I scooped up with my fingers and rubbed on my breasts, for there is nothing so good as sperm for moisturising and cleaning the skin.

'Now Walter had spent so copiously that his tingling prick had deflated as it rubbed itself amorously against my cunney lips, in a last salute as he pulled it out of my pussey. He looked somewhat concerned and said: "Oh dear, Katie, you haven't come yet, have you?"

'I decided to be truthful and said: "To be honest,

I'm afraid not – but honestly it does not matter a bit. I enjoyed the fucking immensely and girls don't expect to spend every single time like you boys can. It's good when it happens but it isn't automatic, more's the pity."

'But Walter still looked worried and he frowned. "Dash it, I think it jolly well does matter, Katie," he said. "I always understood that we are supposed to aim to achieve a climax together and I must be doing something wrong if we don't manage it." The poor lad refused to be comforted until I sucked his cock up to another bursting erection, and this time when he came I assured him that I had spent at exactly the same time. In fact, this was not so very far from the truth, but I don't want either of us to worry any more about a genuinely trifling matter.'

Professor Hammond stroked his chin as he contemplated Katie's problem. 'Buy Walter a copy of Sir Michael Bailey's book for Christmas,' he advised. 'And when he has read it, purchase a copy of Williams & Hartington's *Advanced Copulatory Techniques* for his birthday.'

'All this talk about *les affaires d'amour* is making me deucedly randy,' complained Sir Gerry Newman.

'Let's have some action rather than words,' he added, gently frigging his large cock which was standing up stiffly out of a shaggy mass of curly dark hair. The insatiable Gwendolen was the first to take him at his word as she swung herself over his face so that her luscious cunney was directly over his mouth, and the lusty tycoon frigged her slit with his tongue. Excited by this scene, Celia leaped over his waist and speared herself on his veiny truncheon and began riding up and down upon his thick shaft. They waited until he was approaching climax before jumping off his quivering body.

'You don't want to come too soon, do you, Gerry?' asked Gwendolen rhetorically as each girl took it in turns to lick his cock and balls until Celia lay back and he mounted her, plunging his prick deep inside her cunney, whilst Gwendolen fondled his hairy ballsack and worked a finger delicately in his arse-hole, which excited him greatly. There was just time to bury his great, throbbing tool one more time in Celia's saturated cunney before he jetted a generous portion of spunk inside her.

All this raised the lustful feelings of the other guests. Alan Brooke was busy fucking the lovely Jemima Loughton from behind, doggie fashion, as she bent over the chair of the sofa. How her luscious bum cheeks rotated as Alan drove in and out, which so inflamed Paul Maycock that he ran across to offer the reddish knob of his cock to Jemima's cherry lips, and her little pink tongue flicked out to wash the mushroom dome before sucking it inside her mouth. Penny Arkley joined the chain by kneeling on the floor underneath Alan Brooke and sucking his balls as they moved backwards and forwards as he fucked Jemima. Jonathan Crawford took the opportunity to kneel alongside Penny, who grabbed hold of his sturdy staff and began to frig it deliciously, her hand sliding up and down the thick length of his pulsating prick.

Next to join the chain was Lady Laura Gantshill, who dropped to her knees and raised her full rich lips to Jonathan, and as they exchanged a burning kiss, the explorer cupped her full breasts in his hands, kneading the firm flesh and rubbing his palms across the stalky red nipples.

Professor Hammond completed the chain by lying on top of Lady Laura and inserting his stiff tool into her yearning cunney. The clever girl, whilst still French kissing with Jonathan Crawford, reached across and began to massage the Professor's hairy back, and it was now a question of just who would be the first to spend.

'I think Alan Brooke is about to let loose his libation,' said Gwen to Celia and Sir Gerry who, having just completed a three-way fuck, were in no condition to join the gathering just yet.

'No, no, my money's on Jonathan Crawford,' said Celia, who could see the great traveller's tremendous tool twitching violently under the sensuous rubbing from Penny Arkley.

Celia would probably have won the wager anyhow, for Jonathan was almost ready to spurt his spunk – but to make sure, Celia knelt down and sucked the ruby head of his cock into her mouth, washing the helmet teasingly with her tongue whilst her hands fondled his balls. 'Here we go!' he panted as a veritable torrent of frothy white cream jetted out of his cock. Celia swallowed as much of the pungent juice as possible, but lifted her head to let some of the sticky essence dribble down onto Penny's hand.

Alan Brooke was the second to spend, sending a stream of sperm into Jemima's already saturated cunney, whilst the lovely girl received an equally copious emission of jism in her mouth from Paul Maycock, which she gulped down as she herself achieved the acme of all delights. Alas, Penny and Laura did not reach such heights, although they enjoyed their minor roles in the action and the company repaired to the bar for further refreshment, for a heavy night's fucking needs constant replenishment of fuel for the body as well as the mind.

Whilst they recovered their strength, Jonathan Crawford told the still naked crowd about his forthcoming adventure which would not be in the jungles of Africa, but high in the air above Hampshire, not at all far in fact from Katie and Penny's home of Arkley Hall.

'I didn't know you were interested in aeroplanes, Jonathan,' said Jemima Loughton. 'Will you take me for a flight one day?'

'With the greatest of pleasure,' he said. 'I wouldn't take you up just yet as I am still learning to fly myself. Fortunately, the great French aviator, Monsieur Bleriot, has kindly agreed to give me the benefit of his experience and I am off to France next week to visit him. [*Louis Bleriot (1872–1936) was later to win tremendous acclaim shortly afterwards when he became the first man to fly across the English Channel – RM*]

'Lord Coddrington has constructed an aerodrome on his estate and when I return I shall fly his Lordship's aeroplanes. His Lordship is determined to build a machine that will fly at one hundred miles an hour, and I want to be the man to first fly at this great speed.'

'How exciting it would be to fuck at five thousand feet,' said Jemima dreamily. 'I wonder whether the sensation would be enhanced by the rare atmosphere.'

'An interesting thought, but I wonder whether we will ever be able to fly as high as the upper clouds at speed,' commented Professor Hammond.

Jonathan Crawford held up his hand. 'My dear friend, there is no limit to where aeronautics will lead us. I would not take issue with the writer in today's afternoon newspaper who forecasts that this century will see a man on the moon.'

This brought a hoot of laughter from most of the guests, and only Richard Gewirtz refused to mock the preposterous proposition. 'Why should such a feat be beyond the bounds of possibility?' he protested. 'Look, I have just returned to England from America where only last month Orville Wright collected more than thirty thousand dollars from the US Government. He won this prize for constructing a craft capable of flying at over forty miles an hour on a ten-mile journey carrying a passenger. I was at Fort Myer when he made the cross-country flight to Alexandria and back, at speeds approaching fifty miles per hour when the wind was with him.'

'You can travel faster by train, and more comfortably at that,' scoffed Alan Brooke.

'True enough,' agreed Richard, 'but my father and I had the pleasure of meeting Mr Wright afterwards, and I'll wager a hundred pounds at any reasonable odds that in ten years' time we'll see aeroplanes travelling at more than a hundred miles an hour. For good measure, I'll also bet that we'll soon see flying machines going across the Atlantic Ocean as well.'

[*Richard Gewirtz was remarkably prescient in his prophecies. By 1919, just a little more than ten years on, the first London to Paris passenger service started and in that same year Alcock and Brown flew across the Atlantic at an average speed of 125 miles an hour – RM*]

'There is great scope for improvement in explosive engines,' added Jonathan Crawford. 'The problem now is seventy-five per cent machine, and twenty-five per cent man. But these problems will be overcome and the aeroplane will be transformed from a toy into a commercial success that will become an accepted part of our lives, just like the motor car has superceded the horse on our roads.'

Sir Gerry Newman was impressed by these firm words. 'Perhaps you're right, Jonathan. Tell you what, if you need any capital for your adventure, please let me know as I'd be interested in helping you out.'

Now if a tough, hard-headed businessman like Gerry Newman – far from ungenerous in his personal life, as his munificent generosity to many worthy causes is well recorded – was willing to invest in such an undertaking, it appeared to several of the others that Jonathan and Richard might not be talking through their hats after all. But Celia Debden-Hunte had her mind on other matters when she turned round to her hostess and asked whether she could run a nice warm bath. 'Certainly, my dear, are you getting chilly?' asked Gwendolen anxiously.

'No, no, not at all, but I would like to wash off all the sticky perspiration and the equally sticky other liquids that have recently run over my skin.'

'What a good idea,' chimed in Jemima Loughton. 'May I join you?' And off they trotted, to be followed a little later by Katie Arkley.

Now Gwendolen Bracknell's bath was a large, oval affair and the three girls managed to squeeze in together. The water was nicely warm and they splashed around gaily. But when Katie climbed out and sat on the side with a towel draped around her shoulders, Celia could not resist giving her golden-haired crotch a friendly rub with the palm of her hand. At first Katie was shocked, but the sensation was frankly delicious and soon she was totally relaxed.

Soon enough the third girl joined them so that now, on one side Jemima was caressing her breasts and tweaking her nipples to their fullest erection, whilst Celia began to kiss all around Katie's pouting cunney lips.

Jemima teased her lips around Katie's shoulder, leaving a wet trail as her tongue played all over the soft white skin. She cradled Katie's breasts and squeezed the gorgeous globes as, letting her head fall back, Katie closed her eyes and gave in to the tingling sensation as Jemima's lips found the quivering red nipple which she sucked tenderly at first, and then more hungrily, nibbling around the strawberry stalk which sent sparks of delight shivering through Katie's delicious body.

To add to the excitement, Celia now began to make love to Katie's blonde pleasure patch in earnest. Her pink tongue reached out and explored her wet, smooth dampness. Instinctively, Katie tightened her legs around Celia's head and pushed herself against the probing, exploring mouth. She found her clitty and, as she kissed it, Katie moaned with pleasure. As she licked and lapped at the fleshy little protrusion, Celia worked the fingers of her own hand inside her own pussey which was still under water in the bath. But she kept her mouth glued to Katie's cunney, inhaling the tangy, fresh, feminine aroma of the lovely girl's juices as they began to flow.

As Katie groaned and sighed, tensing towards her release, Celia and Jemima knew exactly what she was feeling with every roll of her slim hips and every luscious flutter of her cunney walls. 'Lick her crack, Celia,' gasped Jemima. 'Rub your face all around her silk pussey and suck her clitty until she spends!'

These lewd words sent the trio into new spasms of desire and with a cry they all came together, gushing, throbbing and crying out in their mutual joy. They shrieked, then giggled and then Katie and Jemima collapsed into the bath to join Celia in the soothing warmth of the water. 'Let Celia and me finish you off, Katie,' said Jemima as they climbed out of the bath and dried themselves with the luxuriously large towels thoughtfully provided by their hostess.

They padded across to Gwendolen's bedroom and, for the second time that evening, Katie Arkley found herself flat on her back in Gwen's bed. Without further ado, Celia stroked the insides of her thighs and gently opened her legs to accommodate Jemima, who licked cleverly along the inside of Katie's cunney lips, not putting her tongue inside the moist crack, but nevertheless sending Katie into paroxysms of pleasure and wanting desperately to be fucked, a request which she boldly made of Jemima.

'It's all right, Katie, I'll do that for you,' said Celia. Katie opened her eyes and giggled when she looked up and saw that Celia had strapped on a belt around her waist which, at the front, had attached a black wooden affair exquisitely shaped like a giant cock, complete with carefully fashioned balls. This was the first time Katie had seen such a dildo (although at school, along with the rest of the Upper Fifth, she had experienced the delights of a hand-held instrument, self-wielded or manipulated by a best friend), and the sweet girl was a little unsure as to what she might expect.

As if reading her mind, Jemima said encouragingly: 'Don't worry, Celia is marvellously skilled at playing the gentleman. Just lie back and enjoy yourself.'

So Katie spreadeagled her legs as Celia climbed on top of her, giving her a passionate kiss on the lips as she reached down and rubbed the heel of her hand against the yielding cunney lips. Then, with a wriggle, she inserted the head of this wooden cock (which, in fact, was wrapped in the finest soft leather) between them. Katie gasped as Celia leaned forwards and the dildo slid into her sopping slit. It took a little while to find the correct rhythm, but once they synchronised their pushing and pumping, Katie really began to enjoy this lewd new experience. Each time Celia thrust forward, the edge of the dildo touched Katie's clitty and at the end of each thrust, when it was in as far as it could go, it rubbed into the furthest recesses and sparks began shooting through her entire body.

Katie felt the first faint waves of orgasm start deep inside her, and they soon began to spread, thundering through her, setting every nerve on fire with intense passion and pleasure. She spent profusely as Celia continued remorselessly to thrust and pull back, until Katie cried out that her cunney had been filled enough. Celia rolled off the quivering girl as Katie's cunney discharged a further copious emission of love juice that dribbled down her thighs.

'Did you enjoy that?' enquired Celia.

'Oh yes, it was heavenly – just like the real thing.

Do you often strap on a dildo?'

'Only occasionally, when Jemima and I are together. We take turns to strap it on and fuck each other, which we like very much.'

Jemima agreed. 'It's funny, but when I strap it on I feel strangely powerful. I know I have a stiff, thick prick mounted between my legs and I am capable of thrusting into Celia's cunt and give her a spend just like a man could, whilst at the same time I often spend myself.'

'It doesn't put you off boys though, does it?' asked Katie.

Celia laughed and shook her had. 'Far from it! But playing with a dildo makes you uncommonly randy. For instance, only last Thursday I was pumping this little friend into Jemima's pussey when Alan Brooke walked in. I was almost ready to spend so I wasn't about to stop what I was doing, so I unbuttoned his trousers, took out his great prick and sucked him off. Then afterwards he fucked us both quite beautifully in his own inimitable style.'

'I enjoy threesomes of any computations of the sexes,' she added. 'I believe that a trio offers the greatest intimacies, for where three are involved one feels one is sharing something very special indeed, without any thoughts of embarrassment. I think two girls and one man makes up an ideal combination, but I'm not too fussy so long as I am promised the use of at least one good, thick prick. On the other hand–'

A masculine voice cut in: '–there's nothing like a straightforward fuck. But then you'll think me old-fashioned.'

The girls looked up to see the handsome young

Richard Gewirtz standing at the foot of the bed, his massive circumcised cock rising stiffly up against his flat belly from the mossy nest of dark hair under which dangled a pair of heavy-looking balls.

'There's a lot to be said for traditional orthodoxy,' said Jemima. 'I saw you fuck Celia just before, and you appeared to give her complete satisfaction.'

'It would be an honour to spunk into your delicious cunney, ma'am,' twinkled the dashing young man.

Jemima returned the easy smile and, for reply, took hold of his iron-hard shaft and gently fondled the pulsating prick, looking with interest at its uncovered, purplish dome and lack of foreskin. 'Do you know, I think this is the first circumcised cock I have ever handled,' said the gorgeous girl, shyly.

'Don't worry, it won't bite you,' giggled Celia. 'I can't really tell the difference once the shaft is lodged in my cunney, but I do think that an unencumbered instrument like Richard's is far prettier to look at. It's easy to keep clean, too, so I never worry about taking such a cock into my mouth.'

'Thank you for those kind words,' said Richard as he climbed onto the bed and lay smiling as Jemima continued to frig his stiff-stander. Then, slowly, he moved on top of the delicious young blonde girl and allowed her to guide his throbbing tool inside her sopping cunney. She writhed excitedly as his cock continued to swell and twitch inside her crack. She felt Richard's lips upon hers, and boldly she thrust her tongue into his mouth as his slim body now rocked in rhythm, faster and faster, his shaft pounding into her willing love-box. Jemima rolled in ecstasy, bouncing up and down as he plunged in and out of her wetness.

He fucked her vigorously with long, sweeping strokes until Jemima whimpered gently. Concerned lest he hurt the poor girl, Richard withdrew his monster rammer so that only the red knob teased her cunney lips. 'I'm afraid my cunney is becoming a little sore,' she apologised. 'Would you mind very much if I finish you off by sucking your cock?'

'Not in the slightest,' said Count Gewirtz's youngest son, scrambling to his knees and offering his glistening, stiff staff to Jemima's hand. She used both hands to grasp the pulsing prick as she, too, leaned forward on her knees to kiss his smooth-skinned helmet before licking up the little pool of pre-spend juice from the 'eye' on the top of his knob.

Jemima sucked his throbbing tool into her mouth, somehow managing to take in its entire ramrod length and letting it slide easily down over her tongue to her throat, just as a sword swallower can, without gagging, take in a lethal weapon between his lips. Richard twisted round and down to complete a *soixante neuf*, and his face was now buried in her damply dense bush, his tongue wickedly tracking through the enveloping blonde jungle of hair to seek out first her cunney lips, which were already open and welcoming to the intrusion, and then her clitoris, engorged and swollen like an answer to his own huge shaft.

As his tongue rubbed over the head of her sensitive clitty and delved deeper into the wetness of her cunt, Jemima began to writhe and shudder. Still holding Richard's enormous cock clamped between her lips, she groaned as her hips bucked ever faster until, in moments, her whole body convulsed and the crashing wave of orgasm surged through her. Jemima's copious libation of love juice filled his mouth as he struggled to hold the trembling girl during the repeated shudders of her passion.

Soon though, Jemima's perspiring body subsided and, ever so slowly, she released his still-charged cock from her mouth and lay beside him. He too lay still as they cuddled together, until her hand reached out to cradle his balls. Shivering slightly, she kissed him lightly on the tip of his still-upstanding prick, hugged him and said: 'I know you haven't spent yet, but I do so want to feel the full majesty of your proud prick in my cunney that I thought it best to leave you temporarily unfulfilled. My cunt is now quite refreshed from your tonguing.'

Richard smiled and said that he had plenty of time and was not impatient to be finished off. Jemima then lifted herself up and straddled the good-looking young man, and lowered herself upon him. He could see his straining staff disappear, inch by inch, into her open-mouthed cunney before she settled down, with a little wriggle to seal the union. Sitting upright, she arched her back so that her magnificent breasts jutted out above him. Putting both hands behind her neck she shook her blonde tresses as, reaching down and taking her weight on her hands, she kissed him full on the lips as she lifted herself so that she was almost clear of his pulsating prick. Again she slowly lowered herself, pausing so that her cunney lips could brush against the red helmet of his knob before she slipped her luscious wetness down the full length of his grand shaft.

Richard could hold back no longer and pushed his cock up to invade her cunney to the brim, and the little love passage opened up and then moved tightly around his thick shaft, swallowing the essence of his being within her. Jemima leaned forward so that the tips of her taut breasts rubbed against his chest and her mouth was open, gasping and moaning. Both of them were at the very brink of ecstasy as the pace increased to a near frenzy.

Suddenly the muscles of her cunney tightened around his shaft as she bore down upon him in a long, rippling seizure that ran from the base to the very tip of his cock. Twice this clutching spasm travelled the length of his shaft and then she relaxed . . . at once the spunk poured out of his prick, hot and seething, jetting upwards into every nook and cranny as gush after gush spurted uncontrollably up, up, deep inside her.

Richard cried out: 'Yes! Yes! Yes!' and thrust up so hard that Jemima clung to him like a rider on a bucking horse whilst she ground her pussey against him, as at last she surrendered to her own climax. Her teeth bit into his shoulder and her breasts crushed against him as he pulled the cheeks of her arse forward towards him, their love juices mingling to flood over their bellies and thighs.

As they slowly subsided, Richard reached down into the dampness and rubbed the love liquid over her succulent red titties. Jemima giggled and did likewise, and in moments they were completely oiled and stickied as they lay entwined in an intimate embrace.

'You'll need another bath,' commented Celia brightly. 'I hope there is enough hot water left in the tank.

'My goodness, Richard Gewirtz, that is a really splendid prick you have dangling over your thigh. It isn't the very biggest I have ever seen, but you certainly know how to use it.'

Richard grinned. 'Well, it's not the size of the wave but the motion of the ocean, as they say in America. Actually, I met a man in Washington with whom my father does business, a Mr Highbury, who enjoys fucking almost as much as I do. He took us to a club *privée* there, The Bees Knees, and we took part in a bacchanalian entertainment. The girls all praised Mr Highbury's prowess with his prick, although I do assure you it was barely half the length of some of the tools that were being flashed around.'

'This proves that the important thing is just how you use the equipment your Creator provided,' boomed out the voice of Professor Hammond who had wandered in.

'Not another lecture, please, Antony,' laughed Katie.

'No, no,' said the Professor genially. 'But I would commend the words of the poet, Alexander Pope, a man small of stature with perhaps an equally diminutive cock.

'You know where you did despise
(T'other day) my little Eyes,
Little Legs and Little Thighs,
And some things, of little size,
You know where.
You, tis true, have fine dark eyes,
Taper Legs and Tempting Thighs,
Yet what more than we all prize
Is a Thing of Little Size,
You know where.'

'Yes, it is too ridiculous to worry about the dimensions of your todger, but you men will worry unnecessarily about being well-hung,' said Celia.

'Are you thinking of anyone in particular?' asked Richard Gewirtz. 'I know one or two chaps who are concerned about what they perceive as their undersized pricks.'

'Other fellows' tools often appear to be bigger than your own,' advised Professor Hammond. 'This is simply because a man is looking at another man's prick from an angle, whereas one sees one's own cock only by looking straight down. This is why it will always appear to be larger, incidentally, when viewed in a mirror.'

Katie coloured slightly. 'I do know that size doesn't really matter, but a really large, well-made prick does excite me and I'm sure that the other girls will agree.'

'Oh yes,' said Jemima. 'But I am just as aroused by a manly chest or the slim flanks of an athlete.'

'I prefer a good rounded arse on a man,' said Celia thoughtfully. 'But as Antony says, it's whether a man has character that counts first and foremost. I take men as I find them, regardless of their position in Society. Indeed, one of my first fucks was with Jed the Gypsy, who was but a humble gardener's boy at our family's country seat in Wiltshire.'

Katie caught her breath as she knew that her own sister, Penny, had been fucking the gardener's boy, Bob Goggin, for at least nine months. But wisely she kept her counsel.

Celia continued: 'Yes, I remember the occasion well. It was a warm summer's afternoon and young Jed was working away in the garden. We called him the Gypsy

Boy, but in fact he was the son of the local publican whose wife came from Romany stock. Jed was only sixteen but he was tall for his age and, as I was to discover, well-built in every way!

'When it was four o'clock he stopped for tea and I saw him disappear into the bothie at the back of the garden. I followed him in there a few minutes after and, though I must confess that mischief was not far from my mind, I had no definite plan for seducing this lovely boy, who was three years younger than me. Anyhow, I opened the door softly and saw Jed sitting bare-chested (for he had taken off his shirt which was drenched from his perspiration). He was looking avidly at a book and it appeared, though at first I thought I was imagining it, that there was a bulge in his trousers. At first he did not see me as he turned the page, and I looked over his shoulder and saw that he was gazing at a copy of last month's edition of *The Oyster*, which featured a selection of prints of the great Kentish artist, Lawrence Back, and I soon saw what had caught young Jed's fancy.

'The scene was set in a richly decorated room and, lying flat on his back in the front of the picture was the Duke of Glasgow, quite naked with his cock standing up proudly as if to salute the pretty nude girl who was leaning over him, squatting in such a fashion that he was able, by lifting his head a trifle, to lick her cunney. Next to this happy pair were a couple who bore an uncanny resemblance to Lord Judd and Mrs Farquhar-Robson. Again, the male figure was lying down but this time his unclothed feminine friend was holding his immense prick in her hands as she took the proud member deep into her mouth. Oh yes, and at the same time nearby another young lady was diddling herself with a cock-shaped dildo, similar to the one we have just been using. No doubt she must have purchased the object as we did from Doctor Nicholas Webb's Surgical Stores in Macdonald Street.

'This lewd scene was proving so engrossing to Jed that it was not till I let out a delicate little cough that he realised that he was not alone. He looked up with a startled expression but I put my finger to his lips and said: "Shush now, Jed, there's no need to be concerned. Why don't we go outside into the glorious sunshine and we can look at these exciting pictures together."

'I led him by the hand to Fisher's Field which backs onto our garden and I lay down in the long grass. I patted the ground and invited him to join me. At last Jed actually spoke as clearing his throat he whispered: "I'd love to, Miss Celia, but I'm supposed to be working on the roses and I'll get into trouble if I don't finish pruning them."

' "I can think of something better to prune," I said, raising my dress to let him see my bare legs – for in the heat I had discarded all petticoats and was wearing only a pair of knickers. "Wouldn't you prefer to see the real thing instead of just looking at pictures?" I raised my dress even higher and his breathing deepened as he fell to the ground beside me.

' "Have you ever seen an actual pussey, Jed?" I purred. He hung his head and said: "I've seen Becky the scullery maid's cunney, and she's let me play with it whilst she handled my tadger, but I've never actually–" "Oh, so you're a virgin," I said delightedly. "Well, I know from my own experience what a tiresome state this can be after the onset of puberty. Let me feel your tool through your trousers. Oh yes, that looks to be a hard, stiff shaft that's ready to be properly placed. My own pussey would welcome it, that is for sure."

'His eyes shone with barely expressed joy. "Do you really mean it, Miss Celia? You're not just teasing me now, are you?"

'For reply I dextrously undid the buttons of my blouse and shrugged off the garment. I was wearing only a thin silk chemise and he was given an excellent view of the firm swell of my breasts. I was unsure at first as to how he would react, but I need not have worried. With a hoarse little yelp he pressed his lips upon mine and we exchanged a most passionate, burning kiss. I slid my tongue between his lips and I think this must have been the first French kiss he had experienced for it sent him into a wild frenzy. We rocked together as he clasped me to him, and I guided his hand over my breast which he cupped very nicely, rubbing and squeezing quite delightfully. Jed was not totally without experience for he let his hand wander downwards to lay over my pussey. He gathered up the material of my dress and, when he placed his hand against my inner thigh, I found myself trembling almost as much as Jed! I reached over and unclipped his belt and with his other hand he unbuttoned his fly. I slipped my hand inside and brought out a beautiful thick cock, as white as one could wish, as smooth as ivory but as hard as marble. His knob had released itself from the confines of his foreskin and his uncapped helmet stood ready for its very first journey into the warm wetness of a cunt.

'For a split second our hot eyes locked together and

I whispered to him to take off his trousers as fucking is far better performed in the nude. He obeyed my instruction with the utmost alacrity, tearing off his boots and socks, and then his trousers and underpants, whilst I divested myself of my dress. He rolled over on top of me and I took hold of his meaty shaft, which was trembling with anticipation, and placed the ruby head at the entrance to my cunney.

' "Now just push forward gently and you will have crossed the Rubicon," I said gently, but this young feller-me-lad was too excited to listen. His cock slewed sideways and missed the target, so I reached down and guided this thick, virgin cock to the mark, pulling his arse towards me so that three inches or so of his knob slipped between my cunney lips. Our lips collided and meshed together as I wriggled my bottom to obtain the full length of his young prick inside me, and my cunney magically extended itself to receive it.

'With a passionate jolt of the loins his cock was now fully inserted and our bodies now began to work together in unison. I gloried in each giant thrust as his balls banged against my bum, and I twirled my tongue in his mouth as I wrapped my legs across his waist. Jed plunged his face between my breasts and sucked furiously at my left nipple, and his shaft moved in and out of my wet pussey even faster. I knew that his first ever effusion into a cunney would come quickly, and I automatically flexed my vaginal muscles, ready to milk the twitching length of cock that was swishing in and out of my love channel. He grabbed my bum cheeks and, with a throaty groan, he emptied his balls, ejaculating a stream of frothy foam into my pulsating pussey.This first fuck produced a shattering climax for young Jed and he lay inert for a few moments as he recovered his breath.

'Eventually he rolled off me, totally exhausted, and I looked down and saw that his copious emission was leaking out of my cunney and running down my thighs. I would have liked the opportunity to suck his prick up to its glorious stiffness, but I felt that we might be in danger of discovery if we stayed much longer. Reluctantly I told Jed that we might get caught if we did not soon put in an appearance, so we dressed in silence, but before he left he gave me a long, lingering kiss and thanked me for a most marvellous fuck.

' "I hope we will be able to do it again, Miss Celia," he said hopefully. "We might, Jed, but don't count on it. I'm sure you will soon find a regular girlfriend with whom you can fuck as often as you both wish. But I hope I can rely on your discretion about this afternoon's little escapade." The dear lad swore by all that was holy that he would never reveal that it was his employer's daughter who relieved him of his unwanted virginity, and I have every reason to believe that he has kept his word to remain silent. So all in all, I was more than happy with this intimate encounter with a member of the working class.'

'One of Nature's gentlemen,' murmured Katie.

'Far more of a gentleman than some others much better born who have tried unsuccessfully to pull down my knickers,' agreed Celia. 'The dear lad has insisted on presenting me with bouquets of flowers from the garden every week that I spend at our country residence.'

'I must admit that there is much to say for this member of the working class,' said Professor Hammond, and he joined in the laughter that his unintentional *double entendre* provoked.

'There is much to be said for fucking *al fresco*,' said Richard Gewirtz thoughtfully. 'Would you be interested in a recent experience of mine?'

The chorus of assent caused him to smile and he began: 'Just before I left for America last April I took a stroll through Allendale Woods, which forms part of the property my father owns up in the Peak District. I was walking along an old mule track coming from Staffordshire into Derbyshire near Mr McDougall's Hall Dale. [*This sixty acre property, along with the neighbouring Hurts Wood, was bequeathed to the National Trust of Great Britain in 1933 – RM*]

'It was a warm afternoon and I decided to take a rest on the bank of a nearby stream. I made a small pillow of my jacket and before long I was asleep; well, not quite asleep, rather I fell into a doze through which I could hear the chirping of the birds, the rush of the water and, after a while, the sound of two voices which were getting louder and louder.

'I was not trespassing so I made no movement, especially when I made out the owners of the voices. Without doubt they belonged to Mary Mulberry and her friend Millie Boughton, both teenage daughters of nearby tenant farmers. They were pretty girls but I never had thoughts of becoming better acquainted as my father owned their land and, as he always maintains, one should never mix business with pleasure. So I decided to feign unconsciousness and kept my eyes closed as they approached me.'

' "Why, look what we have here, Mary," said Millie. "Do you know who this young man might be?" "Oh yes, that's Richard, Count Gewirtz's son," replied Mary, dropping her voice. There was silence for a moment and Millie said: "He is a very handsome boy, isn't he?"

' "Oh yes, and I bet he has a prize pizzle too," said Mary with a giggle. "What makes you think so?" enquired her friend.

' "Well, I heard my father tell Uncle Ronnie that in London, Count Gewirtz has the cream of Society women at his disposal. So he must have a big prick, and you know what they say, like father, like son!"

'I somehow managed to refrain from laughing and simply gave a tiny sigh as I continued to pretend to be in the Land of Nod and, as far as I could judge, my deception appeared to have taken them in.'

' "It would be nice to find out if you are right," said Millie softly. Then I heard the two girls whispering and giggling and wondered what on earth they were planning – but I did not have to wait very long to find out! I felt my belt being unbuckled and then my fly buttons being opened. My trousers were gently pulled down over my hips and a hand deftly inserted itself in my drawers, sliding along, arousing every bit of flesh it touched as it descended to my pubic hair. There it stopped and teased the curls around my stirring cock. "It's very thick," said Millie judiciously, "but look at the end of his shaft, the knob is all uncovered and bare. Have you ever seen such a prick?"

'Suzey explained that some penises lacked foreskins and I learned something new – that English girls differentiated between the two by calling them Roundheads and Cavaliers [*the nomenclature is still used at many British public schools – RM*]

'Somehow I forced myself to keep up the pretence of sleep, even when a soft hand slid under my cock and pressed my balls. Of course my shaft shot up in the air and immediately another warm hand closed around it. Well, that was just too much for any man! I opened my eyes and feigned total surprise and breathed: "For heaven's sake, what is going on here? Mary, what on earth are you doing to my prick?" This was perhaps an unnecessary question as the girl was on her knees in front of me, rubbing my shaft with one hand and cupping my balls with the other, her face just an inch or so away from my twitching prick. Alas, when Millie decided to join in and leaned forward to clasp my cock I could not hold back and a jet of sperm jutted out all over their faces. Most of it splattered across Mary's cheeks, mouth and chin, but this did not appear to distress her as she licked blobs of the sticky cream from the corner of her mouth with her tongue.

'I lay panting as Millie continued to stroke my soft shaft. "I really don't think that I can manage another stand," I gasped."A strong young man like you?" she twinkled, pretending to scold me. "Let's see what will happen if we give you a helping hand!" Slowly at first she gently stroked the sensitive underside of my now slightly stiffening cock, allowing her fingers to trace a path around and underneath my balls which made my whole body tingle with gratification. Then she closed her finger and thumb around the shaft, sliding them along its length as Mary leaned over and took my knob in her mouth, sucking it in lustily between her lips with every evidence of enjoyment. Her head bobbed up and down and when Millie decided to lick my balls, my shaft stiffened up as hard as a rock.

'As soon as it reached full height, Mary scrambled to her feet and lifted her skirt. She pulled down her knickers and climbed over me with her knees on either side, rubbing her hairy slit across the tip of my cock. She slid herself on top of me and I felt my cock slip up into her damp crack as she speared herself on my rampant rod, rocking herself up and down to our mutual pleasure. She was riding me at some speed when all of a sudden Millie lifted her head and hissed: "Careful, there's somebody coming."

Richard paused and Professor Hammond said gloomily: 'Don't tell me, it was one of those clodhopping rural constables. My dear chap, only last month I was in a similar situation in an Oxfordshire meadow eating the pussey of the loveliest undergraduate in my class, when all of a sudden we were rudely interrupted by the arrival of a police officer. Fortunately I was able to persuade him that I was a medical gentleman examining the girl for the rare disease of archeris, which can only be detected by close physical examination.'

'He believed you?' said Jemima incredulously.

'Well, he certainly believed me when I handed him the sovereign which I assured him had just fallen out of his pocket when he took out his notebook!'

Richard Gewirtz grinned. 'That is what I like about your British police – they are the best money can buy! But, no, we were not disturbed by an officer of the law but by a pale young clergyman who none of us had seen before. He sauntered over to where I lay on the ground with Millie firmly speared on my throbbing cock. Fortunately, her skirt hid the fact that my trousers were partially down and that, as he approached, she was busy riding a lovely St George on my pulsing pole. Mary wiped the remainder of my sperm from her face as the reverend gentleman doffed his hat and said: "Good afternoon, my children. Pray continue your fucking, which was so stimulating to see."

'It was hard to say who was more startled, myself or my two pretty companions. We were dumbstruck and looked at him with our mouths agape as he continued: "No, please don't stop on my account, but I hope you will not mind the suggestion, sir, that you release that delicious girl's breasts, which I am sure we would all wish to view."

'I undid her blouse and let Millie's breasts loose. Truly, they were magnificent, and I certainly appreciated the creamy fullness of them as they came tumbling out in glorious nudity. "Are they not superb?" murmured the cleric. "Why don't you rub them for a moment?" This seemed a very reasonable course of action and I took their succulent weight in my hands and, as I gently began to fondle them, as yet untouched, her twin nipples rose in excitement like two sap-filled buds. Our visitor continued to egg us on by commenting that fucking naked was far more pleasurable than doing so when clothed. So Millie lifted herself for a few moments from my erect member and quickly undressed, whilst I now pulled off my trousers completely. Mary too took off her clothes, and I suggested that she straddled my face so that I could lick her pussey with my tongue, whilst Millie continued her ride on my trusty truncheon.

'The girls faced each other so that Mary's lovely

bottom cheeks were inches from my eyes as I wrapped my arm round her to tickle her cunney up in preparation. And as Millie bounced gaily on my cock, the two girls kissed and fondled the other's breasts, making their nipples rise up until they resembled rich, red stalks whilst Millie slid her extremely juicy cunt up and down my cock as I licked and lapped Mary's dripping cunney.

'Now began a short, sharp bout of the most enjoyable fucking. The reverend gentleman unbuttoned to present his bare, stiff prick which he thrust forward between the girls and they lapped at it together to his obvious delight. This was all very exciting and when Millie's cunney muscles tightened gloriously around my shaft, with a gigantic whoosh a second stream of white froth spurted out of my cock into her eager nook. Gush after gush flooded out as she happily screamed her release, and our juices mingled in a tremendous mutual spend and, to complete the happy picture, our new friend sent a fountain of spunk shooting into the air as the girls gobbled his twitching cock and he drenched their faces with his copious emission.

'Mary stretched herself out langorously on the grass as Millie, the reverend and myself dressed ourselves. "I love the warmth of the sun shining on my naked body," she explained and I wished that I had brought my camera, for she looked so ravishingly sensual lying there, her long blonde tresses caressing her shoulders, her big breasts with the large red aureoles and upright nipples looking so exciting, and the golden triangle of her mount with the pouting pussey lips looking so luscious that I could hardly stop myself from dropping to my knees and burying my face in its warm wetness.

'But there was no time for such pleasantries as Millie suddenly hissed out a warning that someone was coming out of the woods towards us. I recognised the grey-haired head of old General Aigen, a well-known country gentleman who owned much property around his house nearby Hangar Lane. "What the deuce is going on here?" he snapped. "My God! A naked woman! Everybody stay where they are whilst I call for the police."

'I was dumbfounded and the girls looked horrified as the General pulled out a whistle to summon assistance, but fortunately our clerical companion showed commendable presence of mind. "My dear sir, there is no cause for alarm," he said soothingly. "The poor girl is well known to me. She is suffering, alas, from a rare skin complaint and her physician has recommended the maximum exposure to the sun as the best cure. This lady is her trained nurse, hired especially to attend to her needs, whilst my curate and I simply arrived here moments before you and were of course about to leave immediately, an action which of course I know you will wish to follow."

'This mollified the General and we turned our backs as Mary hastily threw on her clothes. After he had left us, we thanked our friend for his quickness of thought. "It must be very useful in your work," I commented. "Do you ever preach your sermons impromptu?"

' "No, not really, but then you see I have never preached a sermon." he replied. Mary looked at him in astonishment. "You have never preached a sermon – why on earth not?"

'He smiled and replied: "Well, there are two reasons actually: the first is that I dislike speaking to an audience, and the second is that actually I am not in fact a clergyman. No, don't look so shocked, to the best of my knowledge I have never broken the law as I have never officiated at any services, although last year I was nearly dragged into a church near Folkestone to marry a couple, as for some reason the vicar had not appeared at the appointed hour. Luckily he arrived just as I was being escorted down the aisle, so I was spared any embarrassment.

' "It is a harmless habit," he continued. "I steer clear from offering any religious dogma and so probably do far less damage than many other true Men of the Cloth. However, it is a most useful garb. One gains entry almost anywhere without question and on trains, for instance, one may sit in a first class compartment without having to pay the extra fare. Or indeed any fare at all, for no collector would doubt the word of a clergyman who apologises for having mislaid his ticket."

'We introduced ourselves, which was somewhat ironic as the girls had already sucked his cock and swallowed his spunk, but this was no reason to dispense with formalities. I insisted that the fake priest, whose name was Herbert Holland, and the girls joined me for tea at our cottage which was only ten minutes' walk away. As we trudged our way up the hill Mary said: "You may not be a vicar, Herbert, but you seem to be a connoisseur of the Sins of the Flesh."

' "Hardly Sins, my dear, though like so many pleasures in life, they are indeed frowned upon by Society. My own philosophy is a belief in total freedom of expression and action, so long as no harm is occasioned by such behaviour. *Humani nil a me alienum puto. [I count nothing that is human indifferent to me – RM*]. Especially as far as the fair sex is concerned, I may add. The misogyny of many in religious orders has always concerned me, for I prefer the Persian poet's explanation of the Creation of Eve to that expounded in the Book of Genesis. According to Mustapha Pharte, in the beginning Allah took a rose, a lily, a dove, a serpent, a little honey, a Dead Sea Apple and a handful of clay. When he looked at the amalgam – behold, it was a woman!"

'We continued our rustic frolics after tea. Herbert proved to be most adept and adventurous in his love-making, having studied fucking for six months with the famed Professor Baum of Bloomsbury. His particular favourite method was rear entry into the cunney, an impersonal position, it is true, but one much favoured by the ancient Egyptians. It is also commonly practised by the Eskimos, which may have something to do with their custom of inviting honoured guests to fuck their wives. It was especially interesting to see Herbert fuck Mary in a standing, rear entry method. Mary stood with her head supported by the wall and she pushed out her voluptuous bottom as far as possible. This allowed Herbert to press up behind her and slide his arm around her waist to play with her clitty whilst he slewed his tool in and out of her cunney. Before he spent they changed round so that Herbert stood about a foot away from the wall, leaning backwards so that he was supported by his upper back. Mary stood in front of him, facing away but leaning back against his torso and this allowed Herbert to insert his cock in her crack quite easily from behind. Again he was able to slide his arm around to tickle her clitty whilst she reached back to squeeze his thighs and bum cheeks. They found this method of fucking extremely stimulating and both enjoyed delicious climaxes.

'Alas, Herbert had to leave at five-thirty to catch his train back home, and as I too had an evening appointment I could not avail myself of an evening with these two lovely, willing country girls. But you may be certain that I shall visit them again as soon as I can!'

Richard Gewirtz's saucy story fired the blood of the listeners, and when they trooped back into the lounge, they were further excited by the scene of Alan Brooke and Laura Gantshill lying on the tiger skin rug before the fireplace. Laura had his huge, proud penis clasped in her hand as the pair kissed each other hungrily. Laura's firm young breasts bounced as he squeezed them together in his hands, kissing and sucking them. He then reached out for a cushion which he slipped under her buttocks. The great cocksman paused for a moment as he stared hard at Laura's delicious cunney. He dived between her legs to flick his tongue teasingly along the lips of her parted crack as she shuddered with lust.

'Oh, Alan,' she cried. 'Stick your stiff ram-rod there, I can't wait any longer!' He looked up and grinned before obeying her command. In a flash he was positioned between her legs, the fiery red knob of his monster engine just touching her eager love lips. 'You don't really want me to push in further do you?' he said wickedly.

'Oh yes, yes, I do,' she cried out. 'I want you to spunk into me. Come on, you randy devil, fuck your big cock into my cunt. Nibble my titties, Alan, like you did at Colonel Goldstone's when you sucked one and Ed Fisher sucked the other, whilst you fucked me and I sucked him off.'

She gasped with relief as his superb staff slid into her, and she lifted up her arse in answer to his thrusts, her legs curled around his back. There was no doubt that she was enjoying a delightful fuck as he pounded away, and the handsome couple quickly spent in a delirium of desire and wantonness as his gallant cock slicked furiously in and out of her dripping crack.

The Arkley sisters then joined the fray. Jonathan Crawford drew Katie's hand down towards his stiff, throbbing cock which made her own cunney pulse and throb as if it were already opening wide in lustful anticipation, and Katie knelt down to take his veined shaft into her mouth, licking the red helmet with her tongue as she worked the skin up and down with her hand. She stiffened a little and moaned as Richard Gewirtz (obviously taking a leaf out of Herbert Holland's book) placed himself behind her and carefully positioned his cock between her bum cheeks before thrusting forward to enter her dampening pussey from behind.

Meanwhile, Penny and Paul Maycock were entwined together and as she sank down upon the carpet he was on her instantly, pushing his thick prick between the yielding lips of her cunney as she threw her legs up around his buttocks. Penny thrilled to the rhythm of his frenzied fucking and matched him thrust for thrust.

Sir Gerry Newman now dropped to his knees to lick and lap at Jemima's fragrant pussey, and Celia sucked at her large red nipples as, with one hand, she frigged Professor Hammond's cock and with the other, slid her fingers into Celia's cunt as Celia and Jemima exchanged a passionate kiss.

All this licking and lapping, fucking and sucking delighted Gwen, their hostess, who lay on her back with her legs spread out, rubbing the end of a fresh, foot-long rubber dildo along her sopping slit. Her body jerked as she pushed the rubber prick inside her cunney, working it in and out, sliding it back and forth until her body began to shake and quiver with the onset of a tremendous spend.

There is no doubt that the fun would have continued far into the night, perhaps until the first rays of the rosy-fingered dawn stole through the curtains, but half an hour or so later Lady Arkley called to pick up her daughters as her own party at Lady Bracknell's Belgrave Square mansion had broken up with the departure of Her Majesty Queen Alexandra. Luckily, Sir Gerry Newman had already dressed as he had not planned to stay the night, and the rich tycoon was able to keep the formidable Lady Arkley at bay in the hallway whilst Katie and Penny scrambled into their clothes.

'I trust you have enjoyed yourselves,' enquired Lady Bracknell as they journeyed back to their hotel in their Prestoncrest cab.

'Oh, yes, Mama,' said Penny innocently. 'It was a most pleasant gathering and we learned a great deal from being exposed to London Society.'

It was as well, perhaps, that Lady Bracknell did not pursue this matter further, as the exposure concerned would hardly have been to her liking!